KILL SOME OF THE PRIVILEGED

By Ivan Bering

I0641417

Copyright 2017 Ivan Bering

A Charlie Taylor Novel

ISBN

978-0-9937100-7-0

- 1 -

Acknowledgements

Although I am responsible for the quality of the work and the artistry, I am grateful to my daughter Cathy who started me on this journey and is a ruthless beta tester.

Other Charlie Taylor novels:

Kill most of the Miscreants: first in the series

Kill All of Them: third in the series

Homegrown Killer fourth in the series

Instructions from a Killer fifth in the series

AUTHOR'S NOTE

A work mandated therapy program resulted in my first novel. I have progressed with fewer reckless incidents, but anger and darkness do persist and arrive at inconvenient times, so more writing. Hardcopy documentation makes it easier to detect asshole behavior.

As added pressure, my therapist says my emotional IQ is too low: I'm too inhibited about sharing moments of deep feelings and concerns, my reticence a protective mechanism.

This second novel chronicles the events in our chase of a maniac who harvested body parts and delivered to the neighborhood.

Charlie

Charlie Taylor

Homicide Detective

Sector 14

PROLOGUE

The wheelbarrow was a good idea, but the unconscious man, on a regular basis, violently twitched and almost tipped the barrow. So the trip from the van across the sand and grass was a struggle. The kidnapper's wheelbarrow created a squiggly track from the van to the front door.

Once at the table the block and tackle made it easy to get the victim out of the wheelbarrow and on to the table; the killer quickly attached the restraining straps and positioned a drinking bottle. But it all took time, and his biggest fear was that the man would regain consciousness before he was tightened onto the table.

Finally, he was able to step back and inspect his work; the clothing disguise was heavy, and sweat rolled off his face. He was pleased almost everything went as planned. It felt good to be smart.

The masked man walked, past the small altar with many gaudy statues, to the far end of the room, toweled down, and put on his regular clothing. Next, he sat, cross-legged, in front of the altar, not to pray but to regain control and begin a slow review.

First, the paint....ok all three cans in the cupboard....red, blue and white...each can with its own brush and stir stick......next the compound bow.......where ?..... oh yes in the far corner.....arrows?......still in the van............he'd bring them in when he left......ok all good.

His mind was wandering and thinking about the conclusion, but he kept his eyes closed and focused on the last item. With a massive effort he was able to keep his thoughts from fragmenting:

Last, it was time to edit the recording which would be delivered to the police; they probably wouldn't take it as a serious note, at least not until the body parts started showing up. It had to be perfect. When he finished listening to last night's version, he has some doubts. Maybe he was giving away too much. Maybe best to delete the piece about the Hindu god.

His speculation was interrupted by some moaning from the table; this caused him to smile, and he laughed at his success, pleased with his plan. Fuck the world; He had arrived, a god from a different culture and era.

At this point, his insanity flared, and control left him. He started the chainsaw, and soon he was dancing around the table and signing with a yowling chainsaw providing the music. He thought he looked like an Apache warrior prancing around a fire; this image brought more delight, and he screamed his elation.

CHAPTER 1: Charlie's Log: IT STARTS

It was a computer generated sound, a weird combination of tones, edgy with distorted harmonics. I know it's impossible, but the voice sounded psychotic.

I stood at Manuel's desk, at his request, and impatient to get back to mine. To face me Manuel shifted his entire upper torso; more rehab was required before he would regain normal flexibility and range of motion in his neck and upper body. A few months ago, the Five Star serial killer stabbed him. The stabbing and subsequent recovery drained some of his confidence, the result: a more subdued detective who now frequently asked for direction or permission.

I said, "Again."

Manuel smiled and hit play.

"You may call me Robin Hood. I will be taking from the wealthy and the famous and distributing to the less fortunate. You will know I have arrived when you start finding the body parts. My final signature will be a painted target on the chest with an arrow right through the bull's eye. If you want to stop me, solve these audio clues; it will not be easy because I am the avatar of a Hindu god.

It is Tuesday, August 24th, 2021; you have a few days. Have a nice day."

The rest of the audio consisted of four sound bites, each about 30 seconds long with five-second gaps between each sample:

Giggling: a high-pitched sound, like a young man or a boy, a little wild or out of control,   scared, or perhaps hysterical.

Snorting: an emotional man, taking gulps of air between the snorts: ready to attack or under attack?

Cursing: an older man who was upset or sounding off: a string of unrelated profanity, loud, angry, some words slurred.

Wailing: a young woman or girl, frustrated, almost a screaming, moments of silence and then another piercing wail. A cry for help? In pain?

We played it twice more, but no clear plan or direction presented itself.

Manuel was impressed. "Boss, this is a few steps beyond our regular nuts."

"Where did this come from?"

"Morning mail, addressed to 'The Boys in Homicide.' Do you want me to follow up? I can send it over to the lab see if they can come up with anything."

"All right send it over but not as a priority or we'll have to absorb all the overtime; those boys are too keen to earn the extra bucks. If we add more overtime on this month, the Chief will blow up. Anything else? No bodies with a painted target? No? Right. Just leave the recording with lab. When the bodies start getting delivered, we'll change priorities. I've to go; I've about 20 minutes to finish my report."

I hurry back to my desk. I didn't like this rush nor the recording. Jesus, a Robin Hood in the city. Why do hasty decisions often return through the back door?

The latest stats on the homicide rate in Sector 14 concern the Chief, but why a report had to be written I didn't understand. All I knew: he's been a bear all week, touchy, in a foul mood.

Wes, my senior detective, and good friend, was enjoying the company of some dark- haired woman, both about 12 feet away, standing beside an outside window. In a matter of minutes, a mutual attraction flourished, evident from their endless chatter and bouts of laughter. I didn't know what's so goddamn funny. First: this Robin Hood, the avatar of a Hindu god and now I have to contend with a flirting couple. My report wobbled and halted. I yelled.

"Keep it down.... or.... damn it move."

The dark-haired woman didn't know when to stop.

"Oh, there are consequences for friendly chatter?"

"Yes, I'll put the Jamaican curse on you."

"How will I know the curse has me under its spell?"

"Well first you will feel a little lethargic, but that's not the worst part."

"Alright, smart guy tell me the rest."

Wes should have warned her. He knew I wouldn't let it pass.

"When I snap my fingers, your tits will fall off."

Oh damn, I said that, crude, rude, and stupid. Yes, all of the above. My only excuse: I was trying to write a report and at the same time be a smart ass. As well as being impatient, an expected date, my first in months, had me on the proverbial edge.

Wes guffawed. His lady friend fumed, not used to stationhouse humor.

"I suppose I should have expected schoolyard comedy." She was getting wound up, when the Chief's secretary waved at her, the signal to come; she left, not a word to Wes or me, straight into the Chief's office.

Wes kept the smile; I had to ask, "I give up; it wasn't that funny. Why the big grin?"

"The dark-haired lady whose tits you just destroyed is the new community liaison person direct from the Mayor's office. She's assigned to Homicide for the next three months to assess our operation under the new legislation, our empathy with the public, and our effectiveness in dealing with suspects. At the conclusion of her stay and her report to the Mayor, our budget will be reviewed and revised accordingly."

Jesus Christ, what a way to start a day.

# # # #

The meeting in the Chief's office went better than expected, considering how I'd dealt with Pameela's anatomy.

The Mayor's representative now officially recognized: Pameela Sharma. She was not pleased with me but played it straight as the Chief introduced us and explained her assignment and guaranteed her our cooperation for the three months she would be with us. I only spoke when a question came my way.

I handed the Chief the report he had been so anxious about receiving but now appeared to have forgotten its urgency. Before I got out the door, Pameela gave me her card and requested lunch later in the week. Since the Chief watched, what could I do? I'm going to lunch with the Mayor's rep.

Wes intercepted me. Whenever possible, he became my protector or more accurately tried to cover up my more outrageous outbursts. Before my wife and daughter were killed in a car accident, our families had been close; Wes's wife, who was also a passenger in the car, survived the crash. But, the lengthy recovery proved, among other things, too much for the marriage and the divorce finalized last month, a good two years after the accident. He sensed my mood.

"What's the problem? You got your report done."

"What the hell is the matter with the Chief? After all the noise he made about the report when I gave it to him, I'm not sure he even remembered he'd asked for it."

"Best to take it easy on the Chief; he and Karen have decided to stop, or at least Karen is trying to end it."

"You mean our Karen? They've been playing house?"

"Where the hell have you been? They've been hot and heavy for the last three months. Yes, our single Karen and the married Chief."

I was too stunned to reply; I'd heard rumors but was so involved with different assignments and dealing with my demons, I never pursued it.

Wes continued, "One night we had a late supper, and she told me about the affair; she was confused and upset and wanted to talk. Obviously, she has some strong feelings for the Chief but doesn't want to be responsible for a divorce. I told her: I don't think the Chief will divorce his wife, and it's best if Karen ends it as soon as possible."

Karen was the oldest detective in my homicide squad and one of the best. Our Karen in bed with the Chief? Goddamn it, what a potential mess for both of them.

"You'd better hope she doesn't tell him: you're her lonely hearts advisor. He has a long memory and isn't hesitant about using his position. I've got to go. Take care with Pameela."

###

I rushed to the locker room: time for a shower, a shave and a change in dress. My first date in many months was to be a supper with Emma Collins, sometimes known as Red.

It felt uncomfortable, but I decided to go through with it. We've known each other for some time: most of that time she probably considered me a reckless drunk or something in that general category.

One incident whirled our history into the unusual category. At last year's annual Spring Dance, I, apparently, aggressively pursued her across the dance floor; no, she was not my date, and yes, I'd been drinking (ok, excessively). Now the part, which made Division folklore, is the story I tried to nibble (ok bite) her backside.

Unfortunately, I can only remember arriving at the dance and everything after is a black void. However, it seems extremely unlikely I could pursue someone across the dance floor, at the same time continue to bend down and try to nibble (ok, bite) her in the ass. Of course, logic did not count. The image of me chomping at a woman's behind in front of all the staff and senior management was too salacious. This redacted version survived to be retold many times.

A few months ago, she changed her opinion. At that point, as Senior Medical Tech, she supervised the interrogation and execution of death row convicts at Fort Green prison. During this chaotic process, I assisted a prisoner, Ron Bowen. It appears my sympathetic assistance (my brother, Sam, says manipulation) with the interrogation impressed her; she invited me to call.

I'm sure I never tried to bite her but wish I could remember. I'm afraid to ask.

.

CHAPTER 2: BODY PARTS

Outside the compact cabin, it was a splendid day. The light color of the exterior walls provided an excellent background for the dark green wooden shutters. The wind unlatched two of the shutters, temporarily providing a view of the interior. The shadows of the leaves and branches covered large segments of the south wall and the adjacent walkway. Inside the cabin, a startling change in the landscape prevailed, a repulsive and unfathomable ambiance.

Henry was now fully conscious but not fully aware of his status. In the middle of a log cabin, lying on his back, and naked, he remained securely strapped to a large table, with a drain between his buttocks and knees.

His deep tan, almost black, resulted from many leisure hours on the beach; nevertheless, his muscular build and robust frame would end up being of little value.

Henry Patterson III tilted his head up a few inches and in the dim light saw a series of blue and white concentric circles with a red bull's eye painted on his chest. The loud music irritated him: a familiar tune, but he could not identify it.

From the far corner, a bundle of clothes moved toward him, a gray cotton sweater and pants, topped with a dark green plastic hooded rain jacket, the final addition: a black balaclava. As the abductor shuffled closer, Henry began to recognize some verses; his jailer sang or mouthed the words to a recording.

"Robin Hood... Robin Hood champion.... Robin Hood friend to the poor..." on and on it went, a repetition of praise and a declaration of esteem. He stopped at the edge of the table, the clothing a complete disguise, his voice muffled by the balaclava.

"Do you recognize the tune? No? I thought not. It's the theme song from the old Robin Hood TV series. I don't know all the words, but I like to use my own in any case. I enjoy the company as I go about my work."

His keeper stood at the side of the table and looked at Henry for a long time, neither spoke, Henry still in recovery mode. Finally some clarification:

"Henry, you may think my dress with the accessory rubber boots and gloves means I'm trying to disguise my appearance. Meaning when I release you, there is no possibility of you identifying me; unfortunately, this is not correct. My work results in a copious quantity of blood. It's much easier to shed clothing rather than to try to ensure all traces of blood have been washed off, and no traces can be found.

I must apologize for not introducing myself: I'm Robin Hood, and I'll be removing various body parts from the rich and famous and distributing them to the poor and needy. The poor may cry and complain about the horror of the delivery, but in their hearts, they will be glad to see a fat cat get some payback. Of course, you'll not see their private smiles of delight."

Henry kept shaking his head in a vain attempt to gain some clarity. At first, the entire scenario played like some crazy college prank. But he began to understand this terrifying fashion statement with the accessory rubber boots, aimed to kill him, and it would not be swift and painless. "You're my first and I'm not sure how long I can continue to harvest before you die but I'm thinking with a good water supply, a week seems reasonable. The final act, to provide a sense of closure, which everyone appears to want, will be to remove your head and mail it to your parents. That way they'll know it is over; I'm still wondering about the target I painted on your chest; it seems a little too much.

Should I shoot an arrow through the bull's eye or just forget the whole thing. Ah well, we can discuss it later; I hear you like to talk, discuss, debate and be the center of attention. Sing along with me if you like......
**Robin Hood.... Robin Hood king of this forest, forest..... forest.....
Robin Hood**."

Henry finally regained enough consciousness to absorb, assess and respond to his strange predicament. His friends often commented: Henry acted and spoke like a salesman, a born trader, a true hustler whose talent and array of skills had never been tested. Henry started. "Listen, Buddy, let's talk, money will not be a problem, huge sums, untraceable, believe me, it can be done; there is a fortune for you. Just ask."

Henry's calm opening, no pleading or yelling, infuriated his jailer. "You don't understand, you arrogant bastard. You think that I'm in a quandary or confused, and your gung-ho attitude can make everything better? No, no, no. Now, I'm interested in how long it will take you to understand: there is no hope for you. How many body parts will I have to remove before you realize this is the end for you?"

The music filled the gap as Henry recovered and tried again. "A 15 million dollar present would be possible with no repercussions. Think about it. With that much money, you could start over. Go in a different direction."

No response. Just more off tune muffled singing. The massive table located in the center of the room didn't rock even though Henry shifted his weight and struggled with his binding, not a wobble. His jailer methodically rearranged some tools on a small trolley, previously wheeled up from the far corner. The rest of the room was almost bare; was this a cabin or someone's idea of interior decoration for a recreation room? In some ways, it resembled a large undecorated living room, but the poor light made impossible to see much beyond the table.

"Henry, Henry, Henry, you refuse to believe this is happening, don't you? Maybe it's my calm and reasonable demeanor which makes this appear to be a joke; maybe I should throw my head back and release a manically laugh, howl like an animal. That might scare you. What you have to understand is: I'm insane, but my drugs keep me relatively calm and provide the appearance of a rational person, as long as I'm well rested. If I'm too tired, I can slip in front of my friends, so I'm careful.

What I want you to feel is the hopelessness many sectors of society feel on a daily basis. You, the super-rich and privileged, just cruise along day after day; your biggest decision is: what to do today so as not to be bored. Even now, I can see you're still in denial.

Anyway, tell me how did you get that retro name? Henry….. You must be named after a great-grandfather, the one who used to screw his slaves. Right?"

Henry tried to answer. "Mister, I don't make the rules; I didn't set the table; I didn't……"

"Don't give me that bullshit. You and your group have been setting the table for generations, but now I'm going to do a little payback. See my tools? These are long handle pruning shears, typically used for small branches; they should be good for toes and fingers. Also, I have an array of surgical scalpels that must be handled with care; they are so sharp, if you're not careful, you could cut your nuts off. However, don't worry, I'll do that for you.

And, finally this small chainsaw, that'll be used to remove your head from your body. I told you things would get messy."

Henry, for the first time, was nearly paralyzed, his quick mind unable to deal with the room, the bundle of clothes covering his tormentor, and the hatred spewing from his accuser. He tried to control his breathing, calm his mind, think of an angle, anything to delay the planned attack.

Robin continued; he seemed to have an urgent need to explain. "Finally: since the place is isolated and soundproof, you can scream all you like. In fact, I want some real terror and anguish in your screams; it'll make for a more artistic package when your head arrives. When they identify your head, the sound of your screams will provide a certain flair to the delivery, an artistic touch.

I forgot the bow and arrow; if I use it, I'll have to be about six inches away to ensure the bull's eye gets hit, but you won't care. Without a head what will you know? I think I may skip this last step; it doesn't seem to fit with the rest."

More humming, some singing, and the non-stop music throughout the room, while his jailer sharpened the pruning shears. "Henry where should we start? Any part you feel has not served you with the respect you deserve?"

Henry tried to sound confident and in command. "Why not at least talk to my father? There may be a payoff that'll please you; we can turn this into a win-win scenario."

"I like that win-win. Is that right out of your Business Admin program or Psych 101 course? You stupid shit. You don't understand how much I hate your class and all your privileges; it's time to start harvesting some body parts."

He leaned over to the trolley and picked up the large shears, "These pruning shears should do; how about a couple of toes? Remember I want you to scream, nice and loud and long."

The jailer sang louder and faster as he clipped off each toe. Not satisfied he used a small scalpel to remove both ears. The final product recorded as planned: the constant theme song music as background, complemented by the jailer's singing in praise of the folk hero, and Henry's screaming as the central feature.

Henry's captor gathered the toes and ears, for packing and delivery, and thought about this episode. Disappointed. He anticipated more pleading, begging, whining. Maybe he'd played it wrong, coming across as a control freak, too cool, too rational, not the way to instill fear and terror. Well, he'd just started with Henry. When he came back for more, maybe Henry would be ready to plead and beg. Certainly, when he got to the head and started the chainsaw. Maybe he should use a handsaw; it would be slower.

His original strategy had been to drag it out for a week with multiple deliveries, a part at a time. His primary on the table would beg and plead each day, every groveling encounter a morale booster for him. Each part delivery would force his family to relive the shock; the city's affluent society would live with fear, slowly escalating day after day.

But his control slipped, and he harvested numerous parts on the first encounter; they would be delivered as one consignment. As well, after reviewing the logistics, he questioned how many deliveries were going to be feasible in a short window. Best extend the operation; a two-week window would be better, also more time for the anxiety to mount; the second kidnapping would compound the terror.

 Were the bull's eye and arrow necessary? He committed to the police: the arrow intended as his signature. But it seemed like too much. This speculation and bouts of confused thinking upset the killer. A wrong time to swing from one approach to another.

His daily medication typically maintained his equilibrium and allowed the decision process to be a clear path. Maybe it was time to get back to the psychiatrist. Some days too many voices interrupted; they all seemed to want to direct his operation.

Henry found his voice and began screaming, over the pain. "You crazy bastard…..I'll tear your head off."

It didn't matter. No sound would escape the cabin walls.

The clue about the avatar, had that been too much? If the detectives solve this clue first, Robin's plans would require more drastic adjustments.

CHAPTER 3: FINALLY

To reach the front exit, Charlie hustled down a long corridor and almost made it past the Chief's office. Unfortunately, while waiting for the Chief, Detective Webster and a few of his Vice Squad jammed the hallway. This squad knew all the latest gossip and took great pleasure in using the information, accuracy and validity, not deterrents. An alert Webster pounced. "Gentlemen your attention please: Charlie has a date with Red, and he promised not to bite her. But, he needs some practice kissing someone while he's sober. John, can Charlie give you a couple of small pecks?"

 John was a slim, handsome, dark haired and the new man in Vice. Many thought his appearance and his gay status accounted for his rapid advancement. For past year, the Division aggressively recruited in the LGBT community. "For Charlie anything. Come on over Charlie and gives us some tongue."

 "John, are you crazy? No tongue. It's been a long time for Charlie; he could lose it, and there are only a few of us to pull him off you."

The laughter was loud but good-natured and Charlie, for once, went with the flow.

"Show him the move with the hands."

"John, be careful. Charlie is a hungry guy."

"Does hungry rhyme with horny?"

"Charlie, remember no biting; you can ruin a good skirt............ wait until she has undressed, then be gentle."

Next, some of Webster's squad filled their mouths with those gift shop fake teeth, large white buck teeth, and started chomping; the goddamn clicking, accompanied by the roaring laughter of the Vice Squad filled the hallway space. Webster's crew showed no mercy, and they never stopped, one feeding off the other. They smiled at Charlie like a troop of chimpanzees, flashing broad irritating smirks, and those huge teeth clicking and clicking in the small hallway. The first time, a few months ago right after the dance, the group pulled the same prank, the props all part of Webster's practical joke collection.

Someone in the Vice Squad yelled out. "Charlie, did you knit that jacket? Look at the pockets. Each one is big enough to carry lunch for your entire squad. Is that Monk's old jacket? I bet Monk threw it away; it probably scared the shit out of one of the older parishioners. The Roman Catholic Church insists on higher dress standards."

Even Charlie understood the jacket never rated as a fashion statement, pockets frequently bulging with his paraphernalia, and the entire ensemble resembled a drooping extra-large sweater. But it was his favorite, comfortable, relaxed wear, allowing a quick, easy entry and exit from his car, and yes a good place to keep and carry stuff. His dress jacket was at home in a closet where he had forgotten it in his usual morning rush.

Now for his important date, he would be wearing this jacket, classified near the disaster region of the spectrum. For a moment his peculiar sense of humor surfaced an alternative: leave the jacket in the trunk and wear the bulletproof vest. Wouldn't that add to the myth of Crazy Charlie?

Charlie maintained control and did not run. Instead, he turned his back to them and raised both arms to them a middle finger salute with each hand. A steady pace took him out of the office. Laughter followed him down the hall and to the elevators. This second chimpanzee ambush upset him. How do those bastards know all the gossip?

Even as he walked to the parking lot and his car, he couldn't shake those bloody clicking teeth. As he drove out of the parking lot, to put the prank behind him, he thought about Karen and the Chief; their affair was more explosive than his date. It not only threatened to destroy a marriage, but it could also ruin both careers and bring more ignominy to the Sector.

###

About three months ago Emma invited him to call. Interruption after interruption delayed their date, synchronization of schedules impossible, both dealing with the aftermath of the Dr. Kate incident. For Emma, appointed interim Director of Forensic Division, it meant attempting to enhance the low morale of staff and dealing with shame associated with the former Director's incarceration. For Charlie, it meant soothing the ego of the Chief, who still bristled at the manner in which Charlie received directions from the Judge. This pacification forced Charlie to diligently complete every bureaucratic assignment from creating needless reports to chaperoning visitors from other Sectors.

They decided on a restaurant adjacent to a nearby hotel, not fine dining but a short drive from headquarters, conservative and practical. Both were tense: it became apparent in the little things, a jerky move to grab a menu, a silly exchange with the waiter and pointless laughter.

Emma invited this date with Charlie after he presented a different face when they interrogated the last convict on death row in Fort Green prison. She knew he deliberately led the interrogation away from a juvenile crime. Division gossip had portrayed a different man, a detective with few sensibilities. Why was she nervous?

She looked across the table and saw a tall, athletic man, not particularly handsome but still attractive. He focused on the menu as if it was of grave importance; she decided to lighten up the atmosphere. "Charlie, are the menu contents going to be on the final exam?"

The comment got a chuckle from him. "No not the entire menu, just the wine list. And, I want you to understand I'm ok with one glass of wine, maybe two but that is my limit; beyond that, I turn into an animal and am not responsible for anything I do."

"Yes, I remember the last time I saw you in animal mode; you made me and my date the hit of the Spring Dance and put yourself in the record book."

For some reason, the recollection made her smile. That night her escort, a muscular detective, left her to get some drinks. During his absence Charlie came over for some attention; he tried kissing her bare shoulders and nibbling her ear. She attempted to avoid him and not cause a scene, but he followed her onto the dance floor where he persisted. Her date returned, not prepared to be so forgiving.

After her partner had thrown the contents of both drinks on Charlie, he reached for his neck. But, the drunken homicide detective was impossible to grasp. Instead, Charlie somehow got a hold of one of the date's fingers and without any apparent effort had the muscular man down on his knees. The crowning touch: the band stopped playing when Charlie applied maximum pressure to the finger, and her escort's scream sounded throughout the hall, like a Comanche's war cry. Not a person in attendance missed the view or forgot the spectacle.

She started to giggle at the memory, and then both of them started laughing; Charlie not because he could remember but feeding off her laughter. For him, the night had been and still was a complete blackout.

After ordering, Charlie tried to find some common ground and asked about the security changes in her building. The Forensic Division and the Investigative Division resided in adjacent but separate buildings: a covered walkway joined the buildings, on the third floor. The walkway facilitated the movement of staff and suspects, but the associated extensive security meant staff only utilized the option in inclement weather.

"Emma, I don't understand why your building is using those old fashion, obsolete, keypad locks. I thought your Division was going to upgrade."

"Yes, we did and installed the latest gear, facial recognition, retina scans, the works. Then the frequency and severity of equipment failures forced our supplier to recall his gear; every damn unit was deactivated. Next the crowning touch: no corrections for a least a couple of weeks.

The solution? The keypad locks for as a long as it takes. I don't like it. I'm concerned about the reduced security and our inventory of interrogation drugs. Most people know the interrogation drugs, for the entire Sector, are manufactured and stored in our lab.

Each storage bottle contains a special mixture for a given weight range of the possible recipients. This approach is convenient for distribution, and we can pull a solution directly from the shelf when an interrogation request arrives. The shelf life is short, so we only retain a small inventory. But the Region insists: we must keep tight control on inventory and track each bottle. And do all this without making the Investigative Division wait for any drug request."

"Jesus, let me guess: you have two sets of codes you have to remember before you can get to your supplies: one for your office, another for the lab."

"Almost correct but there is one more keypad lock on the cabinet where the bottles are stored."

"This means you have three access codes you have to remember: not write down or keep in your wallet or pocket."

"There are only four of us who have three unique access codes. I control the generation of the ciphers. And I have a system that makes it easy to remember. What? Don't look at me like that. I won't tell you.'"

They moved on to the various cases. The common ground afforded a smooth flow of stories and problems. The food arrived and set them in a different direction. Charlie reached for his cutlery and was surprised to detect a tremor in his hand, embarrassing, but he couldn't control it. Emma reached over and covered his tremor with her hand.

"Relax Charlie we're going to be fine."

He couldn't remember the last time he'd been alone with a woman he admired. He relaxed; her touch did the job. For the last two years, he maintained control, but now he understood his loneliness; even Monk and his brother could not fill the void. One caress from Emma and he was grounded.

Emma sensed his mood and said. "You don't have to say anything; why don't you let me do the talking." She proceeded to tell him about her background, starting as a freshman at University to her current appointment, omitting a Dr. Jerry King, who had been a significant part of her undergrad experience.

As the meal progressed and the wine consumed, Charlie finally found his footing. They both relaxed and discovered their work provided a multitude of different avenues to talk about and laugh about. After coffee, they walked back to their cars; Charlie accompanied Emma to her car at the far end of the lot. They kept up a constant stream of dialog, a significant difference from the start of the evening. When she reached her car, Charlie waited until she was seated and buckled up.

"You know Emma, I really like you!"

She smiled back and drove away.

Charlie walked across the lot, thinking about what just happened. When he got closer to his car, he saw a giant sitting on his hood.

"Monk, what the hell are you doing here?"

Monk was Charlie's best friend, from Grade 3, through high school, university and many years of football. Monk moved on to play eight years of pro ball as an all-star defensive tackle: at 6 feet 8 inches and over 300 pounds, he was a giant of a man. The big man shocked the sports world with an early retirement to become an ordained Catholic priest, known as Father Ed. But, to Charlie and hundreds of others, he was always Monk.

"Hi, Charlie, good to see you. I was at a meeting across the street and saw you park earlier this evening. Fortunately, my session broke in time for me to see you again and this time with a lady leave the hotel. I rushed over because I need a ride. The good looking woman with that color of hair...... she has to be Red..... Emma Collins...... Right? Good guess? Well.... say something."

"Yes you guessed right; why do you need a ride? Another recall?"

"Yes, another one and please no lecture about a lemon. When I saw you, I knew this would be better than a cab; we get a chance to catch up on your life and adventures."

"Shit, nothing to report but more paperwork and more paperwork."

Monk, a perceptive man, had known Charlie for too long to allow him to get away with this evasion. "Well aren't we the slippery one tonight; I thought with the body language I saw things were well beyond an average night."

Silence. Monk waited, knowing Charlie needed time before he would open up; it would take a few minutes.

"It was way beyond average, and then I pushed it and crossed the line with a high school declaration. Jesus, just as she is getting ready to drive away, I say to her: 'Emma, I really like you.' What a wimpy mundane comment."

"It doesn't sound that way to me. What did she say?

"Nothing. She said nothing. Just smiled and drove away, not a word."

Monk started to say 'lighten up', but he could see the black cloud over Charlie, so he got in the car and said, "Home James."

As they drove, the silence remained, and Monk waited. Apparently, this woman meant a great deal to Charlie. The evening did evolve into a special event, but in Charlie's mind, a few words spoiled the experience.

Monk wanted to be cautious and not add to the stress. An emotional rejection could drive Charlie back to the bottle. Both Monk and Charlie's brother, Sam, had pushed and prodded Charlie to date Emma, and now it appeared the move might have backfired. Could one sentence spell failure?

For the first time, Monk understood the high price Charlie paid for his long self-imposed absence from any female company. Emma had roared in to fill this senior detective's emotional life. The impact of this one evening beyond any reasonable expectation.

Was Charlie that vulnerable?

CHAPTER 4: BACKGROUND

Late August typically signaled the end of summer, but in 2021 the days persisted in being sweltering. Ignoring the weather, two young scientists rested in one of the gazebos located at the far end of Central Research Park, both employed by the Center. They unpacked their lunches and spread a variety of sandwiches, raw carrots, and fresh fruit onto the table. Gary, a physicist with numerous awards, spoke first.

"I had to get out of the building; one more minute with the son of a bitch and I'd choke him. In fact, I think I'll wait for him in the parking lot. I've a gun in the car."

Dr. Max, the topic of conversation created and ran the Central Research Center; he was an international superstar. The research facility had one mission: solve the environmental problem. Global warning and pole reversal remained the dual threats to the extinction of the human race. Max recruited his team from across the world. His team compared to the 1940's crew used to develop the A-bomb.

The difference being the A-bomb development was based on solid theoretical data. Dr. Max's team had to deal with many more unknowns and a global disaster as the penalty for failure. He became known as 24/7 Max, and that was an accurate reflection of his work habits, a demanding, driven, brilliant scientist.

While he procrastinated over his sandwich selection, Rick, the older of the two and also a physicist, wanted some questions answered. "Gary, your plan will fail. He uses a fully equipped suite on the top floor and rarely leaves. And, on to a different topic. Is it true you volunteered for an S1 Interrogation?"

"Yes, as part of my research I requested the session. A helluva surprise. Our colleagues casually refer to that S1 cocktail mix of pharmaceuticals as a truth serum, but I can tell you that is an understatement of their impact. The drugs drive you into a state of euphoria, and you want to disclose everything. Sure it's a painless process but unfortunately also embarrassing, as I found out when I reviewed my interrogation session.

Prior to the start, I submitted two personal secrets which they were allowed to use. Well son of a bitch, not only did I reveal those secrets but spilled everything else, including details about cheating on the Ph.D. oral exam. I behaved like a babbling kid. I'm told there is only one copy of the video, and I can keep it...thank God.

Now I understand why the Investigative Division is solving crimes at a record level. By the way, there have been changes; first, the S2 is no longer used; it was replaced with an enhanced S1 which everyone feels is sufficient."

"Listen Gary, I have one for you, I know about the S3. I was allowed to participate....no...no. I mean I was allowed to see one."

Dr. Max Armstrong received the Nobel Prize for his discoveries: the truth serums, colloquially known as S1 and S2, and the memory probe/scan, known as S3.

His work took place during the time when global warning and north/south pole switching forced a doomsday scenario on the world. Society developed a new psyche which demanded certainty: no tolerance for the legal politics of obfuscation, time too short for the continued coddling of those who refused to cooperate and play the game.

The solution appeared in the form of Dr. Max Armstrong's innovations. The advances meant there was no longer any doubt about guilt or innocence. His discoveries allowed the radical changes to the justice system, soon branded as Justice Reborn.

The novel interrogation techniques, from S1 to S3, were liberally applied, and the accused convicted by his own words or his memory of the crime.

Politicians amended legislation at record speeds. Justice Reborn, demanded consequences for all actions, with mercy reserved for the victims. The universal acceptance of the death penalty even applied

to repeat offenders: the fourth criminal charge became your last, the third for a sexual offense with a minor.

Rehabilitation Farms replaced prisons. The first step of the penitentiary reform, clear death row, used S3 memory scans to release or execute convicts waiting on death row.

The second phase of prison reform meant processing all remaining prisoners. Every prisoner was interrogated with the S1 truth serum and, if required, S3. In the end, each convict faced one of three alternatives: unconditional release, transfer to a Sector Farm, or execution if a murder surfaced.

"Holy shit Rick, they let you watch a live one? How the hell did you manage that?"

"I assisted with some intermittent transmission problems from the probe to the monitor. It was just a fault in one of the transformers, not a big deal, but they allowed me to stay and watch the process. S3 requires significantly more equipment than an S1 and is not an interrogation, in the usual sense; there are no questions and answers.

The accused lies on a table, positioned under a probing device, is almost unconscious, doesn't speak and isn't asked any questions. So why call it Interrogation? I don't know. They probe the brain for memory streams. The first time I saw an individual's memory, you know the retrieval and playback on a monitor, I was stunned; I can't explain the experience. The segment retrieved from the convict's memory displays on a giant screen. The image quality is not equivalent to a TV transmission, and the sound is weird.

But the display erases all doubts. I'll never be able to watch another crime drama without the brutality of that one memory stream flashing in front of me. You should try to get on to a Watcher's list, but this is almost impossible unless you are relative or an arresting officer."

Gary wanted more. "Rick, what intrigues me the most is the movement of the scanner. Ok, they have an event in front of them and know it is not the one they need. How do they decide whether to move back in history or to jump head to a future event?"

Rick had all the answers. "The Watchers control the memory probing: on seeing the image, they signal the technician to move the scanning device: ahead or back to a different time period. A Historian becomes the central cog in the process because his specialized training allows for rapid decisions about each memory segment; this person is a government employee, a permanent member of any Watcher grouping.

The retrieved crime scene provides the required evidence, and the convict is wheeled directly to the execution chamber. In the chamber the Citizen Team waits; three ordinary citizens selected like an old fashion jury, but they operate like a firing squad. On signal, they all press their own release button, but no one knows which release is the fatal dose. I'm told some guys can't wait to get selected and are trying to bribe their way onto an execution.

Anyway, that's how they completed the first step of prison reform and cleared death row cells: the convict's memory proved him either guilty or innocent. The one major complication: if the probing continues for too long, permanent brain damage occurs, not an issue frequently discussed. Not ignored but just not part of most conversations."

Justice Reborn meant we no longer needed prosecutors, defense attorneys or juries. Justice was managed by a Judge, who was assigned a designated territory (a Sector), and a large staff. There were four divisions of specialization: LEGAL where lawyers ensured the legislation was properly applied; INVESTIGATIVE which was the police department; FORENSIC which worked the crime scenes and manufactured and controlled the interrogation drugs; PRISONS which managed the Farms, the halfway houses, and of course the executions.

Both finished lunch and the discussion took a turn.

"Want to hear some juicy gossip? I understand Sally Grovernor is almost finished her sentence at the Sector's Rehab Farm. And when she's out,

Dr. Max wants to get married, if her mother agrees. You look puzzled. Don't remember the girl? Sally Grovernor."

Gary answered. "Sure, it was only a few months ago that Sally and her dad created the enormous shit storm. The disgrace associated with the incident will haunt the Sector for years."

Rick added to the gossip. "You understand they would have gotten away with it except Judge Stephen put detective Charlie Taylor on the case."

"I meet the detective. They call him 'Crazy Charlie'. When he goes after a solution, you do not want to get in his way. On the surface, he appears rather average, but the word is you don't want him after you. The big plus for him: he's the Judge's man."

"I think the Judge deserves a lot of credit for how far we have come with new legislation: establishing an organization, ensuring trained staff and maintaining stability through some rather turbulent times. Justice Reborn is a great name for the revised system, and the public adores it, and the results have been spectacular. Plus, I, reluctantly, have to give Max credit, without him this system is impossible, his science allows it to work."

Both poured their coffees, both given to long stretches of silence, both used to each other, both thinking about their work and events. Gary wanted confirmation. "You said he plans to marry Sally Grovernor. Shit. Is she even legal age to marry?"

"What I hear is for some reason her mother has gone along with the plan. Young Sally gets what she wants which in this case is maybe more than she knows. Her dad, Dr. Grovernor, died at the Farm before serving his full sentence. Max attended the funeral and made his peace with the widow.

It's my understanding they've known each other for years. Max, after graduating, went to work for Grovernor, and they all were close for a long time."

Gary wrapped it up. "Interesting. Our mad genius who has many uncontrollable urges wants to marry. The hard ass is in love.

CHAPTER 5: Charlie's Log: LUNCH

Across from me sat a good-looking woman, between 25 to 30 years old, cinnamon complexion, coal black hair, ivory teeth, all part of an East Indian heritage. Makeup, clothes, jewelry, and accessories all added up to someone wanting to make an impression or someone always conscious of the latest styles. These details were an important part of her persona: Pameela Sharma, the representative from the Mayor's office. Fortunately, my spell had not destroyed her anatomy; in fact, she never even mentioned her tits.

Was she a spin master? Going to try to con me? I found it hard to think of her as a straight shooter, considering her age and elevated position in the municipal bureaucracy.

"I requested this lunch because I'll be with your squad for some time, and it is best if we can work together. I know everyone, from the Chief down, is not pleased with my assignment. I'll be as open as I can with my reports, and then you can decide. Are you going to say anything or just stare?............... Do I pass?"

Intelligence, accompanied by poise and determination. Not someone to make a reckless or thoughtless move. "Do you pass? It's too soon to answer, but you don't seem to be a candidate as a rookie detective in Homicide. You look more like an Ivy League grad ready to mingle with the peasants, then go home: shower off the experience, go out, meet the right people and order a $ 800 bottle of wine to start the meal. I'm sure the entire squad will develop some version of that image. You'll need to earn points to move from that starting point."

I was impressed. She handled all the negative stuff as if employed as a senior clerk in a complaints department: no smirks, no anger flares, and no lifted eyebrows.

"I told you I'll be frank and open. So I trust this is just between the two of us." I nodded my agreement.

"For the most part your summary is correct: I am Ivy League, working toward a Ph.D. in Political Science, and dad paid for the education and all the associated support. He got me an appointment with Sheila Withers before she was elected Mayor. I need this type of work experience before I can go back and complete my degree. Sheila and I clicked, and I became a big part of her campaign team and once elected she wanted me to take on individual projects.

What you have to understand: Sheila is determined to make a success of her term, and one of her concerns is Justice Reborn. She worries there will be too many fishing expeditions and arbitrary arrests; she accepts the technology but, again, concerned about the application; abuses will damage all politicians.

So she wants more hands-on information: how arrests are made, how interrogations are conducted and who are the people directly involved. The Mayor wishes to be able to say: she has confidence in the system and the people who make it work.

Charlie, I'm basically a hardliner; I support Justice Reborn and am prepared to live with the executions. I assume your group will make mistakes but don't intend to report every minor infraction to the Mayor, and she's not interested in that level of detail. She wants assurance people are not taking advantage of the new technology to trample all rights, for example using random arrests and interrogations which are fishing expeditions."

My phone rang, and I decided to answer. I wanted a little more time to assess Pameela and her declaration. It was Manuel. "Charlie, I have the lab people on my ass; they want to know about the Robin Hood recording. They're planning the weekend and want to assess their manpower needs. The question: what type of priority do we want to be put on the analysis of this recording?"

"Manuel, has anything else come in or any crime linked to this recording? Have any body parts been delivered? Or has a corpse with a bull's eye painted on the chest, shown up?"

"No, nothing. It's all very slow and no more recordings."

"We can't afford weekend overtime to process a dubious clue; tell the lab to treat it as a standard request and give it a regular place in the queue. Thanks."

My bright luncheon companion connected the dots. "You don't seem pleased with the decision. Was it that Robin Hood recording?"

"Yes it was Robin, and I'm not comfortable with delaying an analysis, but we're already over budget, and we get a lot of wild ones who fade from the scene without any crimes being committed. I'll admit this one sounds different. Well prepared and determined and yes, rather weird, and I don't like the sound of it."

We talked about budget constraints and risk associated with various decisions to limit spending. All this time I watched her, read her body language, listened to speech patterns. She began to relax. Time to throw the high hard one. "OK, you're on the team but just one condition: don't play with Wes."

This time I set her back; she started to reply and then stopped, and decided to tell the truth.

"You're very observant; I suppose that's what makes you a good detective. Wes and I met downstairs in reception, and within minutes we were comfortable, relaxed and enjoying each other's company. This doesn't happen very often for me, and the instant connection disturbed me. I admit it."

I decided to provide more details. "I'll tell you about Wes. His divorce is final, but he hasn't pursued any female company; the divorce unsettled him. Now he's attracted to you; he starts grinning like a kid whenever you enter the room. I know he needs someone, but you scare me; the social, economic gap is too huge. When you get bored or embarrassed with his position, his dress, his role, and the limits to his social etiquette in the upper regions of society, what happens?"

"It seems to me after an accurate observation you jump to one conclusion after another. Doesn't Wes have anything to say about this? Besides we haven't even been out for a drink."

"Let me try this way. I know the guy; he'll move on you if you give him any encouragement. Wes is one of the two friends I have, and I will protect him. Let me wrap this up. If you play him as some diversion while you're on assignment, you'll find out why I'm called 'Crazy Charlie'. The name I'm sure you've heard."

When I delivered the warning, I didn't smile; she didn't maintain eye contact but finally spoke. "I'm sure you have more than two friends."

Dr. Jerry King, a candidate for the vacant Forensic position, perceived an ambitious manipulator was sitting across the luncheon table; he wondered where this was going, guessing it had little to do with the alleged reason for lunch and the general efficiency of prison reform. Doug Brewster, Director of the Legal Division, did not make him wait very long.

"Dr. King, you understand when we cleared death row in Sectors 13 and 14, we executed over 300 convicts in a few months. If appointed the new Director of the Forensic Division, you will be under extreme pressure to process the remainder of the prison population in 12 months: either transfer a convict to one of our Farms, or release him or execute him."

Doug Brewster held up his hand to wave off Jerry's response. "Let me continue. I know you'll have all the technical advantages of our drug-controlled interrogations, the damn S1 Interrogation, and the S3 memory scan. However, our current procedures call for a 72-hour delay between S1 and S3.

If a convict passes the S1 Interrogation, he is released or transferred to a Farm to complete his sentence; but if he fails S1 Interrogation, we need an S3 memory scan to confirm guilt and to allow an execution. With this 72 hour delay, it'll take many weeks to empty all the prisons."

"Doug, I've given this some thought; I see no scientific reason for the 72-hour delay. I think 24 hours should be sufficient to clear the convict's system of all S1 drugs and allow us to proceed to an S3 memory scan and go right to execution if warranted. The 72-hour rule evolved early in our history, when Dr. Max, for once, decided to be very cautious."

Dr. Jerry read the surprise on Brewster's face; he enjoyed shaking him and wanted to push it further. Brewster thought he was soft, an academic, too left wing, too sensitive to deal with a body count. He decided to drive the point home before Brewster recovered.

"Doug, I realize there may be few errors, a few unwarranted executions, but, on the other hand, a few bad actors will probably slip by and be released. In any case, it will be impossible to confirm. Don't you agree?"

"Dr. King, I'm glad we understand each other. I'm prepared to provide my unqualified support for you to become the next Director of the Forensic Division. But one comment: at your final interview with Judge Stephen, I would refrain from mentioning your plan to drop the 72-hour delay between S1 and S3. As well, your philosophical outlook about the unwarranted execution of a few convicts should remain with us."

CHAPTER 6: ROBIN HOOD

The first session with Henry had not proceeded as he had dreamt. Rather than impress the privileged with his calm demeanor, the setting demanded he allow his emotions to flow and dominate: to scream, spit, swear, howl, whatever surfaced should terrify his captive. He wanted them to beg, grovel, cry and plead for mercy; this had been his dream.

As well his focus kept shifting: struggling with ambivalent plans, changing tactics, and his mind in a general turmoil. What was preventing him from fully enjoying his adventure? Maybe the chainsaw and the anticipated blood and fragments of flesh would push him past a psychological barrier, whatever it might be.

He sulked in the semi-darkness of the cabin, Henry a sleeping, inert companion. Robin thought about the road to this point in his life. Early in their marriage, both his parents became disenchanted with society, lost most of their ambition to a point where they gave up and decided to live at a level which provided the least resistance. This meant, although there was always enough to eat, money became a perpetual issue, options carefully considered before each purchase.

His high scholastic record fell short of providing a full academic scholarship to a top university. Since he refused to settle for anything less than the best, it meant two years of waiting tables and driving cab before his bank account allowed his academic career to begin. The two-year delay afforded enough money to enroll, but he still required outside work to provide the cash flow for daily expenses.

During his undergraduate years his hatred ripened and almost took over; however, he maintained his composure and never revealed his feelings, an outburst could have disrupted to his academic goals. As he saw it, there was one dominant category of students: those from the rich stream resided in a different zone, many entirely unconcerned about grades, money allowing a carefree attitude. It was obvious they belonged, and he would never have admission to their world, someday possibly tolerated but never fully accepted.

Their attitude tore at him on a daily basis. They arrived as, and remained, arrogant bastards, completely oblivious to their impact. Maybe that was the cruelest part of their behavior: their complete unconcern about their attitude and remarks. Their condescension accumulated, month after month, an escalating insult to a sensitive and intelligent young man.

Postgrad work provided relief. The academic demands were intense, and his outside jobs left little time for socializing or even brooding. The fast demanding pace suited him, and his academic work flourished. He evolved into one of the top students in his class, with good job offers and a solid career on the horizon.

Once all the excitement of his graduation faded, and the new job became routine, his old feelings resurfaced. The hatred intensified, and his repressed sexual life compounded the tension. He started sessions with a psychiatrist and tried to control what he revealed, his nightmares now extreme and frightening.

His sex life, long repressed, couldn't be denied. He finally compromised, found a way, unconventional, but it turned out the best for him. Now with love in his life or at least regular physical relief and his lust under control, he reached a different level or state of mind. He was ready to make his dreams reality: make the rich suffer and scream for mercy. As part of his preparation, he stopped seeing the psychiatrist: the sessions started creeping into areas he would never share.

He walked over to Henry and repeatedly poked him until he woke. Henry groaned still in pain, after the removal of two toes and both ears. Dried blood caked around the wounds. Henry, at last, understood his situation and started to plead which pleased his jailor. Robin teased him with a false promise of a release. Finally, he had the game situation he'd dreamt of: a defeated rich kid begging him for mercy, crying at his feet, the balaclava hide the satisfied smile.

"Henry today you'll find out if there is another dimension to our existence or whether this is all there is. What? No comment? Let me cover the essentials. First, the music goes up a little, next I start the small chainsaw, and then I use it to remove your head. Last few steps: the head, after a full rinse, delivered to your parents, the body, also thoroughly washed, dumped some place. The recordings go to the police or I might include them with the delivery of your head. So..........please scream louder than the chainsaw."

Henry knew it was hopeless and pulled himself together; his last act would have surprised both his parents and his friends, fear no longer with him, only acceptance, and a calm, hard face.

"I have nothing to say to you; you're a sorry mess of humanity, confused and insane. Whatever I discover today you'll soon be joining me because with Justice Reborn there is no mercy for killers."

Robin immediately realized his mistake; he shouldn't have played with Henry. He had him when he first woke, but now his captive presented the superior class attitude. This would soon change. He started the chainsaw; the noise roared through the small cabin, and the music blared.

"Goodbye dear Henry, this will be messy but very enjoyable, I'll try not to hurry, but I have deliveries to make today."

The cabin pulsated: the deafening musical theme song mixed with the sound of the chainsaw, and finally Henry's screaming. When the saw finished, there remained a muffled tune.

"Robin Hood, Robin Hood king of something, soon to be loved my all.............."

The jailer allowed the blood to drain, used the hose to complete a full rinse and then deposited the head into a lined cardboard box, along with the recording. Next, he removed all the belts, which had secured the body to the table; he would clean up the room later, in preparation for the next victim. Today he felt rushed: a couple of deliveries would demand care. The bag would help with the body delivery.

The name, Robin Hood, this alias, this stage name, he would continue to use in his communication with the police; however, in the last few minutes, he confirmed his genuine identity. His conjecture had been right, after the removal of the head his singularity became apparent; he was an avatar, a reincarnation of an ancient Hindu god.

He had pushed through the barriers and taken a life, the blood and mayhem of the decapitation in front of him, an overwhelming feeling, and so great a high. He would never be able to stop.

CHAPTER 7: PHASE TWO

Judge Stephen Miller chaired all Sector 14 Board meetings. After all four Divisions had been seated and settled, he proceeded to the main agenda item.

"Most Sectors have completed Phase One of the prison reform projects and cleared their death rows. I will not bore you with statistical details but one fact, which may surprise you, and most critics: very few innocent men were uncovered in the death row cells.

Critics may point out some guilty verdicts and executions were not based on the original sentence but triggered by prior crimes revealed by the S3 memory scan. I doubt the public will be concerned about this distinction.

This meeting is to discuss and formalize our approach to Phase Two where we must decommission all prisons. The processing of the prison population may prove to be a harder task than the politicians expected. Region wants our Sector to start the process and be a leading edge pilot.

This means all the other prisons will be on hold until we complete Fort Green and have established a formal process for handling the prisoners; however, Region still wants all prisons in the Sector shut down within the year. I'll ask Doug to start the discussion."

Doug Brewster, in charge of the Legal Division, was politically astute, incredibly ambitious, image-conscious and in his opinion ready for next step, which meant an appointment as a Sector Judge. Stephen appreciated Doug's legal expertise but worried the man's ambition appeared to be eroding his usually sound judgment.

"Thanks Stephen. First, the obvious: to decommission the prisons we must evaluate each convict and his current sentence. Based on this evaluation, we free him or send him to one of our Farms or in the worst case consider an execution. An administrative review of the formal charges and convictions will not be sufficient; plea bargains distort or conceal the actual crime or the extent of involvement, and for years seasoned criminals talked their way around more serious convictions.

 We will start by conducting S1 Interrogations; if they pass, we can send them to one of our Farms or give them an unconditional release. If they fail the S1, we go to an S3 memory scan, which in all past cases only confirms what we initially uncovered during the S1 interrogation. What this means: if they fail the S1, we can prepare for an execution.

The new legislation did not provide any grandfathering; in fact, it explicitly states as histories are assessed and additional crimes uncovered, the new law will apply and associated sentences used. Let me wrap up by providing some guidelines:

First, in Fort Green we have 153 repeat child molesters; as a repeat offender, with minors, their crime is now deemed a capital offense, and we only need an S3 confirmation to proceed with an execution.

Second, during the interrogations, we will uncover serious crimes, which implicate men, and women who are not in prison. These are threads, which we cannot pursue at this time; this will have to wait until our jails are empty. The recordings will be delivered to the Chief, but I don't want anything to detract from our current efforts.

Third, the other repeat offenders may be the most difficult to detect. Before the S1 interrogation, my staff will review all records and try to identify those most likely to have committed at least three other crimes. However, I'm not optimistic about identifying too many, but you know the public will be furious if we allow a blatant repeat offender a free pass. Bill, any comments?"

The newest member of the Board was Bill Thompson, acting Commissioner of the Prison Division. Stephen surprised everyone with this appointment, formal ratification waiting on Regional. For decades he served as Warden of Fort Green prison, on the verge of retiring, not a fan of Justice Reborn, he didn't present as a potential Board member. His reputation labeled him too soft on the criminal population, and in the yard at Fort Green, the convicts named him 'Uncle Willie'. Stephen anticipated the second phase of prison reform would require someone with Bill's attitude, practical experience, and knowledge to ensure that events did not escalate. The former Warden knew the system and did not hesitate to follow Doug's summary.

"Emma and I have spent a considerable amount of time in assessing our capability to process prisoners, and we've supplied all of you with the details of our assumptions and calculations. The bottom line? It will take at least one year to process Fort Green, and this means there is no way the Sector can shut down all prisons in one year.

The significant issues, which cause the delay: first, we have to wait 72 hours after an S1 interrogation before we can proceed to an S3 memory scan. It would certainly help if we could use the results from S1 as sufficient prove to carry out an execution.

Second, the issue of repeat offenders: I understand the execution of repeat offenders is one of the keys to Justice Reborn. But when we are trying to empty prisons, I question whether this is a realistic objective. Because the interrogator will have to fan out beyond the crime of record, it will entail much probing during each interrogation. Emma, do you wish to comment?"

Emma Collins was the interim Director of the Forensic Division. She had inherited the position from Dr. Kate. Dr. Kate Martinez, the previous manager, now a convicted felon residing in a Sector Farm. Kate's duplicity rocked the entire Sector, but Emma, after years of professional and personal companionship, felt the betrayal a personal insult. For her friends the reason for Kate's action became some solace; her motive: she desperately wanted to assist her daughter and not pull off some personal coup or financial gain.

Stephen knew that Emma was capable of taking over, but her close personal links with previous administration meant her promotions would have to wait: probably not fair but reality. Region's executive group demanded an outside appointment. Emma's respond. "No, I have nothing to add. But I can point out, as you see in the report, I think even the one-year projection to clear Fort Green may be optimistic; it will be a challenging year with little slack for errors or the unanticipated."

Next to speak: Chief Duncan Stirling in charge of the Investigative Division. An established set of rules and regulations allowed the Chief to organize resources and lead the team, an excellent administrator. Crimes and problems which required him to wander outside the boundaries caused Duncan to stumble and struggle. On a couple of occasions,

Stephen had bypassed the Chief and seconded Charlie Taylor to solve these types of crimes; the Chief reluctantly accepted the arrangement.

The Chief had concerns. "I don't think we should prolong an interrogation in hopes a convict will reveal a repeat offender pattern. From my observations of the S1 Interrogations: a prisoner will blabber on about the crime you ask him about. However, if the interrogator does not have a particular focus and begins fishing, the convict will try to help. But the result will be random confessions including everything from cheating on an exam to kicking the family dog. It will be a long, sad series, which in most cases will be meaningless.

I have two recommendations. First, do not make an extra effort to find the repeat offenders. It will only cost us time and not provide any substantial results. Second, we inform Regional the timelines have to increase: show them the math. They may be upset, but it will be better than trying to operate under false expectations and living with daily requests to speed things up."

Stephen allowed his staff to carry the meeting, but he needed some firm conclusions. "Doug, do have anything to add? Any possibility that we could get S1 interrogations sanctioned as the tool and drop the necessity of an S3 to confirm a capital crime confession?"

Doug Brewster, always a lawyer, gave the conventional answer. "Sometime in the future, this will happen, but I think we are at least a year away. Today, for any capital crimes we must live with the S3 and the 72-hour delay before an execution.

Also, I'm not prepared to support the Chief's recommendations: repeat offenders are a key component to Justice Reborn. We have to demonstrate an aggressive pursuit of these cases,"

Stephen surveyed the room and then wrapped up the segment. "Chief, I'm afraid Doug is right we can't afford to neglect the repeat offenders. But, I accept the time constraint calculations and will inform Regional: prison decommissioning needs a revised completion date, a two-year target.

Last, an announcement before we adjourn: one of Doug's seniors in Legal will be appointed Coordination Manager for the prison decommissioning project; this will be Jessie Lopez.

Coordination involves a myriad of tasks: help clear bottlenecks; ensure people serving as Watchers arrive on time; conduct regular project status reviews, provide on the spot legal counsel, and recruit temporary staff as required.

Emma, I would like you to meet with him and bring him up to date with the interrogation process, in particular, the S3 memory scan.

Almost forgot, at our next meeting I plan to announce the new head of Forensic Division and, hopefully, give Emma a more reasonable workload."

The Judge, days later, would reassess this opinion about Jessie and wonder how he had been so naïve and careless with an appointment.

# # #

On one of the city's hiking trails, a brisk wind jeopardized the day, but both walkers kept up a brisk pace. The conversation didn't follow any pattern, a potpourri of topics, from business to home. Finally, Mr. Sharma decided to push. "Pam, what's going on? You seem distracted. Your mind is someplace else."

"It's all the questions coming out of the Mayor's office. I'm beginning to feel like an undercover agent. This was not the understanding when I accepted the assignment."

"I have a hard time believing that explanation. You've worked under pressure on many assignments. Are you going to open up or keep walking around the problem?"

"I hoped you would not press."

"It's a man. Right? What have you got into? You haven't linked up with Charlie Taylor? Besides the Chief, he's the only one I know in the Homicide group. This is not the man you want to bring home to mother."

"No Dad, no…no. I know about Crazy Charlie, and I like the man but would never date him. But I've been seeing another detective, Wes Krause."

"Pam, you're very tight lipped. Does this mean it's serious?"

"Yes, it is. I can't explain it, but we just click; I know how weak that sounds, but it's true. We are so comfortable together. This is very rare for me to find someone, man or woman, who can relate like this….I can't walk away."

Her father was blunt, but they had always been open. "Have you slept with him?"

"Yes. I know you're not pleased…..we are in love. We're not teenagers…this is serious …this is not a one night stand."

"Pam, you know the problems. He's from a different culture, and soon or later, you both have to face this fact. This is the real world. Have you told your mother?"

"No. I would like you to talk to Mom; I know she'll be upset. But, I would like to bring Wes home to meet you both."

"Leave it with me for a couple of days, and I'll find the best time to tell her. I trust you, but I'm worried. The odds are against the two of you."

When the path turned into a steep uphill walk, the conversation ceased as they both struggled to the top of the hill. Within a few minutes, they were at the car park and then on their individual departure routes.

 Pameela was pleased her Dad knew; she did not like keeping secrets from him.

Numerous barriers and objections surfaced in Mr. Sharma's thoughts. His mind in turmoil. He respected his daughter's intelligence. However, he did not see a homicide detective as a permanent member of his household. He knew culture and social status would be bigger issues than Pam was prepared to admit.

CHAPTER 8: THE FIRST DELIVERY

A surprise resided in her freezer.

Lois Jackson followed a regular morning routine: first coffee and the newspaper, followed by a bowl of fruit and yogurt, finally a decision about her evening meal. If the weather held maybe a barbecue: time to check her meat supply. The freezer, too large for the house, was now a covered fixture on her screened and locked front porch. She opened the freezer and started to search for the steaks, in sealed packages, two to a wrapping, one too many since Arnold's recent death. The steaks represented luxury items, which they carefully budgeted for and only used for the occasional barbecue.

A medium sized package sat on the top of her frosty inventory. The frozen moisture made it impossible for her to determine the contents, but a card rested on the parcel. The card only had a bow and arrow, hand drawn against a forest of green trees. Lois carried her steaks plus the mystery package to the kitchen, where more coffee was waiting.

At first, she thought Arnold assembled the package. This was the first time she had accessed the outside freezer since his death. This might be his kind of joke; his sense of humor, generally male slapstick about one degree above fart jokes, didn't connect with her. In any case, it was also washing and cleaning day; the package along with steaks could defrost on the kitchen table while she gathered her laundry, got the first load going, and then moved into the living room with the vacuum cleaner. It still felt like Arnold would be coming in through the front door at any minute. Reality had not caught up with her; maybe she refused to let it happen.

Between all her morning chores and a couple of telephone chats with friends, noon arrived before she got back to the kitchen and more coffee. The condensation still obscured the contents of the mystery package. She used her scissors to cut open the box, and the contents fell onto the table. Lois, generally not given to hysterics, fainting or similar behavior, was stunned and frightened; two toes and two ears stared back at her from their residence next to her thawing steaks.

#

The first responder, a police officer, treated her as an elderly person, possibly suffering from some type of delusion. The neighborhood although not run down, was certainly in the lower economic rungs, with some seniors who liked attention and company. Lois met him on her outside steps; she had not returned to the kitchen since calling 911. The police officer did not pat her head, but his body language and tone of voice left little doubt about his frame of mind.

"Mrs. Jackson, I know some of the kids around here, and my guess is they used special modeling clay and want to give you a scare. I gather you have no way of knowing when the package got into the freezer or heard anyone on your porch."

Lois shook her head to indicate no and opened the door for him. The objects on the kitchen table didn't require an experienced officer to recognize a dangerous situation; they were not modeling clay creations, no kids joke. He made the call to get a full team on site.

# # #

The Chief assumed a body would follow and insisted Homicide be there and take charge. Wes questioned Lois, as the Forensic team went over the table, freezer, porch and then the remainder of the house and yard. Wes took charge because all attempts to contact Charlie failed.

Lois explained: she always locked the porch door and the freezer. Yes, she lived alone, a recent widow, pensioner, long time neighborhood resident. The neighbors look after each other, and if any suspicious strangers lingered, warning calls started up and down the street.

Wes decided to stop any further questioning of the widow; the forensic evidence would tell them more. Manuel and Terry had already started to canvass the area, not expecting much but the procedure a necessity. Everyone wondered: where was Charlie?

The one item, which bothered the entire Homicide team the most: the drawing of the bow and arrow on a green forest; it spelled Robin Hood, the avatar of a Hindu god.

# # #

By late afternoon. The Chief wanted Terry back at the station, leaving Wes and Manuel to wrap up. Their canvassing proved relatively useless, other than the possible presence of a dirty gray van late Thursday night. Wes could not help thinking: why was it always a gray van? Never a bright canary yellow.

As soon as Forensics had completed their work, the reduced Homicide team conducted one last walk around the entire site. Nothing. There was a lock on the porch door, but the door did not even seat properly, and a vigorous push would have been enough to get onto the porch. Wes thought: why use the freeze? The killer certainly knew about the porch and the freezer location, the planting of the package a bold move. Why?

"Mrs. Jackson, how many people know about the location of your freezer?"

"Well, it certainly is not a secret. Just recently, after my husband's funeral I held a lunch at the house, the freezer was used as a table to hold some of the sandwiches. There were too many people for the house, and the porch was used to accommodate some of the crowd. People moved or went where they wanted."

Manuel knew the answers but had to ask. "Ever have any trouble like this before? You know someone getting on to the porch after dark, trying to play a joke."

"No this is the first time the freezer has been used to make a delivery." She was not impressed with the questioning.

Wes's phone rang and provided another direction. He listened to the phone message and then signaled Manuel it was time to leave. As they drove away, he filled Manuel in on the latest.

"A jogger at the edge of Heritage Park discovered a body, and it is probably related."

Manuel wasn't sure what that meant. "Probably…..what the hell does that mean… probably?"

"First glance says the body is missing two toes."

"No mention of the ears."

"There's a problem with that question. The head's missing. You heard right. The head's been removed, and here is the other good part: there is a target painted on his chest, concentric blue and white circles with a red bull's eye but no arrow piercing the chest or bull's eye."

"Son of a bitch. This means that damn Robin Hood recording was the real thing!"

"Where in the hell is Charlie?"

CHAPTER 9: Charlie's Log: MORNING AFTER

When the call came, I was outside on the deck, thinking about her.

It wasn't a long conversation, a string of banality. I'm sure I blathered; that's easier than speaking words of love. She just wanted to hear my voice. Jesus, I was overwhelmed, ecstatic to hear hers, honest to God, like a drug fix. Neither of us spoke of love. Why hold back? Jesus, what a simpleton. She was special, but I'm unsure of myself with these strong feelings

I must have an addict's personality; for months it was alcohol, couldn't get enough, now it's a woman; am I going from one addiction to another?

Time to refocus; it was my turn to host breakfast. I searched for the bacon, but my mind kept skipping around, and I couldn't even find a package in the fridge. Then couldn't even remember what I had been looking for in the damn fridge; six seconds of concentration was beyond me.

Sam, my brother, flew through the front door like an out of control robot. "Brother, brother, I thought you'd be ready, and I brought a guest."

Monk, in his Father Ed suit, followed him through the door; there must be some official business on his agenda because he wore the collar. "Come on Charlie get the lead out. Sam promised me an outstanding breakfast."

"Yah, yah….. give me a minute."

"Well, at least you seem happy. Boy, are you ever happy….wait a minute….. wait a minute….. ..Charlie look at me ……..no don't turn away…… look at me. Can't stop grinning?"

Sam started to laugh. It appears years of study and an extensive psychological counseling practice had sharpened his observation skills.

"Thank God it finally happened; it was Emma…..right? Good, I'm glad……..no more to say let's get going."

We bumbled around the kitchen scrambling eggs, working the juicer, burning the toast. Lots of light banter. Neither Sam nor Monk pressed me; our morning evolved like a regular breakfast session, which Sam and I try to have once a week. We rarely questioned the quality of the results but tore into the food; in about five minutes, we were done. Mom always said we ate like Skipper, who was our family German shepherd, the damn dog wolfed down each meal like a giant vacuum.

Sam rushed around the kitchen. His regular workload enhanced since he now served as the co-chair for an international conference: a big convention for the city, psychologists from around the world in attendance.

"Gentlemen, I'm going to leave the clean up to the two of you. My turn next time. But before I go: Charlie, unless you're going to war and need to carry a week's supplies, get rid of that old jacket or oversized sweater." Before anyone could respond, he tore out the door and into his car. Monk laughed at this hurricane departure.

# # #

When we finished coffee, Monk started. "I can see something bothering you. Want to talk about it? Best you tell me the whole story."

I didn't want to share, not this, not my style. This was too personal, even for Monk. I started slow, but for some reason, the words kept escaping, faster and deeper than I intended.

"Last Friday noon, Red called and said she'd purchased some excellent red wine, and if I picked up the pizza, we could have a great supper at her place. It took a few nanoseconds for me to agree.

I delivered the pizza, and we bumped around the kitchen making a salad…… a couple of tentative get-to-know-you kisses in the kitchen ……… into her small living room …… we turned off the lights…… candles all over the place, background music…. it was great …

……..after the wine and pizza, the kissing became more intense …really intense ….then she got up and started putting out the candles…she wanted to show me the bedroom…the progression seemed natural……. not like an old married couple but more like a rocket launching.

It became the weekend of my life. We were in and out of bed all evening, all Saturday and all Sunday…..you know that nature TV show when the tigers, I think it's tigers, are in mating season and they stay together for a few days and have sex about every 15 minutes… now I can believe that ……..we would get up for a shower or have something to eat ….. a short nap and one of us would wake the other, ready for more. That's how the weekend disappeared, with our pagers turned off. We stayed on our island the entire time, isolated."

I stopped at this point and hesitated. Monk knew. "Come on Charlie it took you a long time to get there; now you have to talk."

I thought I'd gone too far, the rest too private. Monk, adamant, pressed for more. "Charlie you're talking to the guy who has seen you through every imaginable mess in the universe; I'm not sure you remember most of them. Also, hearing confessions is part of my job description, and I'm good at it; I think you have to talk."

Even though I'm a not a believer, his wearing of the priest's collar and jacket provided reassurance. I started the confession. To this day, I can't believe I opened up and told him about the weekend. A stop and go, fragmented confession, but he never interrupted. I couldn't look at him and stared out the window; it was too personal, too everything, Jesus.

"On Sunday evening after supper, I prepared to leave; we were saying good- bye at her front door. A couple of kisses, then she started pulling me upstairs to her bedroom. Of course, I fought all the way up the stairs…...she undressed me, and we started again……this time it was very slow and each touch light and soft …….somewhere in all this, sex turned to love…….no one said the word, but a change took place…… evident in the nature of the touching and murmurs………..she climaxed before me….. I couldn't …….she just reached up and started stroking my face…. soft and gentle and whispering…… looking right at me…… I don't think she said 'love' but it was a powerful moment…...my climax was fierce …..after….within seconds I started crying, and I don't mean a few tears……..I mean hard wrenching sobs, and I couldn't stop….

Emma kept asking what was wrong…..I couldn't answer……she just held me, and I finally stopped. There was a belated awkward exit. She didn't press the matter. What the hell is going on?"

Monk walked around the kitchen into the living room and back. Finally, the walking tour ended, and he started.

"This is my immediate reaction. First, there is nothing to worry about. You're not losing it nor will you probably do it again. But you have a tendency to bottle up the most personal emotions. Remember, a few months ago: the grave site incident when you finally accepted your loss of your wife and daughter and let go. Two years of grief released in an explosive ten minutes.

Now you've been lonely for a long time and needed the kind of company neither Sam, nor I can provide. On the weekend, you're with someone you care for, and she reciprocates.

One thing about sex: it relaxes and drops barriers. With your last act, both of you achieved a level and depth of feeling you've not encountered for a long time. You've been bottling up your feelings and rejecting any female companionship for almost two years.

Suddenly you relax ……all barriers gone and this ball of loneliness and despairs gets released ….you let it all go. It surfaces, and you can't control it …….all your defenses are gone. Red and you destroyed your defenses ……….the release is what you needed…… this is a one-time thing…..it won't happen again."

I'm relieved and wanted to believe this would not be a recurring part of my performance, but the confession left me feeling embarrassed; I didn't say anything.

"Charlie it's obvious you're taken by Emma. Allow me to provide some caution. She's a professional career woman. Even though I don't know her, let me speculate. This weekend may just have been a special treat she gave herself……. a break from a hectic work schedule….after the break she can get back to her job 24/7.

You can treat this as some wild speculation, but I do caution you. Her reaction to the weekend may not be the same as yours; you're almost overwhelmed, for Emma it may be business as usual.

No, that's too harsh. I'll try again. I don't mean it wasn't special for her. I'm attempting to present an alternative: she may have a pattern of periodic intense dates between long stretches of dedicated work, remember she invited you.

You may be special; however, it doesn't mean she's looking for a partner. I could be dead wrong. But, please tread carefully over the next few days. You know: try and be cool and first, accept it as a token of sincere friendship which may end at that level.......listen it was a good weekend for you, just try and keep perspective. Yes? I have to run, OK? See yah."

He left me on the front step, and the grin vanished from my face. Was Monk right? Keep my perspective and maintain a balanced and measured outlook. That's funny.

Christ, I'd already fallen off the truck.

CHAPTER 10: BACK TO WORK

Charlie slumped at his desk; Monk's comments caused more concerns than he probably intended. The emotional high associated with Emma's early morning phone call now converted into a depressing doubt, not anger, just worried about his poor judgment.

Wes hurried into his office. "Boss where in the hell have you been? Your pager broken? You managed to fall into deeper shit than ever before. Yesterday, Chief ordered me to go to your house. Next, I hit your favorite bars. If your AWOL continued this morning, an all-points bulletin was going out. The Chief will tear your heart out."

"Jesus, can't a guy take off for a couple of hours? What the hell is so important? It's been slow, really slow. In fact, Duncan told me to take the weekend off. Hell, he even asked me to leave early on Friday."

Before Wes could answer, the Chief's secretary pushed her way into the office. "Detective Taylor, the Chief wants to see you immediately, and if you know where your bullet proof vest is, best to wear it. The vest may be your only chance to leave his office alive." She raced away, and Wes conveniently faded into the large open area.

Charlie started thinking about excuses, without knowing what happened he knew it was serious; his 48 hours of silence violated department policy. The door to the Chief's office was open, and he stepped in; the Chief sat at the desk talking on his phone, behind him and over to the right side of the room stood Pameela, the Mayor's representative. She looked grim. As soon as the Chief hung up, he started.

"Nice of you to show up. Let me summarize, and when I'm finished, you can correct me and explain. First, a few days ago we received a warning message with four audio clues from someone called Robin Hood. You decided: a crank call and did nothing about it.

Second, on Friday. You know Friday the day you disappeared, a widow calls to say she found two toes and two ears in her freezer. Your great team, Wes, Manuel, and Terry go out there but don't see any connection to any open cases, including the missing person case of Henry Patterson III. You know the man who happens to belong to one of the richest and most influential families in the city.

Oh, the good part. A little card accompanied the fingers and ears. And drawn on the card? A bow and arrow on the background of a green forest. Is there a clue here for you?

Then late Friday afternoon about the time you disappeared from planet Earth, a jogger finds a headless corpse beside a ditch in one of our remote trails. Oh yes, the corpse is not only missing a head but also is missing two toes but does have a large bull's eye painted on his chest. Are we getting your attention?

This morning, about 15 minutes ago, the Patterson family called to say someone delivered a package to their home. Want to guess the contents? The first clue: it complements the corpse in the park."

The Chief refrained swearing which meant he was furious. He thought if he could refrain from cursing this would provide extra control and kept his thinking straight. Even Pameela who did not know the Chief detected his anger, and she became concerned he would physically go at his forlorn detective.

"So how am I doing so far? Nothing to say? Good because I'm so mad, I don't even want to hear your voice. The Patterson family has been one of the real benefactors of the city. I have a meeting with the Mayor in one hour; I'm going to tell her we're going to find Robin Hood before the end of the month. And if you don't find him I'm coming after you with everything I have; I don't care if the Judge is your rabbi. This weekend move equals pure bullshit. Well?"

The news stunned him, each new revelation compounding his dismay. Charlie knew the Patterson family, meeting at one charity function financed by their corporation. Although extremely wealthy with a high profile lifestyle, they were generous and consistently provided community leadership. No doubt, an extraordinary family. This made the events even more devastating.

He stood in front of the desk, his face flushed, his head down, swaying from side to side, the only noise in the room coming through the open door as people rushed up and down the outside hallway. He knew part of the criticism was unfair; every week the department received crank notes and confessions, which only received microseconds of scrutiny, often treated as a joke. Nevertheless, the essence of the dressing down prevailed. As the senior in charge of Homicide, he acted without common sense; the colloquial expression surfaced: he'd been thinking with his small head and not the one on his shoulders.

Charlie raised his head and started to apologize but then looked at Pameela, standing to the right of the Chief. She slowly shook her head; the silent signal was: no, leave it, get out. That was enough for Charlie. He stared at the Chief, nodded his acceptance, turned and left the room. As he exited, the last words he heard reinforced the warning.

"That's no ideal threat. You deliver the son of a bitch ASAP, or you're off the case and the squad."

A subdued detective, in desperate need of solo time to recover, marched down the hall. He walked past his office on the way to the situation room where Wes and the team waited. No preliminaries were necessary. Everyone in the room knew about the session with the Chief, the details not important. Charlie took charge. "I want to run through all we have and our current status. First, the audio clues and warning, any progress on it?"

Even before the Patterson family received the head, Wes established a priority status with the Lab: audio recording, toes, ears, and body: all part of the urgent plea.

Wes reported. "The Lab's assessing the material. Second, our psychologist has a copy of the recording; I think they will both be ready for us in a couple of hours. Except, I'm not optimistic, don't think there is much they can add."

"Manuel, what do have on this first delivery?"

"Mrs. Jackson is a widow living in a blue collar neighborhood, poor but not desperate. The district's seen better days. We canvassed; nothing came out of it except for a possible late drive through by a dirty gray van. Not clunker but no make or model identified, no license number, all vague and no way to even tie it to the delivery.

The freezer sits on the front porch; it's locked, but a high school student could open the lock in 30 seconds. The porch is covered and closed in, and there is a door, but even if locked, one shove would get you in.

Her husband died recently, and she's not accessed the freezer for some time; it will be hard to pin down the exact time the toes and ears found their way into the freezer. But it had to be a recent addition. The package rested on the top of her frozen inventory, and nothing else in the freezer was disturbed. Accompanying the package we have a calling card, a hand drawn bow and arrow with a green forest of trees, no signature."

A silent room waited for Charlie. "Ok, the obvious, Robin Hood is our distributor: taking body parts from the rich and giving them to the needy. Son of a bitch, this means we have a nutcase. Wes, what about the body?"

Wes was ready. "The way I see it the sequence planned by Robin should have unfolded like this: first the freezer package, then the head. All this followed by public family anguish and police running around without any answers, probably the bastard bragging to the media and finally the body.

The reason this didn't play through was a bit of a fluke. The jogger who found the body decided he wanted a change of pace and took a trail rarely used by joggers or hikers; deadfall typically litters the path, with lots of roots covering many sections of the route. So, if our jogger hadn't tried this part of the park, it might have been several days before someone stumbled on the body.

The wind and the rain and sleet pretty well made the dumpsite useless for us, the wind just howls through this section, another reason joggers tend to avoid it. The body as advertised: missing two big toes, a series of blue and white concentric circles painted on the chest with a red bull's eye, no arrow through the bull's eye. I'm surprised to find the arrow absent; everything else is exactly as he warned us, and he seems so precise and systematic. Why no arrow? What changed his mind? Did the jogger scare him off before he shot the arrow?"

Again silence. Charlie did not stop to pursue speculations. "Karen, you've already been at the Patterson house; let's hear a summary."

Karen looked tired, Charlie thought about her affair with the Chief and hoped this would not become an issue in this case, but her voice was firm and confident. "As you can imagine, the family's extremely upset; mother required some medication. The house, itself, appears to be well protected.

The entire Patterson home is fenced, gated, and security cameras cover the entire area. The security video shows: at about 3:00 am a figure with a hood and a scarf across his face deposited a package into their delivery box at the front gate. The delivery area is a cubicle built into the front wall; it is supposed to be a secure box for mail and small parcels; it's covered with a metal, locked door. Robin didn't have a key; he just pried the door open.

Any vehicle, he might have used, was parked out of range of the cameras. First question: is Robin Hood lucky? Smart? Or did he have prior knowledge about the position and range of the cameras?

Just after sunrise the chauffeur, before driving Mrs. Patterson to an early morning appointment, did his mail run. He saw the mail door hanging by its hinge but nothing else unusual and carried the package to the house. It was addressed to Mrs. Patterson; other than the door, there was no indication it wasn't anything other than a regular delivery. The chauffeur says the door sticks, and it's not unusual for an impatient delivery man to damage the portal.

A gruesome recording accompanied the head; it sounds like a chainsaw. The change in pitch occurs as the chainsaw works its way through the different components of Henry's neck. In the background plays the Robin Hood theme music and some muffled signing. The worst part: for a few minutes you can Henry scream as his head is removed. Jesus, what a way to go!

Although everyone treats this a priority, the Forensic Division found nothing of value, and our neighborhood canvass also produced nothing. The homes are spaced a considerable distance from each other, but most have security cameras. I have collected all the recordings but haven't had a chance to watch them, maybe one of them picked up a vehicle in the early morning hours."

Charlie's frustration broke through. "Goddamn it; tell me we have something. OK, let's turn to the one witness sighting.

How many gray vans do we have in the city? Thousands? I suppose we could do some wild speculation. Since our witness said it wasn't a clunker, should we guess and do the first search on all gray vans less than five years old? Do we assume our creep can't afford a luxury model? I think we have to make some assumptions; otherwise, we will have so many hits that it will be impossible to resolve.

Terry, I want you to work on this with the motor vehicles group, you'll have to try some different combinations and see what surfaces. Also, get some pictures of different models and see if our witness recognizes a model or can eliminate some. I know this is a long shot, but we have to go with what we have.

I suggest we all go over our notes, walk through the material and then take your lunch break. We all need some thinking time, and I need some recovery time. After lunch, we reassemble; by then we should have any results from Forensics. As well, by that time I'll have a brainstorm session organized. So be prepared."

Wes waited for Charlie to finish his rather disoriented instructions; he knew Charlie was shaken and struggling, soon the entire Division would know about the Chief's threat and Charlie's dangling career. Wes decided to conclude the meeting. "One last comment; our friendly neighborhood Robin Hood is one mean bastard. Remember: Henry was alive when his head was removed, and it was not removed with a surgical swipe of a sword; our man used a saw to work his way through the neck and spinal cord. Remember: the screaming and grinding sounds we heard on the recording was our guy sawing through the neck while Henry was still alive. The sickest part: at various intervals, he stops sawing and laughs or screams with joy. So we have a rhythm or pattern: chainsaw roars, a stop with the Robin Hood song, then maniacal laughter and it starts again with the chainsaw roars, all of this after Henry stops screaming.

His next kidnaped victim will not receive any kinder treatment; we have to get this bastard before he grabs someone else."

After everyone had left, Charlie thought about the few clues. First the freezer: no one would be wandering around a neighborhood looking for an open freezer to make a deposit. This creep knew the freezer location, and he knew that district.

Second, no one would be walking around the Patterson neighborhood in the middle of the night; he had to be driving, the houses too far apart and too much security to stroll around after midnight. Robin drove and knew where to park, so the Patterson security cameras never filmed his vehicle.

# # #

Judge Stephen's selection of Jessie as Coordination Manager for Phase Two of prison decommissioning surprised Emma. She liked the man but thought he was not an original thinker, nor very creative, too easily swayed by authority, which is why his boss, Doug Brewster fast-tracked him. But, her respect for the Judge meant she would be thorough.

"Jessie, welcome to the team. Judge Stephen asked me to ensure you are familiar with all the operational features of our interrogation procedures. I know you've participated in some cases, so I'll try not to bore you or cover familiar ground. We have to ensure you're ready to deal with the staff. You know they will not be patient with a manager who asks questions about the fundamentals."

"Emma, I understand the intent. I've participated in some S1 and S2 Interrogations. But for the past few months, Doug buried me with research and amendment proposals, hours of work tied to a desk. I understand there have some changes at the fundamental level."

"Right the old S1 and S2 have now been combined into what we now just call S1. We have been able to increase the dosage of an S1 by the addition of some agents, which prevent the violent side reactions. These side reactions used to occur with an S2. I still find it a fascinating experience to participate in a session: the accused is conscious and aware of what he's saying. Unfortunately for him the desire to bond and confess overrides any anxiety about future consequences to him."

"Emma, one question: in all our processing have you ever encountered a case where the S3 memory scan uncovered a different version of the crime than the one revealed in the S1 interrogation?"

"No, never. All the confessions we obtain at S1 have all proven to be valid. It's the death penalty, which has made politicians careful, and they want to be able to claim: no innocent person has been executed. After a few more years, I expect to see us stop using S3 or at least save it for some exceptional situations.

Jessie, no point in reviewing an S1; it is the same as you have witnessed many times. I'm going to give you a recording of an S3 memory scan. This recording contains as much detail as you want from the chemical formulae of the drugs, the binary search techniques, the Watcher selection process, the Historian and, of course, the Citizen Team.

The material contains the actual memory scan for three different death row inmates: two were found guilty, and you can follow their final trip down the hall to the Citizen Team room and the execution. The third and last is a case where the scan exceeded 45 minutes, and although the individual was proven innocent, the extra minutes of scanning proved too much. You'll see him in a care home. This happened during our first attempt to clear a death row; this is where we encountered many duplicates and exceeded the 45-minute barrier a number of times. I don't want to review that operation. All the technical problems have been solved, copies no longer an issue."

- 60 -

"Fair enough. I know the basics. My gaps are in understanding the mechanics of an actual S3. And, I am afraid to ask but can you give me the comic book explanation of a 'binary search', just keep it simple."

"Yes, I understand….let me take some artistic license and give you the simplified version which, in essence, covers the process. Think about an old parlor trick where you ask me to guess a number between 1 and 100. You think of a number, and I have to find the number by asking you a limited number of questions.

Let's suppose you select 68. Well, first I divide the search horizon in half by asking if the number is 50 or is it larger or smaller. You tell me it's larger and I now know it is in between 50 and 100; this I divide again and select 75 and ask the same question. You tell me it is smaller and I now know it is between 75 and 50. This goes on until I get the number.

For an S3 brain scan our horizon is restricted between his date of birth and the current date; from there the search is a very similar process. Once we retrieve the first memory stream, the decisions start, as we search for the day of the crime.

After each display we jump either forward or backward in time; the probing eventually narrows to the event of interest. Of course, the schema for memory storage is more complicated than a parlor game, but the general concept is the same. Although a Medical Tech moves the probing device, it's the Watchers and Historian who decide: jump head or jump back in time."

"Ok enough…. I don't have to understand any of the science. I'll watch what you gave me, but I would like to observe a live memory scan from start to finish. I assume this can be arranged."

"Not a problem. We're currently in operation, with S3 memory scans occurring weekly. Happy to have you on board. I have to run. Call when you are ready. Bye."

She hurried out the door and down the hall. She knew Jessie did not possess a technical background, yet he'd been satisfied with a rather cursory review. If he was going to streamline and expedite, he should've asked many questions or challenged some of her comments. She hoped the Judge would not be disappointed.

After the scandal with Dr. Kate, Judge Stephen could not stand another procedural miss play. Although he had not been demoted or asked to resign, his status at Regional had been severely damaged.

# # #

Back in his office, Sam's mind felt like a juggling act. First, as co-chair for the International Psychologists, he had many people to appease. Next, his wife asserted the trip to India could not be delayed and insisted he pick up the latest set of brochures at the travel agency. Then, Herbie, their big brute of a dog picked up a bug and could not be left alone for more than four hours, unless you were prepared to clean up the floor.

Next, his mind jumped to the most bizarre conversation of the week: an argument with Dr. Max Armstrong. Max wanted to be his patient and voiced his concern. "Sam, I have to control my obsession with young women. I plan to marry and this behavior will wreck my marriage and could destroy my career. There have been too many close calls."

Sam notice Max used the term 'young women' and not 'young girls'. Even this distinction would have been an interesting discussion with the obsessive genius.

"Dr. Armstrong, I understand but as I stated earlier. I'm not the best therapist for you. You and my brother have worked together and may do so again. This may make it difficult for me to be 100% objective. Also, I regularly do work for the Investigative Division. Let me give you two names which I'm confident will help you."

Now Sam regretted the decision: a once in a lifetime opportunity to work with a genius of Max's caliber, a Nobel Peace Prize winner. Damn it. He should've accepted him.

Now, there was Charlie. The weekly breakfast cost him a couple of hours. But Charlie was on the mend, and Sam didn't want to break any patterns, so he took the time to maintain the routine.

Emma sounded like a positive addition to Charlie's life; on the other hand, he sensed Charlie went in with all defenses down and fell in the deep end. Sam hope his diagnosis proved hasty and superficial; maybe Charlie was just in a good mood. But he worried about his brother's emotional swings from 'the hell with it' to 'I'm in love'. Not a good sign.

The last thing Charlie needed was a torrid romance, which crashed after a few weeks. The crash could find him back at the bar, solving all his problems with liquid refreshment. Best alert Monk: tread lightly.

The final puzzle: why'd Charlie want all the travel brochures and background information about India? His wife's research added up to buckets of material, some in hard copy but most in electronic form, lots of information.

Sam knew Charlie did not want to be part of their India trip. So why India?

CHAPTER 11: Charlie's Log: FIRST BRAINSTORM

It had taken a few hours before I recovered from the Chief's explosion and my embarrassment, more accurately reconciled rather than recovered.

For complicated cases, I regularly use a group to participate in brainstorming to bring new insights or a fresh view of the crime. For our first brainstorming, I included Wes, Karen, and Manuel. Terry continued to chase the gray van clue, not a promising prospect.

The only outsider I invited: John Wojecki, who became a regular on desperate cases; John's official title is: Historian which signifies he is the Sector's representative during an S3 memory scan. His education and intelligence mean he recognizes time segments by observing car models, clothing fashions, and a multitude of other trends associated with an era; hence he quickly identifies the period being displayed from a convict's memory bank. Once the time period of a memory segment is established, the technician adjusts the probe, moving forward or back in time.

I allowed them to mingle, get coffee and settle in. This case will need some exceptional ideas to emerge from this session. The brainstorming process encouraged any ideas, outrageous comments, out of the box thinking, anything to spark ideas. The room facilitated our efforts with a wireless network and multiple whiteboards mounted on the surrounding walls. I used my tablet to capture keywords or phrases, which I then displayed on one of the whiteboards, fonts, and colors at my discretion.

"I'm going to play the entire recording received from Robin Hood, in fact, I'll play the series three of four times. After I'll give you the highlights of the report from Forensics."

I started the recording, and everyone concentrated in their way, most with a bowed head and eyes closed, all familiar with each other and comfortable with the setting. All four audio clues pervaded the quiet room: a giggle, a snorting session, a swearing session, and last the wailing.

I started. "What do we know? Robin's central message is a computer-created voice and yields nothing. The four clues present original voices, no computer enhancement or adjustments, the first three male and the last female, all different people.

From the quality of the recordings, it appears the four clues were not recorded on a sound stage. I mean it looks like a concealed recording device captured our sound bites; on two segments, the techs picked up some background breathing. The recorder? Does anyone want to start?

Oh, wait, another observation. Robin dates his recording 'Tuesday, August 24th, 2021'. Jesus, has anyone every received a nut case message created as a business memo?"

Karen, normally first off the mark, jumped in. "What about this? What if it is like one of those contests where you must identify a celebrity but are only given a part of the face, a nose, or an eye? Instead, we hear a small segment of a celebrity's voice acting various parts. The reason I say celebrity because it has to be someone we have a hope of identifying. I mean Robin Hood is playing and doesn't want us to stop using his material. So if we recognize the celebrity, we pass the first step, and more clues will come."

Karen's idea went around the room a few times, then went flat. She acknowledges the major flaw in her idea. "No way…. remember the techs swear it's four different people."

Wes started in a different direction. "You know those arithmetic series, often part of IQ test……… like 2,4,6,8 and you're asked to guess the next number. What if these sound bites form a series and we should guess the next segment? Don't look at me like that; it's just a thought; I've no idea what would follow these four parts. All sections appear to play at the same speed and decibel level; nothing stands out to indicate a pattern. What next a wolf howl? A yodel?

Shit that doesn't make sense….. OK what about this point: he claims to be a reincarnation of a Hindu God? John, anything here for us?"

John responded. "The problem is the number of gods to consider. And I can't think of a Hindu god who ties in with the Robin Hood theme; it bothers me in that it seems like a diversion, it isn't consistent.

Just like the missing arrow, this Hindu God declaration doesn't fit with his precision and logical, cold approach. Makes me wonder if two different people created the tape."

It goes on for another 45 minutes. No one builds on another's idea: just a series of individual outbursts, jumping from one idea to another, a series of fragmented discussions, far from any success. I called for a break.

People disappeared to bathrooms, offices or to the outdoors for a smoke. A disappointing session. We had explored a few good ideas but had not made any progress. We had to jump into a different pattern or break out of our current thinking. It did not take long for people to drift back. I needed to get them on to a different mindset, a wilder track, something outlandish to generate fresh the ideas. I gave it a try. "Here's what I think: we're listening to sex recordings, and Robin Hood collected samples from four different individuals at the various stages from sexual anticipation to the final moments."

For the first time in weeks, Manuel opened up and pumped his fist. "Of course you're right, I think I can record myself, and we can compare!"

Karen could not resist. "Problem is Manuel we need at least 30 seconds of tape; from what I hear that exceeds your capacity."

They all started on Manuel, and I was pleased to see him roll with the abuse. This is what I wanted, out of the rut, wild ideas thrown at each other. The Historian stopped the flow. "One thing is definite: we do have an emotionally charged recording. Emotion runs through each segment, different sounds, but fear, joy or some feeling is present for 30 seconds. Maybe sex but certainly something each individual feels strongly about. Four different people maybe four different emotions."

Wes reacted. "Sure but how does this help us?"

Manuel was serious. "Just go with it, Wes. We're too early into this to know what helps and what doesn't. Let's consider this and follow the path. Let's assume it is about sex and tackle each segment separately. First, we deal with the uncontrolled laughter or giggle.

 This could be a very nervous person anticipating a good time. And he can't control his wild giggle."

I did not want them to stop on one segment and try to solve it in isolation. "Good let's proceed to the snorting."

Then various individuals shouted out ideas. "Well, could be someone getting started and getting into it …so to speak."

"And the swearing could be a release at the climax."

 "Ok, the wailing ….what about the wailing?"

"The wailing sounds like deep sorrow or loss……..may be an extreme reaction after the act…… an emotional letdown or an emotional release expressed."

The Historian, silent for some time, wanted back. "I know I'm reaching, but I think there's another dimension to this recording; as I replay the sound bites in my mind, over and over again, I become more convinced. I think I hear something else."

     He looked at me: he wanted encouragement to go ahead, and I pushed him. "Come on you know that even if you're way off, it still might stimulate the problem solving…..don't hold back."

A reluctant John continued. "I had a brother who was not insane but mentally retarded. He lived at home for a long time before he became too much for my parents. While growing up, I listened to his speech, laughter, whines, outbursts and those of his friend who came to play. What I hear on the audio clues reminds me of the tone and emotion of my brother and his friend, in particular the laughter."

Wes first off the mark. "Robin Hood is too damn smart he .."

John corrected. "No, no…. I'm not saying the recordings are of Robin Hood, I'm saying the audio clues came from individuals who are mentally challenged………….or at least that's what keeps coming back to me ………the patterns, the emotion and the loss of control."

We're all silent. Instead of branching out, we'd dried up. I called a halt. No one was happy with the session. No one bought into the Historian's idea or all too tired to follow up on it. This hadn't been very productive, not a solid idea to chase.

I summarized, "It appears we've not established a unanimous conclusion on any idea. The only theme we seem to agree on is: these segments contain a degree of emotion, possibly an extreme emotional state; this sounds feeble, as you all know.

Jesus, I don't want to wait for the next victim before we've anything solid. But, there's no point in pushing this, let's call it a day, and we will see what the Patterson neighborhood canvassing brings to the table. Thanks, everybody."

Everyone walked out of the room, except the Historian; he wanted to talk.

"Charlie, I know your crew is not happy with my last suggestion, but I had to make the statement. My brother passed away last year..... still, when I close my eyes I can hear him giggle.

I can't explain it, but that first sound bite is like a nightmare for me. When I listened to the first uncontrolled laugh, my immediate reaction was …….my God, it's John and each time I listen I become more convinced, but as I said John passed away last year……I still want to participate, if you want me."

Before I could answer, he rushed out the door and down the hall, an upset Historian. I'm not sure whether it was because of the memory of his brother or because the group never built on his suggestion.

I was also disappointed they did not try to run with his comment, wherever it may have led us. Maybe John still represented an outsider and not someone who belonged in these sessions. But I believe in John, the Historian, one of the brightest people I've ever met, a goddamn perceptive man.

I looked at the whiteboards and the various word captured in a multitude of different fonts and colors: celebrities, arithmetic series, howl, Hindu, sex tapes, strong emotion, mentally retarded. Not a solid thread to build on, not encouraging, the session one of the most disjointed we'd ever conducted, nothing.

I needed the rest of the evening to put together a game plan for tomorrow; the gray van results will be in, the neighborhood canvass completed, interviews of the Patterson family and their long-term staff completed.

Some fundamental questions: How did Robin Hood know the details of the Patterson's property security cameras? How did he know the details of our widow's porch and freezer? Too much for someone to rely on luck, not someone so damn smart. What about the missing arrow? Why change his mind? He seemed so precise; now vacillating, changing his mind in mid-stream: doesn't match the initial impression he left.

All these details and loose ends whirled around and nothing connected. Then another loose end entered and added to the mess: my weekend companion, Emma Collins, had not replied to my voice mail message. Well ok, she sent one text message: no time. Was Monk right?

Jesus Christ, I couldn't believe I let this happen.

# # #

Judge Stephen Miller, the supreme legal authority in Sector 14, the youngest Sector judge in the country, felt anything but young and powerful. Justice Reborn, the radically new system of justice, provided each Sector's judge the responsibility to effectively, and critics cried ruthlessly, apply the revised legislation and use the technical innovations to ensure safe streets. However, Stephen's personal issues for the first time in many years began to intrude and drain his reserves. In a moment, which he now classified as weakness, he confessed to his wife about an old affair; the confession appeared to be accepted until he explained that the relationship might have resulted in his being the unacknowledged father of Dr. Kate's daughter.

Because of Dr. Kate, his Sector lost some of its prestige; she and one of her assistants colluded to beat the S1 Interrogation system through a daring scheme to frame Dr. Max.

Stephen's team, actually Charlie Taylor, uncovered the deception and saved the Judge's reputation, but his reticence during the follow-up investigation and sentencing irritated many of his peers and supporters. Regional Headquarters warned him to be more open and communicate issues, reply promptly and not days after an event.

His disenchanted wife felt second to many facets of his life: his second choice as mate and second to his love of career. The affair no longer angered her, but she sensed Dr. Kate and her daughter survived and thrived in Stephen's mind. She initiated the divorce which finalized last week. It became another blow to Stephen's reputation, another failure. His distractors whispered and labeled him: an old-fashioned academic who struggled with the values and morals of an evolving culture, which championed right vs. wrong, black vs. white, no room for gray.

Yesterday he released his Board's recommendation: the decommissioning of prisons required one more year. This resulted in more calls from angry executives at Regional: even though the arithmetic proved the case, politics often overran logic, and his reputation remained vulnerable to more backstabbing.

To conclude an uneasy week, a friend told him that Doug Brewster had been visiting Regional offices, reason unknown. That son of a bitch with brass balls. Stephen was sure Brewster had some self-promotional scheme in play.

Even though his fast-tracked career seemed threatened, Stephen was not overly concerned with the politics around Regional headquarters. These political games came with the position. He accepted this pressure cooker.

His concern centered on his inability to regain his balance and composure. It was now this personal struggle, which often found him questioning his role and the direction of his life.

CHAPTER 12: FULL BOARD MEETING

The special Board meeting made provision for one deputy from each Division to attend. The extras included: Emma, soon to step down as head of Forensics, Jessie Lopez from Legal and Charlie because the Chief assumed there would be questions about Robin Hood. Judge Stephen, as a standard practice, allowed ample time for all to circulate; he believed this direct interface provided the human contact necessary to resolve minor irritations and possibly prevented the emergence of the bigger issues.

Dr. Jerry King sparkled as the main attraction, everyone anxious to get a little closer, get his measure, and hear his informal small talk. Other than by reputation, no one knew the man and hence he enjoyed an instant attraction like any novelty. Emma Collins made the introductions. One surprise, which surfaced during the presentations: Emma and Dr. King studied at the same University, he at the start of a graduate program when she enrolled as a freshman. Charlie noted this piece of Emma's university experience slipped her mind during her summary at their evening meal.

The Judge typically strove for a brisk business tone, but today wanted a more open air; he sensed there would be numerous complicated and cumbersome meetings in the coming weeks.

"Good morning everyone, please be seated. I promise not to keep you very long. A couple of points from our last meeting: first, Region finally accepted our assessment and agreed to a full year to clear Fort Green plus a two-year target for the Sector. Good news for all, but I know it will still be a challenging goal. However, they did relax their objectives for repeat offenders; the new directive: pursue obvious cases but don't go on fishing expeditions in hopes of ferreting out the guilty.

First order of new business: I want to welcome Dr. Jerry King to our team as the new Director of the Forensic Division. Jerry as many of you know built an impressive career with extensive experience in both North America and Europe; in fact, we stole him from the university in Paris.

We need his leadership as we decommission Fort Green and complete our Sector. For the next two years, his regular companion will be Jessie Lopez, our Coordination Manager.

One recurring problem remains the time delays encountered when we try to contact and bring in Watchers to participate in the S3 memory scans. Jessie recruited some university students to add to our temporary staff pool; this team will be used to expedite the tracking of relatives and arresting detectives.

A heads up: if your Division receives a request to provide people as a Watcher or for any other reason, you must treat it as your priority. Each S3 memory scan continues to be our largest bottleneck, from the additional 72-hour wait to the assembling of a Watcher group."

Charlie thought about the one time he served as a Watcher. These Watchers, familiar with the prisoner's life story, assisted the Historian during the memory scan. The rapid assessment of each memory stream, retrieved from the convict, meant the probe could be moved further into the future or to go back in time. For Charlie, his session resulted in his first favorable contact with Emma.

"Last appointment for today: Since I talked him into delaying his retirement, Bill Thompson has been acting Commissioner of the Prison Division. Yesterday Regional endorsed this as a permanent appointment: in charge of the prison population through this transition. We're lucky to have him and his years of experience. Welcome, Bill."

As the platitudes continued, Charlie tuned out and looked over the new appointments. He thought: how ironic, Bill Thompson, or Uncle Willie as the prisoners called him, an early vocal critic of Justice Reborn now positioned in a leadership role; still, he agreed with the appointment. Over the years, Uncle Willie earned a reputation as a straight shooter, knew the system, understood the prison culture and had the confidence of the prisoners.

When it came to Jessie, the homicide detective hesitated. He knew the man: smart and a hard worker but also very ambitious. The word on the street labeled Jessie as someone eager to please his immediate supervisor instead of dealing with the issue.

Most of Charlie's attention focused Dr. Jerry King. He stared at a handsome man, well over six feet tall, slim, dark complexion, well dressed, articulate, a smile which never stopped, continually dropping French phrases into his conversation. What the hell was de rigueur? Next what about mise-en-scène?

Worse, Emma and Dr. King appeared very comfortable with each other. Just his imagination? They behaved like a couple of high school students doing a shared homework assignment, each invading the others space, heads almost touching, as they formulated replies to the questions from the Board members. Son of a bitch.

The meeting finished and the Judge asked, "Is there anything else warranting some discussion, I want to keep this short because of our workloads?"

Doug Brewster, head of the Legal Division, harbored an unconcealed dislike for Charlie, who reciprocated. Although Doug knew to tread with care because an exchange with Charlie could become ugly in seconds, one inappropriate word would do it; he was not going to let this opportunity pass.

"Judge Stephen, this Robin Hood case should be discussed; it's far from an ordinary murder case, members of our elite society are being targeted. It appears to me we should consider establishing a Task Force to include staff from Legal and Forensic to monitor progress."

The Chief, aware of Doug's intent and his history with Charlie, responded before Charlie could. "You're correct Doug this is special but, on the other hand, we're early into the investigation, still chasing some clues, still gathering facts and so far we only have one victim. We're active and not in a holding pattern. I share your concerns about the Patterson family and the rest of the community."

Brewster was not going to let this go. "Have you considered issuing a general warning about this guy and his targeted victims? A warning would allow people to reassess their security and change some habits. Robin Hood seems to be a very nasty and intelligent individual. We need our best resources on this case; it's beyond a simple homicide."

The Judge intervened. He, aware of Doug and his motives, wanted to end the exchange before it escalated. "Chief I think it would be wise to issue a general warning, nothing extreme which might generate some panic, just an alert. If there're any further cases, you can release additional notices to reflect the new conditions. Other than that, I think we can leave it to the Chief and Charlie to hunt this man and ensure our safety. Now I wish to adjourn and allow everyone to tackle their overflowing job jars. Thank you all."

The crowded meeting room started to empty. Minor traffic jams occurred as staff left through the one exit door. Charlie tried to corner Red, but she shook him off, both with her eyes and a headshake. She left the meeting and walked down the hall with Dr. King. Did he have his arm around her shoulders? Couldn't be. Son of a bitch. Was he seeing things? It appeared Monk was right.

Charlie hadn't been on the wrong page; shit, he'd been in the wrong book.

CHAPTER 13: A LONG SHOT

Charlie collapsed at his desk and felt useless. From the outside, the hustle and activity impressed but reality equaled nothing. Robin left them with nothing except body parts, a body, a head and the audio clues, which no one could decode or understand. A complete brick wall, no meaningful direction, a depressing zero. If another abduction occurred, they would be in the deep stuff clinging to a series of disparate loose ends.

When his phone rang, his pick-up was fast and abrupt; an anxious Historian wanted to talk. "Good morning Charlie, I have a favor to ask."

"Go ahead let's hear it."

"I understand no one in your brainstorming group supports my idea on the audio clues, but I think we should chase it down. My brother spent the last five years of his life in the Complex, which takes care of around 80 to 100 clients. Dr. Reed, the psychologist in charge, became a good friend of mine; we lunch on a regular basis, go to the occasional opera, that sort of thing. Anyway, I think we can trust him......I'd like him to hear the recordings, our audio clues, and give us his opinion.

Dr. Reed works with the mentally challenged crowd on a daily basis; he's a smart man, quick and easy to get along with. My favor: I'd like to take the audio clues out to the Complex and allow him to hear them. His job demands superior listening skills; I believe the nature of his work can help with at least the first clue."

Charlie respected John, but this move meant diverting staff for a long shot with some risk. This psychologist might leak comments to the press. Homicide did not want the audio clues to become public knowledge.

Years ago a few dedicated academics created and promoted the Complex, a combined care facility, and a full-time research center. It was a spin off a university program, which just kept growing until it became an impressive set of buildings and top researchers with an international reputation for excellence. Its original title was one of those ten-word bureaucratic designations, which over time adjusted to a point where now everyone just referred to it as the Complex. Its original mandate was first to provide a home for the mentally handicapped who could no longer live at home. Everyone admitted to the Complex had to agree to participate in their research program which included monitoring development or deterioration as individuals aged. One of their most successful components was the development of exercises, games, and puzzles, which proved to stimulate and enhance the social development of individuals under their care

While John continued to explain the Complex, Charlie waved Wes and Pameela into his office. Finally, he gave into one his to-hell-with-it decisions. "OK let's do it; you phone the Complex and set up an appointment. I'll have one of the detectives pick you up and bring the recordings. Let's make it today."

"Thanks, Charlie."

Charlie, now even more impressed with Pameela's beauty and poise, swung around to face the pair. "Pameela, I apologize for not inviting you to our brainstorming session; I just put out a general call, and you'd already left the building. Unfortunately, you didn't miss much."

"I gave the Mayor an oral report: short and not very sweet. She's upset about Henry Patterson; the family is one of her backers. As well, she knew Henry as a campaign worker, liked him and now the Chief's warning to the public may cause more anxiety. Anything new?"

"To be honest very little. But Wes I'd like you to accompany John to the Complex with the audio clues…"

Before Charlie finished Wes, in an atypical reaction, almost erupted. "A horse shit waste of time, I've better things to do. I know you think he's brilliant but to be able to determine someone's IQ from listening to a 30-second giggle is impossible; send someone else, please."

Wes's outburst set Charlie back; then he noticed Pameela, who must have been briefed about the brainstorming session. She stood next to him and clearly on Wes's side of this assessment. He tried to explain his rationale for the move. "A smart guy? More than that believe me. He is the official Historian for S3 memory scans, dangerous exercises which can end up in a death. He completed months of specialized training, is extremely perceptive, regularly makes quick decisions based on short segments of video from the brain scan readouts, all of this under the pressure of a pending execution. Also, all Historians go to a spring retraining and upgrading sessions each year, not all of them retain their position.

I only participated in one S3 Interrogation, and I can tell you it requires all your attention and awareness. So I know he is quick and unique."

"I know all this; I just don't want the assignment. Why not send Karen? She seemed more excited about the idea than any of the rest of us."

"OK, I'll send Karen. And I understand the odds but what else do we have, except long shots? The gray van? Prior knowledge about the security system? A snooper hanging around a freezer?"

Wes mumbled thanks: then he and Pameela left the office. Charlie continued to be uncomfortable with what he perceived was developing between the two of them. He knew Wes would resent any interference. But this relationship with Pameela could only end one way, and Wes would lose. There was no doubt about this one: Wes would be hurt.

Was he just super sensitive because of his recent experience? Why did he give in so easily and assign Karen?

# # #

A few hours later, Karen and John waited in a very comfortable reception area at the Complex. The sun streamed into the central hallway, shining bright, warm and sparkling; the glistening foyer reminded Karen of a young child after a vigorous scrubbing from a mother. John used to functioning as the Historian, a position of authority, was restless in this setting. He, surprisingly, worried about the upcoming interview and could not control his hand-wringing, a bad habit he couldn't shake.

The facilities impressed Karen, not extravagant but well beyond the institutional design of a research facility or residence: smart staff, well groomed, pleasant with a purpose and direction to their activities. But she wanted to wrap this up and get back to the station; she agreed with Wes but did not share this with Charlie, who she knew struggled with his appalling start to this case. She considered voicing her doubts, but Charlie was firm: go and follow the wild hunch.

The Complex presented a rather bland name for such highly recognized research facility. It started up about 10 or 15 years old, as far as Karen could remember, and still maintained a long waiting list, still difficult for people to be accepted as full-time residents. Its primary targets were the mentally retarded who proved too difficult for aging parents or home care, their strong preference younger patients. The objective was a group which could be observed over a lifetime, as they participated in a variety of programs. Karen did not know much more about the place, and John did not appear to be ready to accept questions or small talk. They sat, waited, absorbed in their own thoughts.

 Karen alternated between the Robin Hood puzzle and her affair with the Chief. In this brief period of silence away from the station, she wondered how to end it, and if she wanted to stop it. Then a moment of panic when she thought about the police grapevine which could devastate the two of them. They allowed this. Had they both been so desperate for affection they were willing to take such a risk? It appeared an uneven contest: biology so powerful it overrode common sense. Goddamn it.

Finally, the receptionist led them down the hall to Dr. Reed's office. He was the Director and John's friend; the young woman stopped in front of an empty room and said, "Dr. Reed has been delayed but will be here shortly; also, his secretary is away today, and I'm handling two jobs, so I apologize for the wait. Can I get you some coffee or water? No? Well, Dr. Reed said you're to go right in and wait in his office."

The room looked like a typical manager's office with a big desk and corner windows; one significant difference: two walls completely lined with books from floor to ceiling. Karen noted a complete library devoted to some aspect of the mind, psychology, mental health and some legal texts. An extensive paper library stood out, definitely a rarity in this age of instant information available online. Dr. Reed may be different. Then she noticed a private entrance.

Karen waited for John to open up and tell her more about his association with the Complex, but the man resided in a different space. Jesus, was he even aware of her presence? She decided to wait it out, besides they, earlier, agreed she would play the lead role.

The private entrance door opened, and small man, about 5 feet 6 inches, with slight build entered the room. The doctor in his late fifties with some classic graying of his temples had a big smile for the Historian. "Hi John, good to see you again and I do remember it is your turn to buy lunch." The two laughed and shook hands.

John said, "Alex, let me introduce Karen Zubik; she is a senior detective with our Sector's police force, and I'll let her explain our mission."

"Hello Karen, please call me Alex unless you're here to arrest me then call me Dr. Reed." He smiled at his joke, and so did Karen. Then she jumped right into the assignment but did note John failed to introduce her as a homicide detective.

"Alex, I'm here to ask for your assistance, but there are conditions. First, you must agree to keep this meeting confidential, second, understand there're limits in how much I can disclose; and last, there are severe consequences if you discuss this case with others. Can you accept these terms? And, please note I'm recording this conversation."

Alex looked at John who nodded for him to agree; he smiled, intrigued by Karen's proposition. "Boy, that's some introduction. Sounds like more fun than I've had so far today; yes I agree and am ready to participate."

Karen started the session. "We came to you because John knows you and states your expertise in the field of mental retardation. But I would like to hear and record a summary of your academic qualifications and work experience."

Karen, always well prepared, already had and read a complete resume on Dr. Reed. Now she wanted to observe him, listen to him and assess this expert, if this goes further, Charlie will want her opinion. Dr. Reed relaxed, looked at both of them, thought about this mysterious visit, conditions, and then started.

"I'm not sure what you're interested in, but I'll start, and you can interrupt and question me or ask for more. I'm sure John knows most of this; I apologize for boring you, so a high-level review: after high school, I attended three different universities to obtain a Ph.D. I did spend some years in between college sessions working with the mentally challenged and the criminally insane. The result, I was a little older than the average student when I received my Ph.D. I'm a doctor of clinical psychology with a specialty in the field of mental retardation."

John interrupted. "Karen, he's too modest; from the time of his Ph.D. dissertation to the present he gets continuous requests for consultation and presentations from across the world; come on Alex more detail."

Alex kept smiling, and Karen thought it must be part of a practiced bedside manner to keep a happy face. "John's correct. The Complex generates numerous inquiries. One of my successes has been the development of activity programs which keep people challenged and happy without causing extreme frustration: both mental exercises and physical games which are modified to match a particular IQ range.

I was also fortunate to be appointed the first and only Director of this Complex; this all occurred during the planning stages hence my input into the general design and unique facilities. John's brother stayed with us for the last five years of his life. I think John can tell you what a difference it can make when we don't have to rely on large doses of drugs to manage people. It goes beyond a reduction in costs; people stay happier and even more surprising….. healthier."

Karen interrupted. "Alex, are you directly involved with selecting occupants, rating them, conducting IQ tests, evaluating their family environment?"

        "I have a staff to do the initial screening, but then I'm the one who makes the final selection as to whether the candidate will be a good fit for the Complex. IQ is rather a limiting term, and we do many more tests; IQ just becomes a quick shorthand assessment, a starting point. It's interesting for how long the term has lived on and remains in daily use, even by professionals."

Karen liked the man. He was obviously brilliant and sincere about his role and the mission of the Complex; he certainly possessed the qualifications they needed.

"Again I apologize for being so cryptic. We have some audio recordings and would like to play them for you and hear your comments ……anything that comes to mind. Are you ready? All right? Good, I'll start the sound unit."

John noticed she never mentioned the sound might have emanated from the mentally retarded community. This is a conclusion, which would have to come from Alex without any prompting. Karen started the unit and watched Dr. Reed concentrate. After the first playing he never spoke, he just gave her a hand signal to repeat the play; this happened four times, and then he signaled for a stop.

"Dr. Reed, anything which comes to mind as you listen to this material? Even if your impressions are vague, even a tentative opinion may help us."

Alex Reed frowned, stood very still and looked at both John and Karen for a long time, his response slow and quiet, almost angry. "I don't know what the hell the two of you are pulling. Some kind of joke? If so, it's not funny."

John spoke first. "I assure you this is not a joke or some game or insult; just believe me. We're serious." Karen thought Alex's temperature dropped a few degrees after John's assurance; she had her fill of this game and wanted to get back to the office. Dr. Reed paced around the room: no longer had angry but still upset. After a few walks across the carpet, he began again, "I know what John does for a living and Karen you are a detective, so I accept John's assurance that this is very serious. But I don't know or understand the context."

He appeared to be stalling; he knew something. What's the problem? What's he afraid of? Even though Karen was impatient, she decided not to push but to wait for him. One more walk across the office and he started. "Karen you asked me 'if anything comes to mind'. Well, it's a helluva a lot more than that, and there may be some legal or ethical questions, which I might be facing. Damn it this is close to home."

There was another long pause. Karen looked at John who also appeared confused. What goes with the good doctor? All they asked: do any of these sounds mean anything to him? An impression on the giggle. John decided to push. "Alex you know you can trust me; we're not trying to trap you or compromise you; there's nothing devious about the request. I thought the giggle might have originated from a mentally retarded individual. Everyone else thought it impossible to assess IQ from a 30-second sound bite.

I suggested you as a potential resource. I thought if you were unaware of my conclusion but came to the same conclusion it would be a reliable indicator I was right and our giggler fit my assessment."

Karen, too late, tried to interrupt; John promised to keep his mouth shut. Now, he'd given Alex the answer. How good would his opinion be now? But, she could see that John's comments placated Alex, and he began once more.

"I believe you and thank you, at least I now understand part of this mystery. Yes, I concur with your assessment about the giggler; in fact, I can go one step further and identify him. The individual giggler on the recording is one of our permanent residents a young man by the name of Barry Cristof."

No one spoke. Karen, who ten seconds ago prepared to walk away, could only think: if Charlie were here, he would say, "Jesus Christ, didn't I tell you the Historian is unique."

CHAPTER 14: Charlie's Log: AN S1 INTERROGATION

Wes hustled down the hall, from one office to the other. "Have you seen Pameela?"

I tried to sound unconcerned. "I think she left to see the Mayor. Slow down. Keep calm." Then I went over the line. "Wes, you know it's best to keep away; give her some space; she's in a different league from us grunts."

Not what he wanted to hear. "I'm a big boy and know what I'm doing; she's just fine, and she knows the score; I understand you already gave her a warning. What the hell are you trying to do? Leave it alone."

After the outburst, he hustled down the stairs to the cafeteria, continuing his search for Pameela. Bloody hell, for sure they'd tumbled into the sack. I knew now: it progressed beyond the point of any rational argument, best to let it play out, regardless of the future pain and disruption. Besides, after my recent experience, I didn't feel qualified to dispense advice about relationships.

# # #

Two hours later, I stood in front of Judge Stephen, trying to get clearance to conduct an S1 Interrogation on our giggler. The Judge read the formal application and requested clarification.

"As I understand the application: Barry Cristof, who lives at the Complex, is the man whose giggle fits as your first audio clue; and, our technical staff confirmed the identification with his voice print. You do not consider Barry a suspect but believe he knows Robin Hood. His parents are dead, and Dr. Reed as his legal guardian is legally in a position to sign the clearance papers. What I don't understand: why is it necessary to use the drugs, if we have a cooperative witness?"

"Judge, a couple of problems: first Barry is very high strung, the nervous giggle is one manifestation of his nervous state. Strangers heighten his condition, so an interrogation with strangers will be a tense situation. The S1 drug mixture serves both as tranquilizer as well as increasing motivation to cooperate."

"I'm extremely reluctant to allow these drugs to be administered to someone who is not a suspect; this could set a precedent and open doors for more extensive use. I view this cocktail as a robust set of chemicals, and I'm not convinced we even understand how they work on our systems.

Oh yes, I know Dr. Max proposed some fine theories, but no scientist has conducted extensive studies on the long-term effects of even one application. It would not be unusual for some unanticipated and undesirable side reaction to surface years after the first administration."

"Judge, he represents our one solid clue. Also, I think Dr. Reed will only give us one shot at Barry. He doesn't want us coming back with a series of repetitive interrogations; Barry is too high strung to be able to cope with a number of strangers probing and pushing him with aggressive questions. Dr. Reed believes the best approach for Barry will be one interview in a tranquilized state; this is why he signed the clearance document."

The Judge got up from his desk, walked to his favorite window and looked down at the courtyard, another warm day and cloudless sky. He made the decision. "The best I'm prepared to do is to allow a half strength mix of the drug combination. If you can get Forensics to change my mind, I will reconsider. But I think with a cooperative person this dosage should assist in calming the participant and maintain his desire to cooperate."

I knew that was the best I'd get; he made his notations on my submission, and I tore out the door. Half strength. Going to work? I knew the Judge, and it would take Dr. Max to change his mind. We did not have time; I would run with it.

# # #

Pameela had requested to be present at our first interrogation in this case, but all my calls went to her answering service; Wes stopped looking but stayed at the station, brooding and in an ugly mood.

When we got to the Complex, Dr. Reed was absent but had arranged for his assistant Dr. Alfred Villa to be our guide. Villa proved to be challenging and different, a rather weird character, a chocolate addict with a mug of hot chocolate glued to his hand: tall, goatee, arrogant, academic asshole.

"I don't understand the need for these drugs. And, second I'm Barry's primary caregiver and should have been consulted, even this half strength approach represents a danger to this young man. I can't allow you access to Barry."

I produced the Judge's directive, which included the clearance provided by Dr. Reed. He eventually caved and called to have Barry brought to the playroom. Karen previously discussed an approach with Dr. Reed and discovered Happy, Barry's nickname, loved soft drinks, in particular, the old fashion bottled Coke. Our Forensic techs put the dosage together and mixed it in the bottle of Coke. We thought a woman would present a softer face for Happy and Karen became the interrogator.

Villa continued with his hard ass attitude. "Detective Taylor, I can only allow one detective to conduct the interrogation and be in the room; you'll have to watch in the adjacent observation room via the two-way mirrors. As well our senior nurse, Helen Demarce, must stay with Barry."

Helen looked about 45 years old, not particularly attractive but a pleasant woman, and she certainly connected with Barry. When she brought him into the playroom, he maintained a strong grip on her forearm. She didn't have a problem peeling off his grip and setting him on one of the large lounges. Happy logged in at 27 years old, looked about 14, a thin beard, jeans, a hoodie, and basketball runners. He never spoke, just looked around with an anxious grin on his face.

I stayed in the observation room; Villa introduced Karen as another doctor who wanted to have a chat. As soon as she handed Happy the Coke, she became his friend. He eagerly gulped his Coke, the conversation light, Helen and Karen talking about the Complex and the weather.

The Complex classified Barry's condition as mild mental retardation; I think that means his IQ ranged in the mid-50s. He, as part of a group outing, participated in regular jaunts to places like the zoo, the park, and the swimming pool. Socially he could be a problem and got excited quickly. Dr. Reed's example: last week, when the main gates at the zoo did not open on time and a lineup formed, Barry literally fought his way through the crowd to get to the head of the line. His pushing and high pitched giggle frightened the group.

Karen sat at his level, and when he reached out to touch her, she held his hand and smiled, no questions, more waiting. However, it did not take long for the drug to take over. Karen let him lie back on the lounge. The relaxing impact stopped the giggles, and he remained silent. Karen beside him started on the prearranged questions. Did he remember anyone recording him? Did anyone approach him during one of his outings?

I found it difficult to understand his hushed responses, but his key answer landed loud and clear. Within minutes Karen signaled: done. Happy was euphoric, so relaxed he fell asleep and slid off the lounge. Nurse Helen bent down and with no assistance had him back on the couch. When lifting heavy weights, the technique is as important as strength, and Helen demonstrated years of experience in handling dead weights.

We stopped because Barry told us: Dr. Villa recorded his giggle.

Villa confirmed the response. He recorded for his students and, in fact, recorded most patients at the Complex, not only gigglers; the recordings captured fragments of conversations, angry outbursts, or whatever behavior the patient exhibited.

As well, his recordings lasted longer than 30 seconds. The recorded conversations or outbursts he linked to the individual's personality and IQ: a discussion point for instructor and students. Villa continued.

"All students in my classes receive of these recordings and have been for some years. These recordings could be scattered all over the country. You know students do graduate and chase employment opportunities."

I wonder why he never shared this with us at the beginning. Also, I realized another alternative: someone at one of the public outings could have recorded his giggle. The entire situation made it impossible to trace a source; too many people, scattered across the country, had copies.

Some small progress: at yesterday's conclusion, Dr. Reed agreed with the Historian: the remaining three audio clues reflected people with emotional issues, but not residents of the Complex. When pressed, Reed guessed: all recordings appeared to be associated with psychological problems. People under the care of a professional? Maybe. But a long stretch for a 30-second sound bite.

Jesus, I hated this Dr. Villa.

# # #

Three of them enjoyed pizza and cold beer: Terry, Manuel, and John, from Vice. The conversation proceeded in a stop and start mode as they dove into the pizza or drank from the frosty glasses. Terry confronted John. "I hear you guys did the teeth scene again."

"Yah. A bloody riot. Webster got word that Charlie had a date with Emma Collins and asked all those who still had the false teeth to bring them; he said we might catch Charlie in the hallway by the front entrance."

"You know he never bit her…just went for a few kisses on her bare shoulders and back."

"Sure we all know, but this is more fun. And, I am curious about your boss. Is he really a crazy son of a bitch, like I keep hearing?"

"Yes he is, but we're glad to have him on our side and remember he has the Judge as his rabbi. And everyone knows Dr. Max was damn lucky Charlie was assigned his case. I think only someone as gutsy as Charlie could have searched in that direction for the answers. I heard the Judge call him an iconoclast......whatever the hell that is."

"I also hear he can drive the Chief to the wall."

"Yes, he can and does on a regular basis."

There was a short break in the conversation, as everyone finished and wiped sauce off their fingers and chins. John stood up. "I have to run guys. Good having lunch with you, and you can tell Charlie he doesn't have to worry about another tooth scene. The Chief ordered Webster to ditch the teeth, or the next bite will be on his ass. See yah."

CHAPTER 15: ANOTHER ONE

A disenchanted group of detectives struggled through the morning; the team was organized and the assignments clear. Unfortunately, all the clues seemed like long shots. In addition, Pameela's absence continued to be a distraction, particularly for Wes. Charlie's plan called for a visit to every institution, which housed, or worked with, the mentally retarded.

Detectives would interview front line staff. The plan: clinic staff would hear the audio clues, with no explanation as to context or reason for the exercise. A simple question followed: do you recognize any of the voices?

Next on the list: visits to private psychologists and psychiatrists with the same routine. Sam Taylor, Charlie's brother and practicing psychologist, vetted the lists of institutions and practitioners.

Wes, in an ugly mood, let everyone know. "What a damn long shot is this? We got lucky once, but this is just crazy, beyond a long shot."

"You might be right, but this is all we have. A slender thread. I'll work with Sam and walk through the list of individual practitioners while you lead the canvassing through the institutions. And, look I need some enthusiasm; you bloody well know this is all we have. In fact, I think we might have to consider the mentally ill which widens the scope. Don't look like that. I'm just speculating; I believe there is some connection. I'm sure the general direction is right ....except I can't put it together......we're on an edge but still too far away.

 Are we dealing with a former institutionalized resident now living on his own? Doesn't make sense; with that background, he could never plan and carry this out. Maybe an old staff member? All pure speculation. If we solve the other three sound clues, perhaps the thread will become evident. But we can't wait for more bodies to provide more clues."

Muddled thinking didn't help Wes, logical arguments meaningless. He couldn't drive Pameela from his mind. Although not pacified, Wes understood Charlie's concerns about their relationship. He knew his affair with Pameela played as a long shot, but he was prepared to pay the price. And, if it all fell apart, Charlie would be supportive and not be in the I-told-you mode. The time to move arrived: Charlie needed support, and the team needed Wes.

"Ok Charlie Ok, we've started. Manuel created copies of the four audio clues but omitted the message from Robin Hood. Karen is harassing the Chief for some more staff, and we hope to be ready within the next 30 minutes. I assume you're going to keep Terry on the gray van chase, and he 'll not be available to assist with the canvass."

"Just go when ready but check with me every hour, and let me know if we get any hits."

After Wes had left, Charlie used the momentary isolation for further reflection. His problem: Emma kept surfacing as an emotional distraction, which he could not shake; was it because he cared so much or was it pride? She walked away from a weekend he viewed as a meeting of the minds, in any case something special.

Relationship issues invaded the Homicide department: in addition to Charlie, Karen, and the Chief struggled with their affair, and Wes could not walk away from Pameela. It would all make for a good TV afternoon soap, almost a comedy if it were not for the fact that in all cases the emotions ran deep.

His isolation didn't last long, within a few minutes the Chief was in his office. "I authorized Karen to put five rookie officers on to an overtime shift for the canvass; I know the odds, but I agree we have to try. Have you read the medical report on Henry's body and head?"

"Yes it's here, and it doesn't help. We have nothing: no fingerprints, no loose hairs, no DNA, a complete bust; he washed the body before release: and, as Wes said Robin is one mean son of a bitch.

Henry was cold sober when his head came off, no drugs, and no alcohol in his system. He was alive, when the head was removed. Doc confirms a chainsaw took off his head. The place of execution must be a blood bath. Jesus Christ you don't want to get onto this guy's radar. Shit, he removes your body parts while you watch him. Son of a bitch."

"We have any better idea of when or how he grabbed Henry?"

"No, nothing. Henry lived in his own apartment, and typically the family only connected about once a week or every two weeks. His mother shopped in that neighborhood and stopped at his apartment. Since he wasn't answering his phone, she convinced the super to open the apartment; the place looked like a typical bachelor's scene, no evidence of a struggle but no Henry.

He maintained an independent lifestyle and bristled at any perceived intrusion; so she waited another day before filing a missing person's report. Medical staff thinks Robin had him for seven to ten days, never fed him but provided the water to keep him alive.

I don't believe he kept Henry for more than a week. This is a well-organized and planned killing. He got the audio clues to us, delivered the ears and fingers to the freezer, got the head to the Pattersons and dropped the body in the park, all within a few days. My assessment: when he makes the next kidnapping we'll have a very narrow window to work with and find the victim, five or six days at the most."

"Charlie, if Henry wasn't drugged and fully conscious during all this bloody cosmetic surgery, he must have been screaming during the entire time. I know I would if someone cut off my toes and then my ears. The screams we hear on the recording are valid and not artificially enhanced.

With the loud howling, let alone a screeching chainsaw where would Robin Hood be working? A regular apartment? Not likely. Even a standard residential home would have trouble absorbing all the screams; at least you would be taking a chance, and I don't think this guy takes those kinds of chances."

"I agree, so we search for an isolated property or some facility which is soundproof. Again we have a clue but no headway."

"You know what is sick? When I described the scenario, I almost said: he would be screaming his head off. "

# # #

The next audio message arrived at the Mayor's office. Charlie, the Chief, and the Mayor sat around a small, low coffee table where the recorder resided: the Mayor completely shaken had trouble speaking. "I don't want to hear this again but feel I must, just in case there is something I can add to assist. Are we ready?" She pressed the start button as if it was contaminated and the horror began to fill the room. The message, again, consisted of a computer-generated voice and some live audio:

"I wish to introduce Pameela Sharma who has been wealthy and privileged all her life; this is about to change because she is now a quest of Robin Hood."

The rest of the recording embodied a series of overlays, an intermingling of sounds, a mixture: first the music from the Robin Hood theme song, muffled humming, occasional off-key singing, and bursts of laughter. The worst part: Pameela's screams which came in waves, at the end her heavy sobs and crying. Finally an abrupt sign-off.

"Later in the week I will distribute some of today's harvest, you know the parts. They will be going to a less fortunate family. Catch me if you can; I believe you have identified the giggler. Good job."

Even after the third replay, Charlie's thoughts refused to coalesce. The son of a bitch knew about the Complex; and how in the hell did he get Pameela? An angry Mayor turned to the Chief.

"How in the hell did you allow this bastard to grab Pameela? She worked with your department, Goddamn it; she was with your staff."

The Chief looked at Charlie to reply; he tried his best, "We knew she had the right profile as a possible victim, but it never occurred to me to provide her with any special protection. In any case, special protection was probably impossible. There are too many people in the city who qualify. She never showed up for work yesterday but since she sets her own hours we never tried to locate her, other than leaving a voice message as to our location and inviting her to join us."

"Is this same guy who killed Henry Patterson?"

"Yes, no doubt ....there's a few changes to his pattern, but he's the one."

The Chief briefed the Mayor on their progress at the Complex and the current canvassing of other institutions and psychologists and psychiatrists; he did not disclose that no other sound bite had been identified. Charlie listened to the two of them discuss the case and then determine who would notify Pameela's family. He knew he had one other arduous task this afternoon: best to get Wes alone, not in front of the squad.

The Mayor insisted that the Chief release a significantly stronger warning message to the public; the Chief agreed but did not mention he'd need the Judge's concurrence. No matter what happened next, the Chief and Charlie knew it was only going to get worse. Unless a miracle occurred, Pameela would be dead by the end of the week, and her head delivered to the Sharma residence; Charlie already started planning a surveillance team to stake out the house.

As they walked back to the station he reviewed his plan with the Chief; both veterans understood the realities of the situation. Although the bastard changed his routine, the delivery of the head was a certainty, along with the body dumped in some remote location.

Why did he deliver a horror recording ahead of time instead with the head, like the delivery to the Pattersons? Did he know about her Homicide assignment? Why'd he not used the arrow through the bull's eye on the chest target of Henry Patterson? How did the bastard know about the giggler? Why select Pameela? Does he know the family?

CHAPTER 16: Charlie's Log: A BAD AFTERNOON

The Chief was in my office and talking loud and fast. "Charlie, this is shit! You have nothing. That bastard will be chain sawing his way through Pameela before the end of the week."

A bad afternoon. It's a day after we found out Robin had Pameela. The Chief turned into a bear, one degree away from getting himself locked up at one of the institutions we were canvassing.

Although I had some doubts about the assignment, I kept a surveillance team, at the Sharma residence, waiting for the delivery of body parts. Robin was a shrewd son of a bitch, and delivery to the Sharma home seemed too obvious a move. Would he make it that easy?

Our canvass of institutions, although not complete, appeared to be a useless exercise. Cooperation not an issue. Many treated it as a game or diversion for their staff and put together a group to listen to the four sound bites; we never interfered with any approach, even those that bordered on horseplay.

We did not want to alert anyone as to how serious this 'game' was; we never revealed the sound bites came from Robin. Next step in the plan was to question individuals who ran solo practices from a single or group office.

I tried to keep Wes close to me, but it proved impossible, at least he stayed in the station and not out in the street. He was a focused and furious man, only a matter of time before I pulled him off this case

I felt helpless; the only useful action appeared to be to wait for the delivery of some part of Pameela. I now realized how much I had come to like her: good looking, smart, and a straight shooter. My personal problems or my one particular problem, Emma, served as a compounder: stirring my black mood and driving it deeper into an ugly zone. I'd been stupid, or desperate enough to leave her another voice mail message; all I got in response was a short text message: no time to talk.

My body chemistry needed rebalancing, and it wasn't going to happen as I sat at my desk. My endorphin levels hit bottom and until adjusted I was not safe. It could evolve into another elevator incident. That's the one when I told the former Commissioner of Prisons to keep his wife out of strange hotel rooms; then I pantomimed how an extensive hose rinse would preserve the hygiene of her crotch. Wes ranked the hose rinse dance as one of my best top ten.

Sam phoned. "Come on home. I'm in your kitchen ready to start supper. My good wife's gone to another India seminar; this damn trip is going to be expensive. She's possessed with the culture.

Anyway, I'm doing all the cooking so you can't say no."

"You're right but give me an hour. I'm going for a swim."

###

I decided to try the west side pool. I rotate my visits to the different pools in the city: before we're done, you will understand why. The city pools are not ostentatious, lots of gray concrete, some soft pastel walls, a utilitarian splendor, just my style. Jesus, I'm carrying attitude today.

I stepped through the front door and saw trouble in the form of a bunch of preschoolers. Shit. I challenged the girl at the reception. "I thought this afternoon was reserved for lane swimming."

She smiled. "You'll be able to swim. The east side pool shut down. So today there'll have to be sharing. Not to worry, this is the largest pool in the city, and they'll only be at one end."

I hurried into the locker room, not convinced, but what the hell. At least they hadn't invaded the locker room, too busy getting logged in at the front desk. The pool is large. But after about a dozen lengths the shallow end erupts into chaos with numerous screaming bodies. I was glad they were all so goddamn happy.

Always flexible, I started going crosswise, you know swim across the width, in the deep section; a couple of others joined me, and we swam in parallel mode. Shit, now three members of the senior community found us; they used shower caps to protect their blue hair, and with their float belts they permanently occupied one corner of the deep end. Time to make another adjustment.

All swimmers shifted over ten feet, and all the swimmers started again, across the width of the pool. A few more laps and another hoard arrived. It appeared an entire bloody school decided this was a good morning. For this younger set, the swimmers were apparently invisible to them. They shot down the slide without a care; and, now a lifeguard provided the rope and ball which led to the Tarzan routine. This means they swung on the damn rope and launched themselves into the middle of the deep end.

I didn't want to get arrested for mugging a child. I got out and headed for the showers. On the way out I stopped at the receptionist front desk; her tag read Sara. I tried to be civil, but I had been a bear when I got up this morning, and the kids in this pool had been poking sticks at me since I arrived. "Sara, you told me I would be able to swim, and that's not true."

She looked up at me from her monitor, a young kid, and smiled. I decided to help. "Listen, Sara, if anyone else phones and asks what the agenda is for this afternoon you tell them: It's a Fucking Zoo."

I had her attention but before she could respond the lifeguard emerged from the adjacent office. "Mister we don't use language like that around here."

Of course, I'm itching for it. "What? Don't you understand the word? Or, do you have a policy of telling lies?"

The temperature went up a few degrees, and his face turned red. I hoped the bugger would come over the counter; he was a big one, but this would make my day. Instead, he just stared at me and shook his head. I turned to Sara. "Sara, do have a pencil and paper?   Good. I want you to write this down as I dictate it: 'It's a   fucking zoo'. Now wait, you people don't know the word...... let me spell it ....ready? ...first ....an..... F .....best to make that a capital ....now.... U C K I N G......good, I can see you have it all."

The lifeguard was in complete shock, and even I was surprised that the receptionist appeared to be writing this down. I continued. "Now when someone calls and asks you know how to answer."

The best part was what came; you will find this hard to believe, but this is not a lie. The phone rang, and she answered. "Good afternoon. West Side Pool. Sara speaking how may help you?"

There was a pause as she listened to the request, then she picked up the paper she had been writing on and appeared to read from it. "It's a fucking zoo." There was a pause and then again. "No sir you heard me right….It's a fucking zoo….good bye."

She hung up and looked up at me with the biggest smile I'd seen in ages; the lifeguard was behind her and couldn't see her face. All my ugliness evaporated, and I matched her smile; I gave her the thumbs up and headed for the car.

Jesus, the day brightened a fraction. I'd send a couple of yellow roses and a note. You have to appreciate the good ones when you find them.

The interior of the car was like a warming oven. As I drove home and to Sam's meal, my euphoria slowly evaporated and turned into despair. I was sure within hours a delivery would arrive: Pameela's head or fingers, depending on how our killer decides to proceed.

Then my hourly nemesis. I couldn't understand Emma and that goddamn Dr. King.

CHAPTER 17: Next Delivery

Clarence always complained the noise of running water woke him, so Bev Sanchez delayed her morning shower. Life had been better before his accident and all the subsequent health problems, which resulted in a significant demotion and reduction in pay. Today he worked the 11:00 pm to 7:00 am security shift. Since they were empty nesters, they could adjust their schedules to accommodate their jobs; she worked three days a week at the hospital: Monday, Wednesday, and Friday from 3:00 pm to midnight.

So not only was his new job a financial blow it also made life an awkward rhythm for them both. She did not blame Clare. It was not his fault; not deliberate, not under his control, just Fate's random blow that forced them to adjust.

Bev prided herself in maintaining a clean and well-organized household, her motto the ancient rallying cry of many mothers: a place for everything and everything in its place. Any clutter, or what she perceived as clutter, got her motor running, and she reverted to correction mode.

She wanted to vacuum but waited; Clare still slept, later than usual, almost 1:00 pm. After starting her first load of laundry, she decided on coffee, her one and only cup of full strength caffeine laden coffee. A small island, in their kitchen, served as their eating table; this is where she started her belated breakfast routine.

When she started on the morning paper, she first noticed the small package on the table. The attached card drew her attention, and she thought Clare bought her a gift, an unusual gesture. No signature, instead on the card: a hand drawn bow and arrow with a background of what appeared to be green trees, a forest. The package opened easily, just one piece of tape across the top lid; she tipped the box, and the contents rolled onto the table.

 Later when she thought about the incident, she wondered why she hadn't screamed. On the table in front of her sat two small ears and two fingers; maybe the lack of blood reduced the shock, ears and fingers thoroughly rinsed. She never touched anything; Robin Hood's methodology monopolized the news, and she guessed the second delivery rested on her table.

First, she called the police, and then woke Clare, hoping he would not be upset and start on her.

# # #

The entire homicide team arrived within the hour. While they waited for the Forensic unit to finish, Manuel and Terry began their routine, a neighborhood canvass. Charlie and Wes walked around the perimeter; apparently, someone had jimmied the side entry door, which was impossible to see from the front sidewalk.

"Wes, alert our stake out teams at the Sharma residence: a second delivery can't be that far off, he doesn't wait too long."

Wes, almost mute, walked back to the car and started his calls; Charlie wanted him off the case but owed him too much to force the issue. Instead, he left Wes and returned to the front entry for Karen's interview of Mrs. Sanchez.

"Mrs. Sanchez is this correct? Your husband leaves for work at around 10 pm, and you don't get back from your shift until between 12:30 am and 1:00 am, correct? Next, you came in the front door, which is your usual routine; you don't use the side door in the morning."

"Yes, that's all correct. I was so tired I never even turned on the lights. I just went directly to the bedroom and asleep in minutes. I never even glanced into the kitchen."

"Mr. Sanchez, can you describe your routine when you came home?"

Clarence Sanchez, a big heavyset man, appeared grumpy, like someone who had woken too early, still trying to recover. "I got home just before 8:00 am; the bus stop is just minutes from the house. I came up the walk and used the front door, had some orange juice from the fridge.......didn't look at the table."

"Did you turn on any lights?"

"No need. Yes, it is a dark house but we have the big city street light in front of our house and our neighbor, across the back alley, uses a large yard light, which everyone complains about. So lots of light for me to get to the bedroom. I can't remember if I even looked at the table, and for sure I never went to the side door."

"Your neighbor keeps that big light on all night?"

"Yes all night, all day, 24/7. He doesn't care who complains. I don't mind because it does light up the back yard and with both of us gone it's good; I thought it might make any punks pick another spot."

Charlie left Karen to continue her interrogation and went to the backyard, all the way to the back fence to check the sight lines from the neighbor's yard to the Sanchez side entrance. After he opened the back gate and walked across the alley, he found Wes. His detective was bent over, hands on his knees, his head pointed to the ground, a string of vomit still dangled from his mouth. He wiped his mouth and face, his face ashen, his eyes red-rimmed.

"Don't say a goddamn thing; I'm staying on this case……. I know she is dead…….I have to be there when we catch him; don't try and stop me; you owe me."

"Alright, you stay until you want to, I'll pull you off when you tell me."

 Charlie knew the risk, uncontrolled emotion coupled with a weapon and badge could result in an incident and irreparable damage to the entire squad. But during Charlie's troubles, the death of his family and his heavy drinking, Wes covered for him and pulled him out of numerous episodes. They both understood the debt.

They stood on the neighbor's back door step. "Shit, the light is excellent, but you can't see the side entrance from here; it's the way the lots are situated. Come on, time to get back to the station."

"Charlie, I alerted all the stakeouts, and everyone reports…..a quiet evening."

"OK, the Chief is up to speed and has informed the Mayor. Next the Sharma family. Jesus, I'd like to skip this one, but they might be able to identify the earring."

One ear had a small gold earring with some unique markings. Charlie wondered: an old family heirloom because all the markings were almost off; it appeared to be scripted in some foreign language. Wes stopped and seemed to gather himself together, fought for control of his emotions.

"I know you warned me to keep away from her, but we clicked plus you can throw in all the other clichés, and you'll have summarized our relationship. It surprised both of us, and we both knew the odds of success, but it didn't matter." He stopped, his control fading.

"Jesus, you're talking in the past tense. We haven't even confirmed these are Pameela's ears and fingers in the package."

"I know it's her earring; she told me about its family history and its provenance; they're her ears and fingers; I don't need her mother to tell me."

Charlie saw all the pain in his friend's face and heard the torment in his voice. He wondered if his own anguish flared more intense because of his recent failed romance.

# # #

Finally, they made time for a late evening meal; between bites, Terry spoke.

"Manuel, you know our place is becoming a romantic soap opera. First, we have Charlie chasing Emma, next Wes and Pameela, and then the Chief after Karen."

"Wait a minute that's just a rumor about the Chief."

"Christ I wish it was because I like both of them. But I saw them the other night. I parked and started to walk across the street to pick up my dry cleaning, and then I saw the Chief getting into his car.

A dark evening with lots of traffic. But the street lighting made it easy to pick out the Chief....... it was him. He walked out of the dry cleaners and got into his car. Karen was waiting in the front seat; he bends over and kisses her. I'm not talking about a peck on the check. I'm talking about a full embrace, no hold barred smack; this was one of those I-want-to-take-your-pants-off kisses. I damn near got run over just watching."

"Son of a bitch, what's the matter with the both of them? A fucking disaster in the works."

"Sure but the real tragedy: Wes and Pameela…..true love. Those two hit it off so fast, hard to believe."

"Charlie shouldn't keep him on the case."

"Why do you say that? Wes isn't happy but appears in control and working his ass off."

"I know this guy. He bottles it up, and when the right situation presents itself he'll explode, and I mean explode. He and I partnered a couple of years ago, right after the car accident killed Charlie's family.

Anyway, Wes and his wife went at it on a daily basis; I heard one end of some rather heated phone calls.

She kept calling during our shift; I don't know the reasons, but it got to the point where Wes wouldn't even take the calls. I didn't realize how irritated she made him….as you said he appeared to be in control.

Then we got called to an ugly domestic killing. This piece of scum shot his young wife in their kitchen, and the sauntered back to the living room to continue drinking and watching the game. He's shot her in the head ……so many shots he almost decapitated her; there was blood and brain all over the kitchen.

The rookie patrol officer first on the scene left the nut in the living room. When we went in to charge him, he stood up and started mouthing off about how she deserved it, and he was the king of whatever. Before I knew it, Wes attacked and drove his head into the coffee table and pounded him with both fists, one haymaker after the other. I needed the help of one of the patrol officers to get him off.

It took all of Charlie's influence and the Chief's sympathetic ear plus a few lies from the patrol officers and me to save his career. It was close."

"So you're saying: given the opportunity, Wes will waste this son of a bitch."

"Yes. In fact, I think he'll go out of his way to make sure he gets the opportunity. I'm telling you Charlie, and the Chief will be in deep shit if they allow Wes to stay on this case. My guarantee: when we get Robin Hood, the first chance he gets Wes will waste him, and he won't care about consequences. No bullshit excuses like he tried to escape or I saw a weapon. Wes will just walk up to him and blow his head off. I guarantee it."

CHAPTER 18: PAMEELA

The pain subsided, and Pameela regained consciousness.

No longer thirsty. A generous supply of water available via a jerry-rigged tube and bottle device. Given her circumstances, a ludicrous image kept flashing: she could not help comparing herself to a drunken football fan with a large can of beer on his head and tube running to his mouth.

Although naked, she was not cold; she felt a stream of air, as the cabin's air conditioning provide a comfortable temperature. Her back and buttocks ached, almost numb from lying in one position on a hard table for many hours. The repetitive, maddening Robin Hood theme music never stopped. She could not lift her head enough to see her captor, but she could hear his humming off to her right, shuffling and humming, a nut case. She thought he looked like a pile of clothes on castors, almost a comic scene, except for the blood splattered all over the front of the costume.

Finally, he appeared in front of her. She could not see him grin but imagined his gloating from his tone and sarcastic, cruel greeting.

"Oh my pet, awake. A good nap? Soon I will provide a longer and deeper sleep, all your worries over in minutes. The problem: the road to this eternal peace will not be pleasant for you; for me, it will be the highlight of the day. For now, I'll start the chainsaw so you can get used to the noise."

Pameela ignored the pain and fired back. "You must realize it's only a question of time before Charlie Taylor and his team catches you. You'd best hope it happens in an open public area and not in some secluded spot or you may be hearing the chainsaw sing to a different tune."

"I love the optimism of you rich, smug bastards; you believe everything in life will fall your way, no road block that Dad's money can't erase. In the next few months, I'll bring terror to your homes. Not a mother will be able to sleep, and every time junior goes out to indulge, to become the spotlight for the press, everyone will have to hope he returns.

There will be many heads delivered, this I promise. As far as Charlie and his team, I sent them the clues, which are valid, but they're going off in the wrong direction, as I thought they might. I enjoy watching that useless chase.

As you probably heard, I'm the avatar of a Hindu god. Can you guess which one? I thought with your Hindu heritage you might have been able to help Charlie; that's one of the reasons I grabbed you next. I wanted you out of the way. You can't guess which God?"

"No. I can't, but I know you'll lose."

"Is that the best you can do? Aren't you going to beg? Try to make a deal? I liked young Henry...... he was fun, so desperate, thought he could overcome all the odds. I enjoyed him; his screaming rated outstanding, and it made for a great audio."

As she listened to this last rant, Pameela accepted this as her final act; she became determined not to provide this maniac with the type of satisfaction he craved. Stoic, she acknowledged her fate; she was not sure where she found her strength. In her neglected religion? In her family heritage? The source of her courage did not matter. She blocked Wes from her mind; his presence would have destroyed her resolve. Her quiet determination irritated Robin Hood.

"I can see your superior attitude surfacing. Don't worry when I start again, you'll lose the poise and will become a begging mass of shit. Allow me to begin with the chainsaw; you can listen and imagine the fun when I start using it."

The harsh screech of the chainsaw filled the room. He kept making feints thrusts with the chainsaw, always close but never touching. As he waved it around her body, she could not control the fear, which ran through her body; she lost control and felt the involuntary wetness between her legs.

Robin saw it all and laughed, his hopes fulfilled.

# # #

The Chief and Charlie sat in the front room of the Sharma residence, Mr. and Mrs. Sharma the other two occupants, the wealth, and elegance of their life evident in the furnishings and the décor. Charlie wondered how they had acquired all this wealth.

Was there a tie back to Robin Hood? Could this be part of some vendetta against the family? Payback disguised as some ritual nut case? They'd best do an in-depth on the Sharma and the Patterson family. During the hectic first hours, no one had considered revenge as a motive.

Mrs. Sharma was mute, able to sit with them but not much else. Mr. Sharma did the talking. "Yes, that is Pameela's earring; one of a set but she made a silly practice of only wearing one at a time. In case she lost one she would always have the other. She was always afraid of losing them; they used to belong to my great-grandmother. My mother brought them with her from India. The markings, as you call them, are Sanskrit."

The man's composure surprised Charlie. "Mr. Sharma your security and our stake out reported nothing out of the ordinary, but we anticipate we'll hear from Robin Hood sometime in the next 24 hours. But now I would like to pursue a different avenue. Is there anyone who stands out as possibly wanting to harm you or your family? An incident which resulted in a financial loss? A firing of an employee? Anything to get someone upset?"

"Mr. Taylor I thought about this since you first asked me and also sent a request to all my senior managers, and they will cascade the request throughout the organization. The problem is the size of my companies and our many locations; an incident which we consider minor may have been the trigger and not register with us. Anyway, the request has gone out, and I hope I to get back to you before the end of the day.

Now, some questions: how much time does she have? I mean after he delivers these gruesome packages, how much time?"

The Chief answered for Charlie. "This is only the second kidnapping, and he hasn't been consistent with other aspects of the case, so we don't know. He apparently provides water, and since Pameela is a healthy young lady, this could go on for days. No way to know."

Mr. Sharma looked at the Chief for a few seconds and then made up his mind.

"Thank you for all you have done, and I will be back to Detective Taylor with a list of potential angry competitors or employees."

That was the signal to leave. Mr. Sharma came to a conclusion and saw no point in pressing for more unpleasant information; he accepted the obvious, the limits of the police a fact of this case.

# # #

As Charlie and the Chief made their way to the car, "What're you thinking Charlie? A possible elaborate case of revenge?"

"I think we have to go down that path. I'll have Karen work with the Patterson family and see if they're aware of any incidents in their history: an ugly incident, more likely a personal insult. Maybe someone wants the parents to pay a price."

"So this becomes a targeted homicide instead of the work of a ritual psychopath, do you think so? It appears rather thin to me."

"I agree. What do I really think? A nut case and he won't stop with these two. But, I want all options open. One intriguing feature of our case is: Robin knows a lot about the families, definitely about their security arrangements. We'll review their security firms and the complete set up including security employees present and the past. You know we only have a couple of days, maybe three at best."

"Yes, I know and so does Mr. Sharma."

CHAPTER 19: UNCLE WILLIE

Bill blurted out his concerns. "Judge, the killings are beyond anyone's expectations."

As usual Judge Stephen was very busy but Ann, his assistant, insisted he make time for Bill Thompson, a man about to explode. Stephen could see Bill's tension, a slight tremor in his hands, an irregular weaving and bouncing of his head; all presented a picture of a man in a hurry.

The Judge wanted clarification. "You mean the executions."

"Yes, yes, I mean the killings. At Fort Green, out of less than 100 convicts we've processed, 32 men have been executed, of course, after failing both the S1 interrogation and the S3 memory scan. But at this rate we'll have a 1000 bodies piled up before we can complete the second stage of prison reform; convicts across the country will revolt."

Stephen waited for Bill to regain some composure; he'd been concerned when Ann presented the first report to him; however, no one at the prison raised the alarm, so he procrastinated.

Bill continued. "The problem: that bloody Dr. Strangelove you appointed; he claims this is only an aberration in the random draw process. I don't buy this; it isn't random. These convicts had finished, or nearly finished, serving their original sentences. Under normal circumstances, most would have been released this month. Their records and crimes cover the spectrum, so in that sense, it is random, but it's not a random sample of our total population.

Dr. Jerry King may be a brilliant academic but useless as an executive or manager, procrastinates with daily problems, many decisions now made by Emma so we can continue.

From the first day, he decided to put his stamp on the process. He forced Emma to start S3 memory scans just 24 hours after men had failed an S1 Interrogation. He insisted the 72 hour waiting period could be ignored, an out of date standard.

I argued with him, but he claimed the drugs used in an S1 would, for all practical purposes, be flushed from a convict's system in a very short time, the 72 hour waiting period only a guideline, not legislation.

Besides, he knows an S3 memory scan has never proven an S1 Interrogation to be wrong. He doesn't know what the hell he is doing. Any remnants of the S1 drug cocktail could distort the memory scan and invalidate the guilty sentence."

The Judge tried to remain calm. "What about Jessie Lopez? He is Legal's representative. I assume he challenged Dr. King and the decision."

"Jessie is a boy, ambitious, hardworking, someone, who wants to get to the top. He intends to move up the organization chart, and he defers to anyone he perceives is on a higher rung of the ladder. He'll not use his position to challenge a so called expert like Dr. King."

The Judge shared Bill's concerns. The 72-hour guideline had been established by Dr. Max, not the most conservative or cautious scientist, in fact, bold and daring would be a more accurate description of Max. And now the Fort Green process ignored the time frame.

Stephen's faith in Bill allowed a rapid decision. "Alright Bill, this is what we do: first stop the interrogation process. Your excuse will be: staff needs a break plus delays in drug production. Try for at least ten days. The ten-day stoppage may attract the Region's attention so I may reduce the timelines, but you start with the ten days. We'll adjust later if necessary.

This must be a secret project, no one to know unless I clear them. First, I talk to Emma: then bring in Dr. Max to assess the damage. Last the Chief and Charlie, will have to review the records of all the men who have been executed outside the 72-hour time limit. I know this adds up to a lot of people for a clandestine operation, but we need answers, fast."

"What about Dr. King? He won't just stand by."

"I plan to send him out of the country. I've been asked to speak at a conference in Germany. I'll arrange for him to deliver the session. I'm sure for an all-expense paid opportunity to flaunt his intelligence he'll be eager to go; we need him out of the way.

The outcome will probably mean I'll have to fire him, but now we need time to assess the situation, without him trying to influence the results. Also, just to reinforce my earlier comment: no discussion with Jessie. I'll talk to him.

Thanks Bill, we need an in-depth investigation, and I hope you're wrong. But no matter, thanks."

Alone in his chambers, the Judge was more upset than he'd revealed. At a recent lunch with Dr. Max, this Nobel Peace Prize winner announced one of his current research projects, a very recent initiative, not ready for publication. Max was charting how quickly an individual's system completely flushed the chemical cocktail from an S1 Interrogation. The results: individual differences were expected, but the range and variation were a surprise.

A small minority cleared the drugs within 12 hours. For most, the drugs proved tenacious and did not even start vacating the body for about 36 hours; a complete flush or clean system took between 48 to 72 hours. Individual results were evenly distributed through this clearance spectrum. Max refused to publish until he ran more tests but was pleased to confirm his initial 72-hour waiting period.

As Stephen saw it: this meant if an S3 took place 24 hours after an S1, the chemical mixture associated with an S3 would be added to a body nearly saturated with a powerful set of drugs from the initial interrogation.

The S3 memory scan drugs protected the brain and facilitated the transfer of images to the computer system and monitors. No one ever conducted a mind probe on an individual loaded with this hodgepodge of chemicals, the results naturally unpredictable.

That damn Dr. King. His doubts about him started soon after he watched him deal with staff and address his peers. After a few interchanges, he noticed the man reiterated many theories, making them sound like his own thinking, knew all the answers but often didn't respond to the original question, like a master politician. His answers always seemed erudite, delivered with a smile and earnest façade. A couple of hours later you realized his answers belonged in the useless bucket, not expert advice, no further ahead than before you asked.

Now for Jessie: the Judge had known the appointment entailed some risk; the young man needed more seasoning, an element of toughness missing. He would talk to him this afternoon.

The bottom line: 32 men had been executed under the auspices of an unauthorized change. How many should have been set free? The public's attitude about criminals was extreme, but even the mistaken execution of one would be considered an inexcusable blunder, relatives, and friends furious.

Stephen would have to live with these errors; since the mass executions started, his nights regularly filled with dreams and images of dead men. Now could he add innocent men?

.

# # #

Near the end of a long day, he finally connected with Emma Collins, a key collaborator. He recognized her stress; she looked fatigued, dark eyes, pale skin, hair combed but not washed, clothes rumbled. "My spies tell me you work 24/7. Not a sustainable pattern."

The tired young woman answered, "I worry too much. My staff, although not green, is struggling with the pace and volume. I've tried to assist with the difficult memory scans. But this proved impossible.....too much happened, too fast."

"Emma, I need you to be brutally honest with me. Some questions deal with facts but some deal with your opinion or feelings. Today I can't afford for you to worry about other people, their feelings or reputations. At this critical juncture, I need your frank insight. All your comments stay with me; you must trust me. Are you ok with this?"

A confused senior technician stared at Stephen and nodded an affirmative; she certainly trusted the Judge.

"First, I want your opinion of Dr. King as head of the Forensic Division?"

She only hesitated a few seconds. "A disaster. Dr. Kate comes out a saint compared to him. Jerry is very smart, but as an administrator, he gets lost in the details. Ever decision involves an endless discussion about all the options, regardless how remote or minor, and often leads to another study. I make many decisions, like which staff to assign to the Fort, order the drug mixtures and other supplies for the project, deal with personality and performance issues, review convict records and prepare the S3 memory scans …."

Stephen interrupted. "You mean primarily operating as if he still resided in France."

"That's about it. The only major decision Jerry made was to reduce our turnaround time between S1 and S3 to 24 hours, but I'm sure he discussed this with you, so this is not a surprise."

"Actually it is a great surprise; I just found out this morning. This is the reason you're here."

The revelation set her back: it took her a few moments to respond. "God, I fought with him about this, almost screaming sessions. He said his mandate was: empty this prison ASAP, maintain a brisk interrogation pace. It's true he never told me you agreed; he just let me infer from his comments that everyone had agreed.

I didn't think he would make such a change without you knowing. On top of this, he is continually pushing the technicians during the scanning process ….. it all adds up to pressure on everyone…..an ugly and challenging situation and I ………."

"Alright Emma, let me summarize for you. I've talked to Dr. Max who he is furious about the 24 hours; he states it is dangerous and irresponsible. OK for a small minority but not most people. I'm bringing him into Fort Green to work with you. The two of you must review all the memory scans of the 32 men, all the executions.

This is strictly confidential; I'm trying to restrict the number of people to involve. Willie will make an announcement: the interrogations stop for a few days, the delay due to supply shortages and staff issues. In addition, I want King out of the way: so I am sending him to a conference in Germany.

While you and Dr. Max review the interrogation recordings of the 32, the Chief and Charlie will grabble with each convict's record and background. Jessie will be told this is going to happen. I'm sure he'll cooperate.

As I see it, we may have executed innocent men. I can't give you and Dr. Max more than a few days. And unfortunately, you're not to involve anyone else that includes the Historian. The Chief and Charlie will access full rap sheets, which goes beyond the actual sentencing documentation; I hope this provides the original charges before a plea bargain resulted in a sentence. I'm sorry I've been rambling, not giving you a chance to comment or question."

"Judge I'm Ok. For days I've felt harassed and always worried about the reduced time lag before a memory scan. The body count seemed high.

These scans proved difficult. Their S3 memory scans caused a variety of problems: memory retrievals were often transient, at times almost overlapped one image on another, and then often disappearing before a firm image could be established. The rapidly decaying images meant the Watchers had to be quick.

The Watchers moved the interrogations along, but there were many complaints, even the Historian bitched; did the complaints trigger your investigation? Or did Willie complain?.... Good, I see he told you; I'm glad you appointed him head of the Prison Division.............so when do I start?"

"Dr. Max would like to meet at the Prison this evening. I've to warn you about his work habits; you might wish to catch a nap before supper because after supper it may be too late; it will be a world wind of non-stop action. And thanks. I will deal with Dr. King when he gets back."

"Judge, one last comment. I like Jerry. He is an excellent academic; it's just that this position requires a particular skill set or personality and that is not him. I'm surprised he accepted the appointment. I do miss Dr. Kate."

When she was gone, Stephen poured his last coffee and walked to his window. He thought about Emma's parting comment: I do miss Dr. Kate. She wasn't the only one; he thought about her every day and monitored her progress at the Farm. She may get an early release but still faced a massive number of community hours. He needed to maintain his distance, at least until she finished her sentence.

He also thought about a daughter who could never know him as her father. Sonja, a daughter he never found out about until Kate's confession, was now a regular part of his habitual musing.

Next decision: when to report to Regional? His reputation of holding back information and trying to solve problems without their assistance irritated some of the senior staff a headquarters. Should he delay again? Yes, delay for a few days. If he reported today without a conclusion or solution, he would be flooded with instructions or even expert visitors prepared to conduct their investigation.

 If innocent men had been executed, even one convict, he would tender his resignation along with his report of the incident.

# # #

 As soon as he returned to the Complex, the idiotic receptionist told him: earlier in the day detective Karen visited and spent time with different staff members. He pretended to be indifferent to this flouting of his orders and with a casual toss of his head walked away. He controlled his anger until in the privacy of his office.

Now in his office at the far end of the hall, the most isolated spot in the Complex, he exploded: that goddamn bitch. He'd ordered her out, but the bitch probably waited until he left the building and then hustled back. The bitch was as irritating as her boss that bloody Taylor, who thought he could control Barry's interrogation.

What had the detective heard? He knew gossip flew around the Complex: a bunch of goddamn women could not keep their mouths shut. Did anyone know? Helen could keep her mouth shut and be discrete: not even allowing any touching or personal remarks during working hours. However, some of the bitches around here were masters at detecting even the most subtle anomaly.

His head ached, and a migraine loomed; he was over medicated and would have to live with this one, without any more painkillers. Any additional meds and he would sleep for the rest of the day. Not possible, too much to do. Now, he needed to stop that son of a bitch of a detective from coming back.

Villa knew his affair with Helen left him vulnerable. If tight-ass Dr. Reed found out, he would demand a resignation. Tight-ass would not understand love versus a short-lived relationship. Helen agreed to marry him; it was just a question of timing: new jobs to be obtained and a new city.

Although Villa loved her, he'd not revealed all, one secret remained. He thought she would understand: her experience plus her work with the Complex residents meant she'd not lived a sheltered life. She's faced many variations and aberrations of the human psyche.

The immediate task: get that bitch detective off his back and away from the Complex. He might as well start at the top; he understood the Judge was relatively easy to contact and kept a sympathetic ear for anyone who could demonstrate a bureaucratic abuse. A few fucking lies and he would sink that bitch detective.

He also hated the goddamn Taylor, but that would be for another time. Now he had to hurry, lots to do today.

Jessie Lopez sat across from the Judge and confirmed he'd accepted King's decision to reduce the time between an S1 Interrogation and an S3 memory scan to 24 hours. Stephen maintained his composure, but strain crept into his voice. "A couple of things you will have to help me with: first, we've been operating on a 72 hours lag for some time, so why agree to a change like this? Second, why was I not informed about this change?"

Jessie understood this could escalate to a place he did not want to be. "Well Judge, the drug manufacturer states 24 hours should be sufficient and the 72 hours is only a guideline in our procedures. It didn't seem to be a significant departure plus Dr. King is a renowned scientist who is in charge of the science associated with interrogations. And I assumed he would inform you."

"Goddamn it man, you represent the Legal Division. You're to be an independent body at the scene to provide a check and balance, to ensure all the legal steps are followed. This means arguing, if necessary with Dr. King, Willie or anyone else who steps over the line.

The drug manufacturer's statements must be your idea of a joke; an S1 uses a cocktail mixture of a series of different drugs, not a single drug.

You bloody well do not report to Dr. King; you were appointed as his peer for this project. Your role: to ensure the prisoners were treated according to Justice Reborn legislation and the Sector protected from any unwarranted criticism. Is this getting through?"

The Judge's anger silenced Jessie, who began to understand his situation. He thought he should respond, but Stephen quickly continued. "Just be quiet. I do not want to hear a word from you. I know you're an intelligent man, and I used to have big plans for you. At this point, keep your mouth shut about what transpired, and that means no midnight discussions with Dr. King.

I've started an investigation; Emma, Dr. Max, the Chief and Charlie are going to determine what happened and if we've killed some innocent men. If asked, you'll give them immediate assistance, no questions asked. If you breathe a word of this, you'll be fired and never work as a Legal in any Sector.

You may leave and hope all the convicts executed deserved their fate because if not, you and the good Dr. are in serious trouble. Now get out and do your job."

It had been a long time since the judge vented his anger; although he was upset, he still believed Jessie would mature, and he wanted him to feel the heat. Stephen hoped Jessie could move on and prove he could do the job.

Later in the day: the scene resembled a segment of an 18th-century religious oil painting, a small slice of hell. Robin kept the music blasting and the chainsaw roaring. *Ring Around the Rosie* became the game; as he danced around the table, he recited some verses but often lost control and just howled with delight. At times Robin walked, at other times he did the strange dance, and at random intervals, he sped up the saw and thrust it close to her neck, a fake head shot. He alternated singing his song and releasing his maniac laugh; the terror he inflicted on Pameela supreme enjoyment. It was Ring Around the Rosie as played by a very disturbed man, but for him, the exercise was an unexpected bonus.

His original plan had been to harvest and deliver more body parts, but once he discovered the impact of the chainsaw, he abandoned that idea. When he brought the saw next to his kidnaped victim's face, the screech of the saw and smell of the oil impregnated chain delivered intimidation, no heroic backtalk, just pleading. No need to proceed with more deliveries and the associated risk.

Chaos, terror, and madness simultaneously blended in the cabin. Pameela sobbed most of the time but only screamed when he brought the chainsaw too close. Robin sang his favorite melody with interval recitations of *Ring Around the Rosie* as a change of pace.

CHAPTER 20: THE CHIEF

When the Judge first explained the problem to the Chief and Charlie, they tried to deflect his request: Legal could do a better job. Both men wanted to stay focused on their killer, but their priority didn't match Stephen's. Their protest was useless; the Judge was firm. Once Max and Emma released the results, the detective and Chief must drop everything; they could not use other staff, results within two days.

They would have to review case histories for each convict and determine if the individual committed a capital offense or was a repeat offender who warranted the death sentence. When they left the Chambers, the two angry men thought: another screw up by Forensics, which required their resources, again bad timing.

# # #

By the next day, the Judge greeted an unexpected visitor, a pleasant surprise.

"Emma, how did you manage to get results so quickly?"

"As you warned me the man is unbelievable. We worked all night; we started when he arrived and wrapped up this morning. Dr. Max isolated 15 cases, which concern him; he analyzed the blood samples we retained and reviewed the recorded memory scans. A formal report will hit your desk by noon.

For these 15 the S1 drug mixture never cleared their system in 24 hours; S3 introduced more drugs into a saturated system. The net result they acted like people in a deep sleep. I've never seen people this far under, like a hypnotized state.

So far under the memory scans appear to be picking up dreams and fantasies; the images were short-lived and quickly shattered like kaleidoscope images. At other times images slowly dissolved into an electronic fog. If the technician was patient and waited long enough, the incident pictures could be captured.

Nevertheless, the question remained: a real memory or wishful fantasy or maybe a dream? Jessie sent the records of all 15 to the Chief."

The speed of their investigation pleased Stephen, an unanticipated bonus. The rest would be up to the Chief and Charlie. He asked her to pass on his thanks to Max and then asked her about the current rumors.

Emma, an exhausted researcher, smiled at the question and relayed Max's response to the gossip. Yes, he planned to marry Sally Grovernor; he understood their age difference would cause him more bad publicity. So what? He remained convinced it would work.

Stephen initial reaction of dismay, at the behavior of the Sector's resident wizard, slowly transformed to admiration. The Judge realized he had begun to respect Max, who lived his life as he saw it, took the blows from his distractors and kept on going. On numerous occasions, Max demonstrated his exceptional mind, and Stephen knew society needed the expertise of this unpredictable and outlandish man.

#

They sat in the Chief's office, each with the list of 15 names. In addition to Max's report, Jessie Lopez provided details of each criminal record, and Emma gave them access to the memory scan archives. The criminal records were in paper form for security reasons, besides the Chief preferred this format. Charlie wondered what the Chief would say if he knew Charlie had refused the Judge's initial request unless he included the Chief. The detective remembered the last time the Judge excluded the Chief, the scars still fresh. The Chief spoke first.

"I've isolated six which should be easy. They've been through our doors many times. Ready?....... I'll read off the numbers."

As the Chief read off the figures, Charlie compared them to his assessment; Charlie added two more in that category. "I also have Maguire and Adams; they're numbers 11 and 15 to put on the easy list. Wes and I have arrested them numerous times, both slime balls. How'd you want to do this? Do the easy ones first?"

"I'll take these first six plus the last two you just provided and see if I can convict them from their rap sheets and known history. You go after the remaining seven, if there are other jurisdictions involved it'll become more difficult, but the Judge has provided access to a National database. Cautious with your research. Remember these convicts have been executed and any questions about them could stir up some interest which we have to avoid.

I'm hoping I can complete these easy ones fast and get the Judge some early good news; the tension in his office is unbelievable. As soon as I'm finished, I'll come and help you. There is no grandfather clause…….. and remember the original charge, not the plea bargain, is what we compare to the memory stream display.

For these memory segments, Dr. Max wonders if it is an actual memory or a dream fantasy. The Dr. proceeds each questionable memory stream with his comments and opinion. If we get a memory display which matches our records and photos of the crime scene, it should be safe to assume it's a real event: otherwise, how would the convict know the details? But if we can't find anything in his records to match the memory slice, then we concur with Dr. Max and treat it as a dream."

"Jesus, Chief the two days…… that's not enough time."

"We don't have any choice, and in case you're wondering ……..I'll still have to yell at you and berate you for lack of progress on Robin Hood, anything less would raise suspicion."

In some ways it was the worst time but, on the other hand, he and the Chief had been working as partners for the last couple days: maybe he could get away with it.

 "Chief I want to talk about something else not related and very personal. You ok with this? Promise not to shoot me?"

"You son of a bitch. What kind of trouble are you in?

"For once it is not me it's you, and it's very personal."

The Chief blushed, plainly guilty. "I don't have to be told. My bonehead move and it's not getting resolved. How far has the news traveled?"

"I'm not sure, but certainly everyone in Homicide knows and I think the Vice squad….their senior detective, Webster, knows everything. Karen's work hasn't suffered……no one can complain about that front."

"Shit, can you believe this? Someone at my age, over 50, a hardnosed cop all my life and now in love, like a fucking teenager. I know I'm not movie star quality; but, on numerous occasions, I've had it thrown at me. I always put it down to the uniform and position…" Each phrase was punctuated with a short pause as he allowed his concerns to surface, but the words were soft and quiet.

"Chief, I don't have to hear this, I'm just.."

"Never mind you started this …… some damn women …..whether it's an aggressive rub at a Xmas party dance or just a touch …..too brazen with inviting eyes….I never accepted …not once…wavered a couple of times ….I'm not going to tell who these women are. But you know most of them. Jesus, it was close a couple of occasions….. two of us in a car……late, both too much to drink, but I always made an awkward exit."

Charlie tried not to listen, didn't want to hear, too personal. In any case, the Chief was not making sense, just blurting out random phrases of frustration.

"Then Karen. You, of course, can't believe an old bugger like me could fall in love. No need to shake your head. We clicked ……never happened to me before. At this point, I'm not talking sex. Ok, ok too much. I just want you to understand this is not a quick roll. I want someone out there to defend me when the shit starts to fly. So do think you can throw in a few kind words for me?"

"Chief you know you're asking the wrong man about personal relationships. Except I like the both of you and will defend you both. But I hope it doesn't come to a full-blown scandal."

The openness surprised Charlie. Apparently, the Chief needed to vent. When he ran down, Charlie pressed. "Chief, you're not going to break up your marriage. You are only a few years away from retirement, and then you can go south and go golf crazy and sail every day. You want to go out on a high note with all the honors and not viewed as someone who coerced a staff member, used his position to ..".

"I don't want to hear the details; I've been over it many times. Since you are so concerned, here is what I will try. I'll try and break with Karen. We've tried in the past but it just takes one call and we're back. But I'll try and now bugger off and get to work."

Charlie gathered all his material and left, thinking the Chief cannot do it. If it's love or lust, it does not matter: he's not convincing, and he'll not do it. This meant Charlie would have to talk to Karen.

Then his life intruded, Monk called. "I visited the central pool today and talked to the supervisor; he knows both of us and wanted me to tell you no more cursing or spelling lessons with his staff. I said you're under enormous pressure and apologized. But it appears the entire staff thinks it's funny, so no problems.

And some more good news. St Michael's Hospital's administration sent me some framed thank-you photos of us and all the kids on the third floor; there are copies for you and Wes. They're pleased with our visit and want us back. I said we would come next month. Now, if you're free tonight, I can come over with the photos and some pizza."

"Monk, I'm ok with going back to visit the kids but for once I have to refuse the pizza; my working zoo has turned into a hurricane."

"You're not replacing me with a redhead are you?"

"Don't even mention her; I've decided to walk away from that lady and feel better for the decision; you're right about the weekend and her. All she has had time for are a couple of text messages which say: I'm busy leave me alone.

So that's what I'll do. But maybe next week or the weekend I'll be ready for a killer workout but this time back to the old gym."

The short conversation ended on that note. Charlie had been abrupt with Monk who understood Charlie and did not take offense; there was nothing he could do. It had only been one weekend, but Charlie's long stretches of self-induced loneliness had left him vulnerable to the intense encounter. He now appeared desperate not to let it slip away.

Charlie would have to ride this one out on his own. Emma hurt him more than he was prepared to admit.

CHAPTER 21: Another Delivery

The body arrived: headless, two missing fingers, a target painted on the chest, no arrow in the bull's eye, naked and washed, like Henry.

The corpse lay in a ditch on a relatively low traffic secondary roadway, not on any of the running trails in the parks, not at the Sharma residence. Their stakeouts at these locations became a waste of time. No jewelry decorated the female body, no identifying marks or scars, but they all knew.

Charlie ordered Wes to stay at the station. But Wes refused, and now he stood at the periphery of the crime scene, bent at the waist, convulsing silent sobs. Their friend's grief permeated the setting, many of the Forensic team fought off tears.

She had been a beautiful person, beyond her physical appearance: empathy and an upbeat attitude were all part of her persona, so genuine it was rarely questioned or doubted. Charlie walked Wes to the car, sat him in the back seat and left him, without saying a word. The senior homicide detective and jilted lover knew his emotional edge could tip at any moment. The finality of Pameela's body amplified his feeling, but the investigation demanded leadership, grief an unacceptable luxury. The team huddled on the side of the road as they waited for Forensics to finish, prospects not good.

"Karen, you go to the Sharma residence; don't try and deal with Mrs. Sharma. The last I heard she is bedridden and heavily sedated; Mr. Sharma will work with you. Although it may be premature to put him through this, just tell him about the body, no need to force him to view the body. The head is going to arrive within hours.

Manuel, I want you to organize the patrolmen to canvass the area. There aren't many homes around here, but there might be someone who uses the highway as a regular route. Don't stick around for any observations from Forensics; I'll wait and talk to them."

"Terry, Karen's already started on the staff employment search, but I'd like you to go back to the office and continue from where she stopped. We need a thorough review of the employment records for both families. Go back for the past three years.

We want anyone or any company both families utilized which would give them knowledge about the security systems and the damn cameras. And drive Wes back to the station; try to get him to work with you. Good, let's get started I'll be here if you need me."

They all gladly left the scene; a brisk wind threw loose debris around and cooled off the day. Charlie still wore his ugly jacket and enjoyed its warmth, hands deep into its large pockets. He paced up the road and then back; his mind filled with dark, inchoate ideas: Robin Hood, obviously, intelligent enough to break his delivery pattern when he guessed stakeouts might now be in play.

 For most cases, Charlie could develop and juggle numerous different theories about a crime and his adversary. He would use his brainstorm sessions to surface new ideas and to test alternatives. The result: a continual process of rejecting or aggressively pursuing different avenues. Today, although his team hunted in a variety of different directions, he wasn't pleased with the progress, already worried about the next victim.

Was his personal strife the cause of cluttered thinking? Even though he had walked away from Emma, was his unconscious mind and his ego not willing to accept the rejection of his affection? Maybe he had to run a marathon to clear his mind.

 The time now an issue. Another victim on the horizon. And Charlie was convinced Robin resided in the area: he knew the terrain, knew the residents and their respective social status, was aware of traffic patterns, and the running and hiking trails. All this knowledge allowed supreme planning to establish the timing and decisions on the routes to take for each delivery. No doubt, a resident. Where was the bastard working and living? Surely exceptional weird or aggressive behavior would get reported. Or do peers just ignore it? Best not to get involved. His phone stopped all further speculation.

"Charlie, meet me at the Mayor's office ASAP; the head's been delivered. No questions just come."

The Chief's call left him numb. The head was not a surprise, just the delivery address: no stake out at the Mayor's office, this delivery to the same location as the first greeting another change in his routine. Robin

Hood was more than lucky; he went for maximum impact, knowing the friendship between the Mayor and Pameela.

# # #

Charlie walked directly into the Mayor's office: Forensics already on the scene, the Mayor and the Chief the lone other occupants. The Mayor exhausted, holding a glass of scotch, not talking just watched the Forensic staff. The Chief filled Charlie in. "A regular FedEx delivery. This box along with the rest of the parcels left in the drop-off zone. Security scanned and cleared all the damn packages; this one was marked 'personal and confidential' so the Mayor's secretary just put it on her desk."

Forensics signaled Charlie to come over: taped on the lid of the cardboard box sat a hand drawn a card with bow and arrow plus a forest of green trees, inside the washed head of Pameela. The head appeared to be severed with a saw and not a sharp blade. Charlie knew when Forensics finished, it would prove to be the same saw used on Henry; there was no point staring at the head. The medical evidence would tell him what he needed. The Chief kept talking.

"Before that damn audio set, the Mayor has never received any threats or calls from Robin Hood, but he apparently knew about the working relationship and friendship. Have you been able to tie Pameela and Henry together in any fashion? Any connections?"

Charlie told him the little he knew. "Nothing yet, but we're trying to link the families through contractors or hired staff. Pameela and Henry were both extremely wealthy, well-educated, but they didn't move in the same circles, the exception being the high-profile charity events where both families contributed people and money. But so do a lot of families; so why select these two?"

The Mayor sipped her drink, recovered enough to ask a question, "That set of audio clues. Any success? Any further progress?"

Charlie again the man on the spot. "Nothing of any real value. I keep thinking we might be missing the obvious? What? I'm not sure we're using the clues correctly or interpreting his damn recording in the right manner. Maybe there is a different direction we should be pursuing." Charlie realized he was rambling and sounded like a desperate man: best to change the subject.

"We're pursuing the gray van, a feeble lead. Next, it's unlikely we'll get an eyewitness from the dumping of Pameela's body. That roadway is a light traffic secondary highway with only a few homes in the region, and most are about a half mile off the road. About ten seconds to unload the body and take off with no one the wiser. Sorry for the rambling but this killing is personal and hard on the entire team."

The Mayor ended her silence. "Gentlemen I'll go to the Sharma residence and spend time with them; please arrange for the body and head to be together; can this happen in the next few hours? Yes? Good. You know they're going to want to see their girl.....goddamn it ....goddamn it ....I can barely hold it together..... please leave .....and...... get the body assembled."

The Chief nodded his assurance, and he and Charlie left the office.

"Chief I'm going to reassign Wes; I'm afraid that if we get close, he'll do something reckless."

"Why not wait? He is a good detective, and you need him. He'll come around. We need all the manpower we can muster. We need a driven detective, and he'll be willing to work the hours........ you know we need him. Yes, I'm afraid of 'reckless', but I work with it daily. You should be aware this."

The Chief broke away and walked to his car, leaving Charlie a little confused.

#

A strange quietness settled in the bright hallway. Three EMS type stretchers with casters lined up in front of a large set of double doors.

The top half of each gurney sat in a vertical position with a guard to control any movement; each was occupied by a convict, sitting up and strapped in, fully restrained. The lineup formed a queue for an S1 Interrogation in Fort Green. About every 60 minutes, the double doors would open, and a stretcher would roll out with a sleeping convict, smiling, oblivious to his fate, the gurney supports now horizontal to accommodate the tranquil man.

Within seconds, the next stretcher at the front of the line rolled through the doors. The convicts never spoke, the guards only uttered the occasional order; hence the most prevalent sounds in the hall were the rolling wheels of the stretchers and the odd squeak of leather as a convict adjusted his position.

Mallory waited at the head of the queue, stoic as always, a reflection of his nickname: Snowman. He was in his mid-40s, a small man, with a face that belonged on people the city pound hired to euthanatize dogs and cats: at least this is what his ex-wife said, mean and without mercy. His hair turned white before he hit 40, and this appearance was often mistaken as the reason for his nickname. But, it was his ability to maintain his composure and think clearly when under pressure which earned him the Snowman title. This poise also accounted for his promotions in the car theft ring.

His nicotine-stained fingers craved a cigarette. While waiting, he thought about last night's session with the group in the yard, a trio of concerned prisoners.

"Goddamn it Snowman, too many have been executed. What the hell is going on? Are these bastards just making up the law as they go? We don't stand a chance."

"Time to organize a fucking riot. If we don't get an explanation and fucking soon, it's going to happen, an explosion."

Mallory tried to calm his friends. "At this point, the execution rate might be valid. You know they're looking for repeat offenders and for that first group, I don't think 30% is that far out of line."

"Screw that Snowman. Wait until you're waiting for your turn at an S1. You may change your mind. That fairy King dropped the 72-hour time limit between S1 and S3…down to 24 fucking hours!"

Once they wheel you out after the S1 Interrogation, within 24 hours, you could find yourself having a brain scan and just as fast end up with an injection and then the big fucking fire. Once they strapped you on the stretcher for a memory scan, it'll feel like a greased slide into the furnace, it'll happen that fast. King is a maniac, and he doesn't give a shit if he happens to make the odd error as long as he finishes ahead of schedule."

"I know you're right I don't like it. I've complained to Uncle Willie, and I hope some changes will be made."

Now as he sat waiting his turn he wished he'd talked to Willie as soon as the first statistics surfaced. When he closed his eyes, images of bodies sliding into a furnace flashed in full color. Damn it. A guard broke into his thoughts. "Alright Snowman, your turn, hold on, time to go."

The gurney rolled into a room: almost bare, three hardback chairs, two men in suits, one woman in a white lab coat, the recording equipment focused on the stretcher location. The guard locked the wheels and said, "Good luck Snowman."

A severe, officious setting, no introductions, all business, a job to be done efficiently and quickly. The woman started.

"Mallory, first drink this solution. Then I'll adjust your back support to about 30 degrees; the S1 Interrogation lasts from 30 to 60 minutes, when finished, you'll be taken back to your cell. It's okay to be very relaxed, and at the conclusion, most people have a deep sleep and wake up very refreshed. These two men represent the Legal Division. While I monitor your vital signs and reaction to the drugs, they'll conduct the questioning. Do you have any questions?"

"No? Good, let's get started."

He tipped the glass and swallowed the drugs. The woman immediately attached a couple of electrodes to his chest and adjusted his back support. She walked to a wall mounted monitor and signaled the suits with her arm extended and the five fingers of her upright hand. Mallory thought: unusual for a drug to be effective in five minutes. But soon he started to relax, even began to smile, and felt at peace with the world. He knew it was happening, and he felt like 'Joe Schmuck', but he couldn't control his growing feeling of happiness or keep the idiotic grin off his face.

The suits recognized the first impact. They patiently sipped some coffee; they reviewed his case files while they waited, knowing this could be a difficult case for them to assess. Mallory felt like humming or whistling. Ridiculous. He wanted to be friends with the entire world, to please everyone, to cooperate, be open, knowing they would understand. Then the one with the navy suit started with some easy questions.

"Mallory, this was your first conviction and prison time. Guilty as charged?"

"You goddamn rights. I ran two chop shops, a million dollar business. It was challenging and exciting and the pay a helluva lot better than my mechanics wages."

Mallory could not believe his outburst, like a gushing hose. Although he was aware of what he was doing, all was overridden by his desire to be friends and share and hope they liked him, cooperation the key.

"Would you mind telling us how you got started in this business? Where you involved in other criminal activity before car theft?"

"I started early. In high school a friend got me going. We stole a couple of cars every weekend, made enough money, never got caught. Then I meet my ex-wife… she forced me to get out. I got my mechanics papers and a good job. Ok for a while maybe a year or two …shit…., people always need or want money…no kids just wanted to do more, you know go out, buy more ……..so I went back on a part time…..basically took orders for the model, year, color of car…..not too many orders and still worked as a mechanic but now a lot more money. Sylvia, that's my ex, she caught on but by this time she enjoyed the extra bucks too much and let it ride.

My next break came when they wanted me to work in the chop shop as a mechanic and floor supervisor; I quit my other job; the money was fucking great."

His dry mouth forced a short recess. As he drank the water, he tried to regain control, take the edge off his confession. It never happened, and the words continued to spill out of his mouth.

"I worked like that for about five years, and then the manager was killed in a car accident…… ironic right? My luck…I'm now the new manager of the entire shop. I was born to it: a combination of business, mechanical problems, a multitude of cars, logistics and the pressure of maintaining our volumes plus running the legitimate part of the shop ….all one helluva high with millions under the table. For the last six years I managed two shops, Sylvia left before this; she couldn't take the hours or the stress of a possible arrest.

I figured no one got killed; insurance companies picked up the costs, so we're just stirring up the economy and providing a lot of secondary or spin-off work. In all this time …no arrests…not even a police visit….no interrogation. Then we got unlucky; the cops nabbed an aggressive drunk, and this new technology drained all the information from my drunken mechanic."

The suits walked to another side of the room to confer. A tired Mallory needed help. "I'm getting sleepy. Is it ok if I nod off?"

"Sure go ahead Mallory we've your record and your comments this should do; thank you."

The Snowman felt the technician lower his back support to the horizontal position, and now he understood why those who exited the room smiled, whether fully asleep or not. What a happy time; he confessed. It felt good were his last thoughts before sleep conquered him, and the guard wheeled back to his cell.

The navy suit started. "I consider him a repeat offender; he is like a swindler who defrauded many people over many years. He caused a lot of heartache and hardship for many, and I don't hear any remorse; if released he will be back at within three months."

The second suit disagreed. "He is not a repeat offender; he has never been arrested or convicted, never informed he must change or suffer severe consequences. I mean ….if he had been arrested a few times and then went back to the car theft ring, I would agree.

He just coasted along rationalizing his behavior as a big business with a bit of an edge; he never faced the consequences. As for remorse, I think that is a stretch; you know how hard it is do anything besides smile under those S1 medications, everyone is happy when they tell us about their history. That doesn't mean there is no regret. God, some even laugh through the entire process, can't stop giggling."

The navy suit walked around the chairs a few times and then frowned at his colleague.

"What I hear is: no agreement. I think he should go to an S3 memory scan and disclose an unrelenting full-time criminal ……..the type society doesn't want to set free.

You, on the other hand, see someone who has not been forced to recognize his criminal activity and when forced will reform. Hence, he should be sent to a Farm, where he will become a solid citizen.

Ok, I'll stop. We can't agree that's why we have Jessie. He only wants a summary of the interview; he can cast the deciding vote for Mallory. Then we will see if the Snowman melts this week."

His partner agreed, and they signaled for the next convict.

CHAPTER 22: Charlie's Log: THE RECIPIENTS

I'd called an early morning meeting; detectives drifted around the room, coffee a natural diversion. A couple lingered over the tray of fruit, chatter at an all-time low; this hard-nosed crew had adopted Pameela in her short time with us. The grief for her coupled with our lack of progress added up to a depressed group of detectives. I sat in the same boat. Wes looked depleted, but I'd stopped debating with him and decided to let him stay on the case. We desperately needed a change in direction. I decided to share my doubts with the group.

"We're missing something; this asshole can't be that smart. Are we looking in the wrong direction? Let me throw this out, and you can feed off it. My first question: let's reconsider the people who received his distributions. Was this a random selection? Alternatively, did he select them because of an easy access to their homes? Or, even better were they chosen for a different reason or purpose?"

Karen started. "You mean Robin Hood selected these homes for a reason, and we haven't even considered that possibility ……..basically ignored them as a clue?"

I kept going. "Look he sent us a cryptic set of audio clues. Why? He enjoys playing with us, thinks he is superior and likes the excitement of being chased. Otherwise why any clues at all? Maybe there are more clues, and we aren't seeing them. This asshole enjoys playing games; I think the distribution is part of his game. I think our focus should switch to that segment. Are the recipients linked in some way?

Goddamn it, I'm convinced he knows them or of them. How the hell else would he know about their work schedules, freezer location, side entrance door, etc.? Even more puzzling: how did he meet them? In the same social circles? It's easy enough to isolate the lower middle class in the city, but then you have to select people from a large population segment within that district.

What do you do? Knock on doors? I don't think so. What do we know about them? Manuel you first…let's hear it."

Manuel was brief. "Ok the first delivery: Mrs. Jackson a recent widow, long-term resident of the city and that district, lives off her husband's pension, apparently not well off.........certainly not retarded, like our giggler, as normal as my grandmother. Sorry, not very much but she wasn't considered a suspect."

"Karen, what about the second delivery?"

Karen had little to add. "Mr. and Mrs. Sanchez both work, she only part time, not really poor but appear to be on the financial edge, only been in that house for about 10 years, again not retarded........ Christ, they seem normal and a well-adjusted couple."

I was not pleased; it was too superficial. "Too damn thin; we know nothing about them or their history. Go back and dig deeper. Do a complete work up on both recipients. Shit, let them listen to the audio, and see if they can identify the sounds or if anything in those sound bites rings a bell. I'm convinced they're not random selections from a poor district. And I want to meet right after lunch with the results. Manuel, you and Terry do Mrs. Jackson; Wes you help Karen with Mr. and Mrs. Sanchez."

Karen was surprised. "You serious? You want us to play the recordings for them?"

"Yes, play the damn things and let them listen. I can't give you a reason, but I've convinced myself the deliveries are a link to our killer. How? I don't bloody know. Just let them hear the audio. Thanks."

No more arguments. Not because they agreed, more like they were just too tired to debate. I couldn't reach Monk, but I left a long message to cancel our regular Thursday night supper, and our weekly workout.

Last, I rushed over to the Chief's office, and we hustled over to the Judge's chambers.

"Damn it, Charlie, why do you always make me late?"

#

And yes, the Chief and I were the last to arrive, Emma and Dr. Max already seated and waiting. I knew the Judge would not waste time on casual greetings or a warm up.

"Dr. Max why don't you brief us on the current situation?"

Max was ready. "Judge, I've reviewed our guidelines. If we revert to a 72-hour wait after S1, an individual will enter the S3 memory scan with a clear system, there will be no lingering interference, and we can obtain valid memory segments. In other words, the original 72 hour waiting period is sufficient and will not cause any problems with a memory scan.

Next, Emma finalized all the equipment upgrades. I know you didn't request this, but we thought it would be an excellent opportunity to ensure there would be no further questions about the process. So now, all Fort Green scanning units match the equipment used in the downtown interrogation center.

Last, she exploited this short delay to work with the new staff, put them through a few dry runs; they are now a more confident group. During our restart, I'm prepared to be an observer should anything else arise to stop us or slow us down."

Judge Stephan continued. "Chief, you and Charlie are the second part of this recovery project; we need your report."

The Chief experienced at verbal debriefings began. "Of the 15 questionable cases, eight were easy to confirm as valid executions. Charlie and I reviewed all the records and on a couple of occasions spoke to the original arresting officers. Not to worry we both know the officers and they'll be silent. In all cases, the convicts were repeat offenders who had plea bargained their way through the system. In every case, the unofficial records document a trail of violence and brutality. Their last sentence to Fort Green another plea bargain accepted in the name of efficiency; with a crowded docket, the prosecuting attorney needed make a deal.

The other seven men confessed to crimes, which were never solved. The pattern here is intriguing; in each case, during their S1 Interrogation, they revealed details about the crime, which had never been made public; so they were either present or did commit the crime.

When we turned to the S3 memory retrieval recordings, it became difficult. The memory segments are of a very short duration, and in some cases multiple images overlay each other. The images certainly look like the crime scene; it appears these men participated. But the memory streams are impossible to use.......we can't get a stable picture......the flow keeps jumping to different frames....a mixture of various scenes ....many not related to the crime."

For these cases, we spent significantly more time with original case detectives. When we presented the details gleaned from the original S1 Interrogation, these investigators were convinced; the cases were solved. Unfortunately, this was only true for five cases.

This left two confessions where we could not confirm guilt or innocence. We feel confident that they were part of the crime but can't prove they are the killers."

Silence filled the room; we all knew this was not the answer the Judge wanted. Dr. Max restarted the conversation. "Judge, the Chief gave me a heads up on these two extreme cases, and I went back to the memory scans. The scans are like the quality of an old fashion movie, and we get streams of memory displayed at 15 frames per second. I focused on what looked like the exact murder scene and converted those streams into individual frames, basically photographs; and, these I was able to edit and enhance.

I worked with the individual frames, like a series of old fashion photographs. Now I could drop the random images, which were interwoven, into each stream; it was these unrelated frames, which made the viewing of the original scans almost impossible. I have to say it was a boring and tedious chore with massive amounts of still photos to handle. You see even with stream displaying 15 frames per second, a short 30 second streams means 450 still photos.

I'll put this collection of stills into Emma's hands, and she can file them into the archives. I can see you're all waiting...............All right, I'm happy to report; there is no doubt both men were guilty. The images are stable, clear enough.........pictures of the crime with our convicts as killers. And I refuse to do that again."

Stephen smiled. "Thank you all, I'd appreciate this discussion remaining in this room, at least for the next week. I'll submit a covering report to Regional and let them know we're back on schedule."

What he did not say: his ass could still be in a wringer. The boys in Regional played for keeps: the Judge was the man who selected Dr. King. This after Dr. Kate betrayed the Sector, just months ago. We all started to disperse; as I left, I heard the Judge asked Emma. "How is Jessie?"

Emma seemed pleased. "He is a changed man; he's taken charge; he's now a Legal representative and a resource for the entire team. He's anticipating problems and getting ahead of them, working long hours, covering all bases. Even Uncle Willie is impressed. Jessie has turned into the man you wanted when you first appointed him."

As the Chief and I made our way out, I heard Stephen ask Ann, his assistant, to get Dr. King to his chambers plus arrange an appointment with Regional. I did not have to be part of either meeting, thank God.

I never spoke to Emma; in fact, I never spoke throughout the entire meeting. I knew the 15 convicts were important for the Sector, but they had drained my time, and I needed all my energy to deal with Robin Hood. I got the impression Emma wanted to talk, but I wasn't in the mood to listen to her bullshit. But then again I was the one so far off base because I'd read too much into a casual weekend. Dumb shit. Really pathetic.

As you can see, I was not in a happy place.

CHAPTER 23: Audio Results

Back at the office and Charlie was impatient. "Manuel, you first."

"I'll start with an embarrassing apology. When I first questioned Mrs. Jackson, there was nothing of interest, all ordinary, dull stuff, years of married life, now a widow. Everything normal that is until I played the audio clues. When the snorting played, she became very agitated and demanded to know where I got the recordings. Of course, I didn't tell. This was difficult for her: finally said the snorting sounded like her dead husband. But she didn't want to talk about him or the snorting.

An angry or embarrassed widow. I couldn't understand what was bothering her. The boiling water allowed her to walk away and declare a coffee break. The instant decaffeinated variety her choice. Next, she surprised me by pouring some liqueur into both cups; her cup got a colossal shot of Baily's Irish Cream. Mrs. Jackson knew she would have to tell me but wanted time to get there. I decided to back off and drink my coffee, a patient detective, pleased with my patience.

 I talked in generalities about our case and our problem with a void in clues, and eventually, she relaxed enough, or the Irish Cream did it for her. She said an explanation to a stranger was disturbing, hard to open up and tell all.

 It seems when they had sex, as her husband climaxed he went into a different zone and started snorting; it was loud, fierce and upset her to a point she considered a divorce. I didn't ask why the sound bothered her; I didn't want her to stop.

About that time, the University maintained an extensive postgraduate program for psychology students; they had committed to giving back to the community and at the same time give their students some real life problems. You qualified for their consulting sessions, if you had a unique problem. The Jacksons were accepted, and a young man began working with her husband; he asked her to record her husband; he wanted the sound bites as part of the therapy. He used the recordings in combination with some type of feedback process.

She never knew much about the sessions, and her husband could never remember anything of substance since much of the time he was under hypnosis. It would seem strange to include house, freezer, and the porch as topics of conversation but who knows. Except and the bottom line: she swears the second recording is her husband. The student who worked with her husband was a Harold or Harry Mesko; and sorry ……..no pictures."

"Son of a bitch." Karen exploded. "I've got the same guy."

Chaos, everyone became energized, questions from all corners. Charlie brought order back to the room. "Hold it, hold it, guys. Karen, let's hear it?"

"When I got Bev and Clare Sanchez back together, all the questions got nowhere; everything appeared straightforward. As my wrap up, I turned on the recording and played the audio clues; when the swearing played, they both straightened up and stared at me. Like Manuel, I didn't tell them about the origin.

Bev didn't hesitate to tell me the story: until about ten years ago Clare worked as a truck driver, and then a serious accident resulted in severe brain damage. Although not classified as mentally retarded, he could no longer function as a truck driver. Also, a strange side effect showed up; whenever he felt pressure or became tense, he began swearing: yelling, a loud string of curses, which didn't make sense, just random curses. The company paid for the remedial therapy: conducted by a University professor or postgrad student, a Dr. Harry Mesko.

Mesko used to record Clare's swearing segments and worked with some feedback mechanisms; he wasn't entirely successful. He reduced the frequency of the outbursts and had the volume dropped, but the swearing continued, loud and distinct enough to recognize most of the words. The company moved Clare to a job on the night shift as a security guard. The reduced pay put her to work and forced them to move to that house and neighborhood.

Bad news…….. no pictures; Clare describes Mesko as bald, slight build, black goatee, pinkish complexion, dark rimmed glasses, very polite, good interface with patients."

Manuel jumped in. "That's the guy, same description Mrs. Jackson got from her husband. Do we have him?"

Charlie started to organize the approach. "Wes, I want you to go the University; I'm sure they'll have pictures, they're always taking pictures of students and profs. Even if he was only in the grad program for a few years, they're bound to have images.

Manuel, there is a national registration process for psychologists, call my brother Sam he will give you the details and help with the search.

Terry go back to the gray van search; you now have a name and also search motor vehicles for licenses under that name…..try everything within a 100-mile radius. He'd to have a license; it would be too dangerous not to drive without one."

Karen was not satisfied. "One piece doesn't fit: our giggler, Barry, under Stage 1 Interrogation drugs never mentioned Dr. Mesko, in fact never talked about anyone special. Dr. Reed and Dr. Villa certainly don't fit the description of Mesko. So how does Barry fit into the puzzle?"

"Karen you're right. But we never sent anyone back to see what else he might tell us; you're the best choice to try and talk to the giggler. I'm sure the Judge won't let us put him under again.

Best wait until Villa is out of the building; the guy is a real asshole. In fact, if you can't talk to Barry, try the rest of staff and focus on Villa. I'm sure he knows more than he has told us."

Karen accepted and never revealed she had already been back. And, she had waited until Villa left, then went in for a pleasant but nonproductive talk with Barry. Karen spent most of her time with the staff who were willing to share, gossip being a universal sport. Going back a third time would be pressing, and she would have to tread lightly.

The room emptied quickly, new energy in everyone's step, enthusiasm in the air. Charlie finally found a moment to himself; sat back and thought: maybe they'd found the missing clues.

He reviewed his messages for missed calls: one from Sam, another from the Chief but nothing from the Monk.

#

Hours later the same crew gathered in the same room, but now the attitude had turned 180 degrees. Charlie sensed: bad news. Wes started. "There're no pictures of Dr. Mesko at the University, Oh yes, he was part of their grad program and even stayed for a couple of years after his Ph.D. Problem? ....A fire in the Psychology department along with water damage destroyed all the pictures; only individual grades and other academic material stored in a different building survived.

A couple of profs remember him, sort of, but this was over ten years ago and people retire and all that shit. Sorry Charlie.

The best I could get: Mesko is remembered as a loner, brilliant, hard worker but definitely not a joiner.... got his advanced degree...... didn't make any friends. He never shared anything about his background or family. Their verbal descriptions were useless. Our police artist wouldn't have enough to get us a decent picture."

Terry followed. "Well, no Dr. Mesko in a 100-mile radius....no driver's license and no vehicle registration. As well, Manuel couldn't find him in the national registry for psychologists. We used the system to spit out the best 75 closest pseudo names to be derived from Mesko. Manuel and I'll go back and redo our searches based on these potential alias names. Sorry Charlie."

Karen shook her head. "I got access to our giggler, but I'm empty handed; Nurse Helen worked with me. We tried to establish a quiet family type session to see if Barry would talk about the past; he did talk. A rambling nothing; Helen's good with him and kept him calm but in the end: nothing.

The more time I spend with him, the more pessimistic I become. At this point, I don't even think another S1 Interrogation would help, and with his IQ there is no way you could subject him to an S3 memory scan. If he lost five to ten IQ points, it could be ugly.

But I do have an idea: Charlie, I wondered if you could talk to Emma or Dr. Max. I mean maybe there is a way to conduct a memory scan and guarantee no damage."

Charlie didn't hesitate. "Nice thought. But no way. The Judge almost never allowed the first interrogation. There is no way he would allow us to scan someone like the giggler; he's too vulnerable and not even a suspect."

No one could believe their new status. Charlie was not easily defeated. "Karen I know Clare Sanchez is not a candidate for S 3 because of his brain damage but what about Bev? She arranged Clare's treatment and must have a memory of the damn Dr. Mesko. A memory retrieval might deliver a picture of this bastard."

"Good try. As I was driving back from the Complex, I had the same idea. I stopped in at the Sanchez house and spoke to Bev. Here is an interesting part of Dr. Mesko's routine: he only dealt in person with the patient. He used the phone, without video, to deal with relatives and friends; she never saw him. And I bet if you call Mrs. Jackson you will find the same thing; a sly reluctant psychologist that she never saw and only spoke to on the phone."

A dramatic turn. How could a university graduate, a Ph.D., disappear in this society? Impossible. He had to be in the Sector and driving a vehicle. Maybe the alias search would deliver. It seemed too easy. This maniac was too smart to be caught because of a driver's license.

# # #

Karen trudged in, the end of long day, a promising start, and a dramatic crash. The Chief was on the phone but motioned her to be seated. Generally a composed person but since the two of them started their affair, she felt uncomfortable in the office of the headman of the Investigative Division.

"Hi Karen, I don't have much, and it's a bit awkward. There's been a complaint."

"Shit. What now? Surely it wasn't Charlie."

The Chief laughed. "No, no…you're one Charlie's favorites. It came from the Complex. Dr. Villa phoned the Judge's office to lodge a complaint, and the Judge transferred him to me."

"Villa. What the hell did that asshole complain about? Oh, wait Charlie isn't here. This means Villa went after me. Right?"

"Yes, you're the one he lodged the complaint against. According to him, you hang around the Complex, sneaking back in when he leaves. You, according to Villa, stir up gossip, in particular about his love life and his interactions with the Complex staff."

"The son of a bitch."

"Villa screams loud and is hard to shut up. He says you imply he used his position of authority to force staff to have sex with him, and you try to get the staff to tell you tales. You dislike him because of the manner in which he curtailed your interview with the giggler."

"Yes, I listened to his staff…..trying to find out about the operational issues and it's true I wandered around and did some fishing……and yes, the staff gossip about a sex angle but nothing spectacular, just innuendo, vague and useless, so far. Why so protective? I'm sure he knows more.

And Chief, sorry to screw your day, but Charlie had me return to the Complex today. And I did spend time more time with the giggler. Wait until Villa hears about this visit. Your phone will be vibrating very soon."

"Karen, I get it. No need to go on. This guy is a real bag of trouble …a loud mouth who doesn't care about accuracy. I read your reports, and I know what happened, but I guess you hit a sensitive button. With his reaction, I assume he wants to conceal an affair with his staff.

I'll let Charlie know when he returns or you can warn him about Villa. I have to record this on your file but will put in my assessment that the complaint is without merit. Just make sure you minimize your contact with this idiot and don't get him stirred up."

"Some complaint……sort of ironic …isn't it? ……considering the two of us …a supervisor and a staff member…...and Villa worrying that I want to uncover an inappropriate relationship."

Karen never told the Chief she intended to go back to the Complex. If she couldn't secure a memory scan, she would try Barry again. The happy giggler babbled, and if Karen could keep him going long enough, maybe he would leak something. As she walked out of the building and to her car, Karen wondered was she becoming the female version of Charlie, ignoring orders and challenging authority.

# # #

Wes's murderous rage started to subside a few days ago, the morning after Monk's visit. Monk arrived in the early evening, not with a Bible but with a case of Guinness and a bottle of Irish whiskey.

They stayed in the detective's kitchen, not a big room, and Monk seemed to fill the entire space. A strange evening. It evolved into a two-man wake, the drinking and talking easy and natural. Wes did most of the talking with just the occasional nudge from Monk to keep going; Monk did not leave until dawn. Wes woke around noon and rushed back to the station. Later in the day, he realized Monk drank very little, and he'd consumed most of the alcohol.

He knew Charlie was watching and looking for any sign of uncontrolled behavior. Any deviation would get him pulled from the case or sent home on compassionate leave. Now he felt under control, his hate no more than he carried for any other killer.

He never read any of the literature or research, which debated the 'nature vs. nurture' argument, but clung to some strong opinions. After years of dealing with violent behavior, he decided the genes controlled action, and no amount of nurturing was going to change a criminal. As he saw it, the violence embraced by those at the extreme end would never be flushed: the death penalty the only way to protect society.

In previous years, he simmered when a career criminal was presented as a product of his environment who made one small error in judgment, an unintended accident. An early lack of nurturing negated any possibility of blaming the individual. This rather tendentious analysis provided by psychiatrists swayed some the media. Today Wes appreciated the attitude shift which resulted as numerous memory scans leaked to the Internet.

Of course, she swapped his thoughts: Pameela would not leave him. This pain would go on for months. Their time together had been short with only a few intense moments. Didn't matter, memory after memory floated through his mind: a relationship unlikely to ever happen again. He'd helped Charlie go through a grieving process, and Wes knew he would not be alone.

His phone brought him back to the present: the Chief. "Wes, the Mayor has agreed to give Pameela a police funeral, and Charlie suggested you be part of the organization team. You ready to do this?"

"Thanks, I want to be part of the process. Chief, tell the Mayor I appreciate her support."

After the conversation, he walked down the hall to thank Charlie; Wes knew who'd pushed the Chief and talked the Union into making an exception for this type of funeral. Pameela, who was a civilian, didn't qualify.

.

CHAPTER 24: Delivery for Charlie

The Chief wasn't convinced. "Charlie, you sure this is the guy?"

"If he's not the guy, he's a solid link, a connection in some way, and the only connection between the two deliveries. This is all we have, but I feel good about this one: for once on this goddamn case, we're on the right track.

He made the recordings. Did other staff make copies of the same material? We tried to trace his work record back through the psychology department, but we may never get answers from them.

Mesko's direct supervisor is dead; the other two senior people who may be familiar with his work have retired and moved away: besides, they never had more than incidental contact with Mesko. It was a long time ago, and it appears a fire destroyed most of his history and water damaged the rest.

Whatever the fire and water didn't destroy their sloppy technician crew wrecked in trying to recover from the backup databases. An unbelievable mess, an embarrassment to the university and a few people lost their job. None of this helps us.

What it boils down to: their entire Social Outreach program, including all of Mesko's community cases, are destroyed. Jesus, there is no way to track his work. Also, the grad school records for his era are wiped out; we have no grades, application letters or academic records for these students."

"You mean you can't find the name, Mesko, anywhere in the Sector?"

"Another blank…. no luck. My guess: a name change; we can't find a Mesko in any other University as a psychology major or in any other undergrad program. Did he change his name before he applied to the grad program and then again after? Why? That's my current guess."

The Chief knew Charlie and didn't think his guidance was necessary, so after a few more comments he went back to his office. Within a few minutes, the front desk came up with a delivery for Charlie, a package marked 'urgent' and 'personal'. Charlie stared at the box for a long time, a package too small for a head but the return address: a hand drawn bow and arrow and some green trees. He put on his gloves and yelled.

"Wes, get the Forensic unit up here and call the rest of the squad."

The woman from Forensics did her job in record time and opened the package. No ears, no fingers, and no head. She brought the detectives an audio recording. Karen loaded the unit and hit the play button. The same computer generated voice, unmistakable, Robin Hood:

"Hi Charlie, I have the big boy; I know he doesn't exactly fit the profile, but he does represent a segment of society which is richer

than it admits. And the church has been ass kissing the elite for centuries; it is filled with arrogant, superior, smug, over- feed bastards; maybe they won't sleep as easy tonight. I wanted you to appreciate the rationale, nothing personal about Monk.

I like the big guy; he is one tough fellow, but I can't make any exceptions; besides the first delivery has already been achieved. I think I will keep him longer than the other two. I'm not sure how to make him scream without using the head routine. The chainsaw is my favorite. Bye for now. Say hello to Karen for me. Bye, bye."

A cynical, hardened room never uttered a word, the recording a horror film scene. Finally, Charlie erupted with a string of questions. "How does this bastard know Karen? And the relationship between Monk and I? Christ, how did he know Monk? How long has he been planning this? It's like he bugged the station or worked with us."

Every detective knew they needed a big break for Monk to survive.

# # #

News about Monk reached the Judge's office within minutes, another high-profile kidnapping, no progress, the Sector close to panic. This latest development added to Stephen's hectic office.

In the past 12 hours, he'd fired Dr. King, who proved to be an unpleasant person; next, he underwent a panel review by the senior executive at Regional headquarters. The appraisal focused on the 15 convicts executed with the questionable S3 memory scan interrogations. The Panel concluded no innocent men had been killed, no public statement or declarations were necessary. They concurred with Dr. Max's conclusions, which supplemented the Chief's assessment of criminal records.

The Region did make a surprise decision: after the prison decommissioning, a small team would be appointed to work with Max and assess the feasibility of dropping S3 memory scans as a necessary step prior to an execution. The objective: establish S1 Interrogations as the sole procedure of proving guilt or innocence.

Although Stephen's career had been saved, his status suffered from what many viewed as two irresponsible staff selections: Dr. Kate and Dr. King. The latter he acknowledged as a bad decision, but Kate served many invaluable years before her one slip. Fortunately, a change in attitude appeared to be developing, and a minority of Regional executive began to understand her value, not someone to bury in a rehabilitation Farm. They needed her and the rumor: Region's spin doctors were developing a politically acceptable rationale for an early release.

Stephen knew Dr. King was probably the last irregularity they would accept before asking for his retirement. Any more deviations from policy guidelines would be more than frowned upon; anomalies would be viewed as originating from someone who could not accept direction or someone who wanted to operate as an independent, an unacceptable situation.

He stood in front of his favorite window with a mug of coffee, stared down at the ailing trees, gusts of wind tore at the leaves and threw around loose debris, the streets almost bare, a strangely quiet front yard. After returning from Regional headquarters, he felt the tension drain from his body, a surprise because he had not been aware of how apprehensive he had been.

Monk's kidnapping changed all that, Cardinal Belak first to express his concern, followed by the Mayor. Stephen never met Monk, but had watched him play, and knew of his friendship with Charlie, even some of their escapades had reached his office: the basketball breast incident still made him smile.

He knew Charlie would be furious and emotional. Would this turn into a reckless operation, something that required careful monitoring? Should he call the Chief? No, it would be too obvious.

He thoughts came back to Dr. Kate Martinez; it was possible she could be out of the Farm very shortly and be assigned the extra weeks as community service. As soon as she completed that phase, he planned to contact her. His Sector's prison decommissioning would be completed and his role slipping into a more normal phase, some routine returning, less pressure. How would Region react to his establishing a relationship with a convicted criminal? This kind of move could reinforce the loudest knock against him: some perceived him as arrogant.

Last, he thought about Dr. Max, a man who lived as he pleased and absorbed all the arrows along with the accolades. The Dr. did what he thought was right, and continued to serve the community, but his terms of reference upset many. Now he was to marry a teenager who had been convicted of falsely accusing him of statutory rape. The marriage would occur as soon as her rehabilitation wrapped up; she almost destroyed him yet he understood her: she was the one.

Max's behavior seemed to give Stephen the resolve he needed. He decided if Kate responded, regardless of the consequences to his position, he would pursue a relationship. He would see how reality would play out, time to take a chance; he also knew she was the one.

Ann, his assistant, knocked and entered, "Best to take this call. It's Charlie claiming an emergency."

As soon as Stephen accepted the call, Charlie was off. "Judge, I need you to authorize an S3 memory scan on someone who is not a suspect. And I'll need Dr. Max's assistance with this one; the lady we want to interrogate is a disorganized schizophrenic, very smart woman but still a schizophrenic."

An astonished Judge recovered quickly, and he didn't ask any of the obvious questions.

"I'll have Ann get Dr. Max here within the hour. He just left for lunch; this will give you time to prepare your request and bring your material; you know how difficult this will be; there are risks for this woman. I can't ignore these risks. We'll meet in an hour."

After he had hung up, he asked Ann to chase Max and Emma Collins. He stopped and reflected. Jumping right back into the fire? Regional's reaction would be severe unless they had a substantial reason for risking this woman's intelligence.

A disorganized schizophrenic. Where did Charlie get this woman?

# # #

Seeing Charlie back in charge and pushing the team, boosted the entire squad, and Karen was especially happy to see Charlie back on a roll. A significant difference from a few months ago when alcohol dominated his life. She'd hoped Emma would evolve into a fixture of his life, but word around the Division dashed that speculation.

The Villa's complaint about a workplace affair embarrassed her. The Chief, Duncan Stirling, was the most decent man she'd ever worked with. He didn't have the imagination and quickness of Charlie; however, he was solid and knew how to run the Division.

She believed his confession of an unhappy marriage. And obviously, they both relished and hungered for physical affection. But, and this was the big 'but': would he leave his wife? And, just as big a question: did she want to be responsible for a divorce? When busy, she ignored all the doubts and questions. As always the slow periods or the quiet time at night caused all the anguish.

Any prolonged gaze by any detective in the squad whirled into a suspicious moment. Paranoid? Then, a few nights ago she thought Terry saw them kissing in Duncan's car. On the way to her apartment, they made one stop to pick up his dry cleaning. Before they pulled away from the curb, horns blared from behind Duncan's car. When she looked through the back window, she spied Terry. He stood in the middle of the road shaking his fist at a truck, which moved inches away from his hips. The exceptionally bright street lights cut through the darkness. She was sure Terry saw them, probably in full embrace. She never told Duncan.

Time to end the affair? Could she?

CHAPTER 25: Charlie's Log: A DISCONNECTED MIND

The best and most promising lead we uncovered to date triggered my call to the Judge.

In less than an hour after the Monk audio, dispatch called. Someone from the west side reported a suspicious delivery, same neighborhood as the others; Wes and I arrived at the home in minutes, breaking every traffic rule we'd ever enforced.

Another modest neighborhood, another modest house, the pattern remained, and we knew what to expect. Cora Clark and her husband, Gene, came home from grocery shopping to find their side door jimmied open and a small package residing on the kitchen table; they lived about eight blocks from Mrs. Jackson but did not know her or Bev Sanchez.

The box looked identical to the others. Gene had opened it to find the two fingers and two ears, no blood, contents washed, no note, just a bow and arrow on the outside of the package. The contents looked large, even for the so-called little finger. Monk? I couldn't identify the fingers, but I sensed this third delivery belonged to my friend.

We didn't waste any time; Wes went outside organizing a canvass, hoping for a gray van. I directed my attention to the couple. "Mrs. Clark, have you or your husband ever been under the care of a psychologist or a psychiatrist?

The question seemed to bother her, and she appeared to hesitate. "No neither of us have.."

Wes interrupted before she finished. He pulled me outside, excited. "We got a gray van in the vicinity and the time frame fits; I made sure there was no prompting...... so a solid unsolicited citing. The guy, walking his dog, saw the van, never got the plates, and never thought anything was unusual. We will get him downtown and maybe we can closer to a make and model. Oh, and here is a copy of the audio clues, you ran out so fast you left them on your desk. I'm going to take the guy downtown; you ok with this?"

"Go chase the van. I'll go back in."

Cora and Gene Clark waited at the kitchen table, the sun shone through the one large window and cast shadows on the table, and steam from the fresh coffee came off the cups. Cora poured a cup for me; I restarted. "I'd like you both to listen to this short audio and tell me if you recognize any of the sounds."

They agreed, so I turned on the recording, letting it play through all segments giggle, the snorter, the cursing and finally the primal wailing. The first parts caused the usual shaking of heads and exchanged glances. As soon as the wailing started, Mr. Clark came right out of his chair and looked at his wife. "For God's sake, Cora that's our Lynn!"

His wife looked at me and nodded. "I tried to tell you our daughter has been diagnosed as a disorganized schizophrenic; she was diagnosed some years ago."

They then provided the details about their daughter. She had always been a high achiever, very bright, an IQ between 130 and 140, pleasant with an aptitude for music and art. Sometime in her late teens, the start of her second term at University, the problems surfaced. The incidents at first were always short lived, and she would be back to normal. The incidents varied but most often she was unable to focus on a single idea, couldn't express herself; her words and phrases spoken as random, unconnected segments. This resulted in frustration, which manifested with the primal wailing and pounding her desk and walls.

As a university student, she knew the Psychology department offered free assistance, if your case qualified. At that point, she managed enough control and awareness to understand she needed help and just walked into the Psychology front office and asked for help.

The department assigned her to a young postgraduate student, who already had a Ph.D., a Dr. Mesko. He spent about two or three sessions with her, asked her to tape her wailing and attempts to talk coherently; finally, he recommended she see a psychiatrist.

"We never saw Dr. Mesko; he just phoned us and said we shouldn't wait and didn't sound optimistic. Well Lynn did see a psychiatrist, and she now lives a group home; the home keeps staff on the premises 24/7, but residents are still permitted lots of freedom. So this combination of drugs, group therapy, social skill training and play acting allows her to live a pretty normal life."

"Any pictures of Dr. Mesko?"

"No, nothing like that. As I said, our only contact was over the phone."

"Did you ever see him? You or Gene?"

"Of course Lynn saw him at every session. But we never saw him, and the last contact was that phone call; I think he left the University shortly after his time with Lynn."

Son of a bitch. Close but still nothing. I had to push. "You said your daughter is brilliant; how do you know her IQ?"

"The first tests took place in elementary school. Then, Dr. Mesko, as part of his assessment, completed some of his own tests …so we end up with a number between 130 and 140."

I explained, with some omissions, our desperate search for Dr. Mesko and the possible death of Monk and then ended. "The overriding issue is: we can't find Dr. Mesko, and there're no pictures of the man."

I was in a sympathetic kitchen, which was comforting, but not of any use, I pushed harder. "I have an extreme request of your family. I wonder if I could get the both of you and Lynn to agree to have her undergo an S3 memory scan. With the brain probing process, we may be able to retrieve a segment of Lynn's memory, which contains an image of Dr. Mesko. Once we collect a picture we can age his appearance………. morph it to his current age. This is the kind of break we desperately need."

Neither spoke, I thought sympathy left the room; I'd been too fast, too blunt, and too desperate. Gene finally broke the silence. "Am I right there is no pain, but there is a possibility of permanent brain damage? Is this correct?"

"You're right on both accounts. I assure you Lynn will not be in pain at any time. Brain damage typically only occurs if the probing and scanning exceeds 45 minutes. For Lynn I intend to bring Dr. Max Armstrong, the Nobel Peace Prize winner who perfected the process, to supervise the interrogation.

Still a risk but I think Dr. Max can minimize the risk. In most cases the damage amounts five or at the worst ten IQ points; this loss can be a disaster for people who have low IQs; they can't afford this loss."

I realized how this sounded: Lynn can lose a few points, and it'll not matter to her. You know she is outside the mainstream in any case. I never said this, but I implied it. Shit.

They both listened and measured every word, serious people, wanting to help, not strangers to hardships and disappointments. After a long silence, Cora spoke. "The Robin Hood character killed Henry Patterson and Pameela Sharma, right? The Patterson family financed and built the group home where Lynn lives, and they heavily supplement the operating budget.

Gene, I think we should support this request. If there is some minor brain damage, Lynn will still be above average and still have many other problems, not related to IQ points. Gene, I think you should go to the home and explain it to her. She trusts you above all people; if you recommend it, she'll cooperate."

"You're right Cora; I know we owe the Patterson family. As well, the priest should be saved. If we don't help, even if there is some risk to Lynn, it will be difficult to live with that memory. Come on Detective Taylor you can follow us to the home and meet Lynn."

Jesus Christ, I wanted to kiss them both.

CHAPTER 26: A DECISION

A crowd gathered in the Judge's chamber: Stephen, his assistant Ann, Charlie, Emma, and Dr. Max Armstrong, Ann the surprise attendee. Did the Judge want a witness? The group, more or less, arranged in a circle, and the Judge gave Charlie the nod.

"Judge, I'm sure this Dr. Mesko is our guy; however, somehow, after completing his post-grad work, he managed to vanish. No id exists, no photos, no job history, and no vehicle registration as if he disappeared to a remote island. But, he presents the one common thread to all three deliveries and the audio clue set. We desperately need a picture; with a picture, we will get the face sent across the world in minutes. Since no photos exist, and we are desperate, I believe we can retrieve his image from Lynn Clark's memory. Lynn and her parents have agreed to an S3 memory scan."

The Judge, who recently received a reprieve from Regional, knew he was being forced back into a vulnerable position. If the scan failed in any way, the consequences would be severe, too many unusual incidents, too many unorthodox moves under his jurisdiction in the last year. The girl's family, if she suffered brain damage, could quickly turn, in their guilt, and claim they were pressured and did not appreciate the risks. He started his questioning. "Charlie, is the girl capable of comprehending the risk?"

"Her family and her psychiatrist think so. Although she lives in a supervised group home, she holds a part-time job, which forces her to interact with the public. Judge, she is all we have, and I think the Monk's head will be delivered within the week."

Dr. Max decided to add his support. "Judge before coming here I spoke to Dr. Wassant. Lynn has been under his care for over seven years. Dr. Wassant is a recognized expert with a solid reputation; he designed, or I should say redesigned the supplemental therapy sessions. These sessions significantly enhance the standard behavior modification programs or the social skill training and are now part of most programs in schizophrenic treatment centers across the state.

He claims if the worst happens and she loses between five and ten IQ points her lifestyle will not suffer, and her occupational skills will not be degraded; Lynn is an incredibly bright young woman.

Schizophrenics are often categorized as falling into three groups. One-third of the group never experiences another psychotic episode – after the initial occurrence. Treatment results in significant and permanent improvement.

The middle third, with the proper treatment, will experience improvement except for intermittent relapses and will experience some residual disability; their occupational level possibly decreases or they may become socially isolated.

The remaining one-third, unfortunately, experiences severe and permanent incapacity in all facets of their lives. They remain chronically ill and worse often don't respond to medications.

Lynn falls into the middle third; she is a disorganized schizophrenic, and although chronic, she is atypical in that her behavior regression stabilized, and because of a disciplined medication agenda, she maintains contact with reality. Her anti-psychotic medication allows her to function, cooperate, and participate in group therapy, and to even hold a part time job.

Last, I'll point out: Emma is the best S3 scanner in the region; she's mapped numerous memory patterns under extreme conditions. We've discussed the problem, and we propose to limit the S3 Interrogation to 35 minutes. It may appear that cutting back ten minutes is not significant, but I assure you the process is very time sensitive, and the closer we get to 45 minutes the risk escalates. If we go over 45 minutes, brain damage will occur; it only becomes a question of the degree of the damage. Therefore, the ten-minute buffer establishes a substantial margin. Emma will conduct the scan, and I'll monitor Lynn's vital signs and any outward manifestations of discomfort. Plus her own doctor will be present."

It sounded like a robust and practical approach. But why did these plans always encounter the unanticipated, the universal: Murphy's Law? It did not appear Stephen was convinced: previous foolproof plans and good intentions lingered as part of his consciousness. He looked at Dr. Max.

"Thanks, Max I appreciate your efforts, and I know Charlie does. My concerns with S3 are: we are operating on the cutting edge, and regardless of good intentions and theory, we're on the edge, and the risk is high. Regardless, I'll sign the authorization, but first I'll have Ann set up a recording session for Mr. and Mrs. Clark and Dr. Wassant.

Our session with them will be brutal and blunt; it will make the risks apparent, and there will be little chance of them claiming they never understood what was about to happen."

Charlie thought that son of a bitch; he'd developed a plan before the meeting started, which explained Ann's presence, so she could hear and grasp all the implications. Stephen continued.

"If I understand the group around me, you probably have Lynn in my reception area waiting to start. Am I right?"

Emma smiled and answered for the group. "Judge, you're close but wrong. She is across the square in the interrogation room; there a medical technician is explaining, answering questions, and helping in any possible way. John Wojecki, who will be our Historian for the session, is briefing her parents as to how the process works and how to play their roles as Watchers. Lynn's doctor, Dr. Wassant, waits for us in the Forensic building. Dr. Max and I have about a ten-minute walk, and we will be ready to start."

"Just remember Ann gets the clearance signatures first after the parents watch an S3 full video. Then I sign, then you begin; that is the sequence and no short cuts. And good luck to us all."

# # #

It took more like an hour than ten minutes for everything to be completed and the process to get started. In the meantime, Charlie returned to the station; the Chief needed briefing, a gap in communication not an option at this point. Dr. Wassant, Lynn's doctor, patiently waited in one of the small adjacent observation rooms.

John remained with Lynn's parents in the Watcher stations; they both appeared to be comfortable with their role. But, John, the experienced Historian, worried about their reaction when live memory segments flowed in front of them. If the first retrievals were profoundly emotional laden scenes, would they freeze or not respond quickly? This probe, with the 35-minute limit, demanded fast responses. He stressed the situation with Cora, who appeared to be a better candidate as a reserved detached viewer.

"Cora, the memory segments displayed often upset relatives, but our technicians can't control or edit the content. Each retrieved segment will be shown as experienced by Lynn. Some images may be a complete surprise to you or even a shock. Don't judge or become involved; you can cry later. Now it is critical for you to determine the date or time period displayed on the monitor: the key to deciding: is this before or after Lynn saw Dr. Mesko?"

"John, I know. I understand. The full training images we saw took away most of the shock of such an intimate retrieval. I know what's at stake; Ann was very blunt and honest."

Emma and Dr. Max sat with Lynn in the scanning room; Lynn had been administered all the S3 medications and was only partially conscious, almost a sleep state. Most people could respond to commands but felt no desire to chat and, of course, there was no need.

A strange site: Lynn firmly strapped to the table, with the scanning device clamped on her head; her scalp shaved to ensure a firm fit. The central component of the scanning device resembled a football helmet with a multitude of attached cables, numerous wires entering the helmet and one large cable exiting, serving as the feeder to a computer system.

"Max, I think I should be a more stringent editor than I normally am; I mean there could be images which no parent should see; you know the type of situations we could encounter."

"Emma we can't afford the time for you to select which memory streams are suitable for parents. If you get a stable image, you just release it to the Watcher room. John and I've discussed this, and he has warned the parents; we've to go with it; let's start, everyone is ready."

She did not argue. Her routine began. The first sets of images were always retained in the control room so Emma could calibrate focus and adjust to the physical dimensions of the patient's skull. Max started screaming almost immediately. "Goddamn it Emma! Is the unit broken? What the hell is this?"

The retrieved images, which flashed on their monitors, were transient images, one after another appearing and then disappearing in an explosion of fireworks. Emma felt she was riding a bucking horse at a rodeo: it became impossible to retrieve a memory stream and have it display as a contiguous set. Images appeared in a random fashion and disappeared as quickly, no stability, chaotic strings of meaningless videos. Every direction Emma moved the scanner, the results never changed, an incoherent view of the world: bounding from one image and unrelated segment to another.

Emma thought she understood. "Max you know what we're seeing? Goddamn it. It's a disorganized schizophrenic view of the world; we're seeing, a disconnected mind, nothing makes sense. This is how Lynn sees the world and tries to relate. This is either from one of her early episodes, or this is her current world, she can't focus, not able to process her world. We can't move in a meaningful way without being able to establish reference points in time."

"Shut it down; we can't afford any more time on this introductory session. I'm going next door and talk to Dr. Wassant. Join me after you set the unit into a waiting stage and tell the Watchers we need some time, no reason just say time."

Max burst into the waiting room where Dr. Wassant was just finishing a phone call. From this smaller secondary observation room, he'd seen the preliminary results but still appeared calm.

"Dr. Wassant you told us Lynn was stable and taking her medication. What we see is far from stable."

"As soon as I saw the images, I called the home and spoke to the staff. It appears over the past week Lynn has been exhibiting some symptoms. I must stress nothing severe, trouble expressing herself, minor problems in concentrating on the task at hand, some inappropriate giggling, minor episodes like that. Staff thought it was due to the pressure of her new job and increased public contact."

Emma entered the room and saw a furious Max, almost out of control.

"Dr. Wassant isn't this rather fucking late for you to be providing this information. Is there anything else you or staff cares to reveal about Lynn?"

Emma thought he might strike Wassant; she tried to intervene. "Is there anything you can suggest? She is your patient, and you know her medical history. How would you proceed, if she wasn't under the S3 medication?"

Dr. Wassant may have been careless about Lynn's status, but he was certainly confident and calm under pressure, never muttered, never mumbled, and never fidgeted. He spoke in an authoritative voice.

"I've seen this on a few occasions, and I think I know what happened to Lynn. What the staff saw and failed to report was not due to the stress of a part-time job but episodes of psychosis, of very short duration; Lynn controlled the outward manifestations, so staff did not detect the changes. Yes, she has been taking her medication. It appears she is one of those patients who has developed a tolerance for her medication. An exceptional situation but I'm convinced it started last week and so the drug a derivative of ziprasidone has slowly been losing its efficacy over the last six or seven days."

Max continued to fume, so Emma continued. "Assume you're right. What would you typically do at this point?"

"Obviously I'd switch her medication. But now, for her at this juncture, I would recommend some high doses of valium to bring her down, provide some stabilization until I can research another long term medication."

This time Dr. Max broke in. "For God's sake she's been living with this goddamn ziprasidone derivative in her system for years, and we've just saturated her with the S3 drug mixture, and you propose we introduce another drug. Fucking asinine.

We have no way of knowing how she'll react to the addition of another drug. Goddamn it, we can't do that; the risk is too high. It would take me days to study all the interactions with all those drugs and the electronics of a brain scan. Unfucking believable."

Wassant, not ruffled, persisted. "An alternative is to wait 24 hours for all drugs to clear her system and start all over using valium to stabilize her."

"Listen you stupid shit; you've no way of knowing if 24 hours is enough time to cleanse her system. And a 24-hour delay means we might as well print up Monk's death certificate."

Emma wondered about Dr. Wassant: had he known about Lynn's condition before they started? Had he just been curious about Stage 3? Did he just want to see streams of disorganized schizophrenic memory retrieved? Did he just conveniently forget about Lynn's recent problems?

It did not take him long to come up with tolerance theory. Maybe this well-respected professional wanted more glory, another bullet point for his vitae curriculum.

She exchanged a look with Max, his feeling all over his face, and she knew she projected the same frustration. Who would call Judge Stephen? Another example of Murphy's Law? Who would tell Charlie?

CHAPTER 27: DR. MESKO

The amputation wounds throbbed, and a numbness settled into his buttocks.

Monk was conscious again; thirst abated, hunger a dull need. Some of the discomforts reminded him of his years as a defensive tackle, when it took a couple of days to whirlpool away the pain of a tough Sunday afternoon. This afternoon a symphony of pain and discomfort competed for his attention: ears, fingers, butt, like an ugly merry-go-round, a reminder of his hopeless position. The music blared, on a maddening non-stop loop; on occasion, his jailer would break into song, 'Robin Hood' being the only phrase the lunatic consistently verbalized. His jailer advanced to his side and studied Monk.

"I can't believe your pain tolerance. To be truthful, it's rather irritating; the screaming is part of my enjoyment, and definitely an enhancement to the audio productions. I'll have to come up with a different part to amputate next time. What I mean is before I do your head.

I need to record a magnificent scream. What is the matter with you? Don't you ever talk? Took a vow of silence?"

Monk wondered how to deal with the maniac. One thing he believed: the other victims begged or tried to reason with him, and that failed. Until some other plan or strategy came to mind, he decided to be mute. His stoic loss of the ears and fingers even surprised him.

"Why don't you bless me? Try to convert me? Get me off this evil track. Hell of a priest you turned out to be. Not even willing to work with a poor sinner."

A variation of this mocking challenge continued for some time; he wanted a reaction, a pleading outburst. Next, the killer shook the table in an attempt to aggravate the wounds. But Monk's professional football legacy of living with a multitude of injuries and his faith provided the buffer to deal with the maniac's antics. When he played even his teammates used to remark about his ability to play hurt week after week.

"You stubborn bastard. I'm going to run. Work to be done. Work that finances my extracurricular activity. I'll be back, and then we'll have more fun; I always save the saw for the last cut. I'll turn it on before I go so you can think about it.

Now pay attention, I'm positioning this drinking tube by your cheek, if you want a drink just turn your head a few degrees. I don't want you to die on me, not until I'm ready. Good-bye big man."

Robin went to the far corner of the cabin and began the unpeeling process, layers of clothing, gloves, and a mask. For the most part, he was pleased with his executions and deliveries, all well planned, clockwork precision, the product of a superior intellect. One aspect irritated: his own inconsistency, at times last minute decisions and changes. Upsetting behavior. Why did he not shoot the arrow into the bull's eye? Why did he deliver Pameela's head to the Mayor's office and not to her home? His original plan called for a rigid sequence of events with the deliveries and discoveries in the proper order.

For the priest: where to deliver the head? To the Cardinal? Charlie? Neither poor or in need. But, the priest was more symbolic. Best to go to the Cardinal, the delivery site already scouted, no need to change and go to an unknown area.

After the big guy, best to change and move on. After a while, he could start another series, same genre but a different script. He wondered if Charlie had discovered Dr. Mesko. Did not matter he would never find him.

The solitary detective surveyed the room.

Monk kept this as his private sanctuary. The Forensic team finished earlier in the day; now Charlie remained on a straight back chair. He desperately searched for any anomaly, anything out of place, a possible clue as to how Robin captured Monk.

In Monk's room: a single bed, a desk with a computer, a big lounge chair, and two straight back chairs, a few books, clothes in the closet and a large dresser, a small rug on the floor, the walls almost bare. He thought the damn place looked a monk's retreat and smiled at the weak joke. Forensics had analyzed the computer, scanned the security tapes, and reviewed any paper correspondence, all resulting in nothing, absolutely nothing.

The only connection to this case was that Monk, on occasion, did visit the Complex where the giggler lived. He tried to set up a regular Sunday service, but it appeared Dr. Villa opposed the idea and influenced the rest of the staff. However, Monk's last visit took place weeks ago.

How in the hell had he been snatched? It seemed impossible someone that large could be abducted without a trace. Surely someone he trusted, someone he knew and when he understood the mistaken belief, it was too late.

Charlie walked around the room. Memories of all their times together from elementary school, through years of football, to the present surfaced in a rather random fashion. The day dreaming highlights brought a smile. He thought about Monk's pro career, a regular all-star, a hard, tough man, giving no quarter and, of course, asking for none, a complete opposite to his persona off the field. A damn cliché. The proverbial gentle giant his best friend for years.

Charlie played and lived as the emotional and quick-tempered partner, needing immediate satisfaction and ready for a reckless move to achieve it. Monk had been patient and a steady rock throughout the years. Was Charlie going to fail him?

Charlie reviewed all the loose papers, even the sticky notes plastered on the desktop computer. He was wasting his time, a useless exercise. How did Robin select Monk? If he hated the Catholic Church, why grab Monk? Was it because Monk had such an extensive profile in the community? Or did he know Monk? No good answers surfaced.

No more clues, other than Dr. Mesko. Soon he would hear from Emma and Dr. Max; he needed that image retrieval from young Lynn's memory scan.

# # #

Judge Stephen spoke in an even voice, despite his concern. "Dr. King wrote a formal letter of complaint, with copies to all members of the Regional Committee. In his grievance, he accuses you of recommending the change to our standard waiting period of 72 hours between an S1 Interrogation and the S3 memory scan."

Doug Brewster, a lawyer for many years, familiar with accusations, knew all about intense questioning, and nasty insinuations. Besides, as soon as he heard about Dr. Jerry King's firing, he guessed the little prick would strike out, and he would be an obvious target. So the call to the Judge's office had not come as a surprise, and he arrived prepared.

Doug considered his lunch with King as one his better moves: the manipulation of this academic close to a masterpiece. For a brilliant scientist, the good Dr. had been easy. Maybe this is what con men meant when they said: if people want the result, they will believe and ignore even obvious risks. King wanted recognition, and a record fast clearing of Fort Green would have done that for him.

"I don't suppose he has any evidence, like a recording or written directive, of this alleged recommendation. Does he?"

"No, but he claims this happened at a luncheon before his final interview with individual members of our Board. As well, he states you coached him as to how to conduct himself during his interview with me: a detailed and convincing letter."

"This doesn't surprise me. A high-end achiever, fired from his first job outside of an academic setting, is lashing out at anyone. Yes, I did have lunch with him prior to our interviews; I wanted to get to know him ......in an informal setting, beyond the structure of an interview. After our problem with Dr. Kate, I thought we needed to be extremely cautious with the next appointment.

During lunch, he came across a trifle harsh. When he started talking about the process of assessing convicts before making decisions about their fate, I suggested high emotions didn't belong in the process. We needed cold logic, and this is what most members of the Board would be looking for in our candidate. Now if that is what he means by 'coaching', then I guess I am guilty. Nevertheless, I certainly never told him to reduce the waiting period to 24 hours.

Stephen, we both know this can't be resolved. If we go any further, it will become a huge public relations nightmare of: he said…..I said and everyone enjoying the spectacle except our Board."

"Yes, I know. I'm informing Regional no evidence exists to support King's accusations, and I'm not prepared to go any further. However, I'm putting his letter on file.

I know you're an ambitious man, but I caution you to be patient: your turn will come. And I also advise you to stop underestimating me."

An unrepentant Doug Brewster left the Judge's office. He did not feel intimidated. What the Judge did not know: Doug's wife's cousin was a recent hire at Regional headquarters. This family connection provided the type of support that the Judge was lacking. This last appointment along with his other allies placed him in a position to deal with many complaints and bullshit letters.

The Judge, on the other hand, teetered on the edge, King his second consecutive disastrous appointment to a pivotal position. How many more times could Stephen bring his unorthodox decisions to the attention of the Region? One more incident and Region might ask the Judge to resign: at least the prevailing gossip whispered a firing.

Stephen consistently proved too damn naïve, regularly forgetting that not everyone played by the rules.

CHAPTER 28: THE RESULTS

The manner in which Dr. Wassant reacted or failed to react impressed Emma.

He appeared to ignore the obvious: Emma and Dr. Max were furious with him. Dr. Max continued with a non-stop tirade broadcasting his opinion about Wassant's competence and integrity. An ugly scene. Emma, for the first time, witnessed a Dr. Max tirade. She guessed part of his frustration resulted from an obligation he felt for Charlie and his work in uncovering the Dr. Kate-Grovernor conspiracy. But she also knew he detested incompetence. Wassant sat quietly, chin resting on his hands, thinking. Finally, he spoke.

"On other occasions, I mean in an emergency, when I worried about a medication change and the possible side reactions, I continued with the same drug. But doubled the standard dosage of the same drug; usually, the results were swift, and within minutes the patient stabilized, was cooperative and able to communicate. The risk is minimal, only a one-time occurrence; at worst the patient becomes so relaxed she goes to sleep.

And, because Lynn's medication is in everyday use, I carry the liquid version of the derivative, and this version will be absorbed much faster than her morning meds."

Dr. Max thought for a few minutes then responded. "Dr. Wassant get the dosage ready for Lynn; we'll go with your recommendation; this sounds like our best alternative. While you prepare her, Emma and I will be in the next room discussing the scan restart."

Once alone, Max instructed her. "Phone Charlie and get him to call the Judge. This is a departure, and we should get the Judge's clearance. I believe Wassant, and we'll not be introducing a different drug into her system. But I don't trust the bastard, or maybe I just don't like him."

Emma reached Charlie in seconds and explained the dilemma, his response a shock.

"No, I'm not calling Stephen, and I suggest you don't either. He's already hanging too far out on this interrogation. If there are risks, the consequences belong to Dr. Max and you. It's a medical decision, and you're the experts. Make the goddamn decision or prepare for Monk's funeral." Then he hung up, his intense anger hard for her to fathom.

Dr. Max listened as she relayed the response, and he agreed with Charlie: this interrogation left the Judge vulnerable, an easy target. Emma continued. "Ok Max let's leave it, but maybe we should talk to the parents and get their agreement."

"No, let's get Dr. Wassant in here and proceed with the meds. I'll go on record as making this my decision and only mine, no one else. I owe Charlie and Stephen; now it's my turn. In any case, I honestly believe there'll be no harm to Lynn. My concern now: if this doesn't work then we won't have any choice but to wait 48 hours for her system to clear before we can try and stabilize her with the antipsychotic drug."

As they waited for the additional dose to take effect, Emma thought about the last few minutes. Why was Charlie so angry? Was she the reason? How did Dr. Wassant happen to carry the additional drug dosage? Dr. Max's behavior also delivered a jolt, not only his anger with Wassant but his feelings for Charlie and Stephen, the first time he'd acknowledged the work of Charlie and the Judge's support.

No more time for speculation. First, John was told about the restart so he could resettle Mr. and Mrs. Clark back to their stations, these two still not informed about the drama with Dr. Wassant. She looked at the clock monitor and saw they'd only devoured five minutes of their target time. The clock control was integrated with the scanning unit and counted the number of minutes and seconds the probe actively intruded on the brain. They now had 30 minutes left to find Dr. Mesko's image in Lynn's memory.

Lynn Clark, after the new dosage, progressed to a relaxed state, not fully asleep but very close, a smile on her face, a happy woman. Emma signaled ready, and John responded ready. Dr. Max sat in the control room, as the silent monitor. He knew Emma to be the key person from this point forward.

The memory storage patterns were more enigmas than a science. Chronological sequences often gave way to some twisted folding roller coaster sequences that Western logic could not solve. Even Emma could not explain how she visualized the evolving patterns; it was this visualization which allowed her to move the scanner around the physical dimensions of the brain. For many participants, the memory schematics seemed to evolve quickly, and Emma would move with ease. For other scans, a problematic pattern made the probing a more difficult task and they, on rare occasions, came close to exceeding the 45-minute barrier. She functioned best when she relaxed and allowed the subliminal components of her mind to direct her hand.

Her calm comments got his attention.

"Max it looks good. I'm getting stable images….. they're holding…. her family…. has responded they recognized the first set of memories. It's good….. Max, it's good."

Then Emma was lost to him, as she worked in conjunction with the Watchers. She moved the probe back and forth trying to find the correct period, to locate the segment of Lynn's memory, which would yield the scene they needed. As the image retrievals continued, Dr. Max relaxed for a few moments.

The elapsed time on the clock monitor flashed 22 minutes. Emma struggled to consistently find a coherent template, which would allow her to feel confident about the next scalp location of the probe. Each new move of the probe began to feel like a gambling exercise, a shot in the dark, a random move. Often when Emma thought she'd isolated the next sequential memory module, it turned out to be an unrelated segment. But the image quality persisted, and Cora Clark proved to be fast and not distracted by pictures and memories on the screen. No bizarre behavior was retrieved, all frames regular but erratic, making it difficult for Emma.

Without warning, the main display screen flashed a classroom, which looked, like a university lecture theater. Could Emma locate a session with the psychology group? She tried to relax: let her subconscious make the next minor adjustment of the probe; she couldn't recall making so many miniscule probe shifts. Then a buzzer noise filled the control room, and John's voice announced the success.

"Emma, we have him. That is the guy."

A perfect hit. On the screen: in a small room, like an interview room, a young man was talking to Lynn. He was bald, goatee beard, horn rim glasses with an olive complexion and the soft features of an academic. Emma heard his voice, definitely dispensing advice. Max was urgent. "Emma please stop and capture the images."

They obtained 12 different images, all various aspects of Dr. Mesko's face; all were immediately forwarded to Charlie. Smiles all around, Lynn now peacefully asleep; the clock monitor read 27 minutes.

A stunned Dr. Wassant walked out of the observation facility and to his patient; the entire procedure had gone beyond his expectation. He'd known the risk in allowing Lynn to go forward; her symptoms had bothered him throughout the week, the reason for the liquid dosage in his bag. Unless Dr. Max went after him, his duplicity would be forgotten and never questioned.

 Max stopped swearing at him once the memory streams began, erratic time switches but stable images. Still, Dr. Wassant realized it would be some time before he could relax and stop worrying about the wild bastard; he'd heard about his sexual prowess but not his explosive temper.

# # #

At the completion of Lynn's scan, Dr. Max abruptly left the building and drove back to the Central Research Center and the safety of his office on the top floor. He paced the interior of his office and then around the full perimeter of the floor; the deserted floor furnished the seclusion he wanted. The man cursed, swung his arms in frustration, and occasionally banged counter tops as he raced around the facility. The frightened scientist was furious at himself for allowing the memory probe to proceed, jumping into the unknown, ignoring the risk.

 Max could still visualize a helpless Lynn: sedated with the S3 drugs, in addition to her regular derivative of ziprasidone. Then for Christ's sake, he allowed that bloody Dr. Wassant to give her more of the fucking derivative. Wassant insisted the worst outcome: Lynn would lose consciousness. What pure bullshit. The entire memory probe a calculated guess. Double the damn dosage!

If any harm came to the young woman, he, along with the Judge, would pay the price. He needed to monitor her: best to send one of his more supportive colleagues to see Lynn and keep checking for the next month. Goddamn that Wassant. However, to be honest, Max knew he wanted to help Charlie. He certainly owed the detective and, of course, the Judge, who assigned him to Max's rape case. A rare occasion for him to succumb to an altruistic act, but that damn rape charge and the prospect of an S3 memory interrogation had terrified him.

As he made another circuit on the floor, his thoughts diverted to the Farm, a regular distraction. Maybe he should visit the Farm again and spend some time with Sally Grovernor. What a woman: still a teenager but smarter and tougher than any of his previous conquests. The surprise: her mother agreed to the engagement. It appeared Mrs. Grovernor had enough of Sally, and if Max wanted the responsibility, she gladly acquiesced. Besides after the big family scandal – a wedding to a Nobel Peace Prize winner would get her back on the top of the social scene.

He guessed what the Judge's view of his engagement would not be favorable. Stephen would be upset and would find it hard to believe. Could the older man be jealous? Not of Sally but because Max acted on his desires, something the Judge could not do. Max did not know the background behind Stephen's fascination with Dr. Kate. However, from the time she came on the Board Max sensed a strong attraction, and if there was one thing he understood, it was male-female bonding. Would the righteous Judge ever muster the courage to follow his own instincts?

Once more around the research lab and his mind seized another idea. The retrieval of segments of memory from the disorganized schizophrenic, Lynn, started to intrigue him, beyond Charlie's case. There was a significant piece of research in front of him. The idea: retrieve relevant memory streams from different types of mentally ill people.

This harvest would create an unbelievable inventory for more advanced research. Once the streams were captured and cataloged; the analysis could begin. Reality compared to the scene as perceived by the mentally ill person.

Max thought about the range of different mental illnesses and the possible scenarios, which could be retrieved and analyzed. It would be a bitch of a project. First, there was the danger of permanent brain damage to all people subjected to the S3 memory scan. What would be a safe time limit? 30 minutes?

Would he have to take them off all medications? Moreover, for how long? Yes, they would have to come off their medication and be off long enough to revert to full-blown psychotics. Otherwise, he would not be capturing the images he needed. Last, would it be possible to conduct repetitive scans, say every six to twelve months, in associations with different treatments? Repetitive scans undoubtedly increased the risk of permanent brain damage. Many barriers and unknowns.

It intrigued him: the idea of capturing a slanted, insane view of the world. Max would capture reality as perceived by a deranged subject. What to expect when the mentally ill wrestle with reality? What happens when they return to their medication and see the distorted retrieved images? He had to find a psychiatrist to become part of the project.

This scenario had the potential to become a milestone in the treatment of the mentally ill. Max could not complete the thought process: did not know where it would lead; his mind raced in a multitude of directions. May not work for all types of illnesses. Did not matter. He believed his selection pool was so large he'd be able to obtain many volunteers, and his reputation should ease the funding campaign. Lynn's possible problems faded and disappeared from his mind.

One exciting question remained: has any man ever won two Nobel Peace Prizes in his lifetime?

CHAPTER 29: MORPHING

Wes and Karen waited while Charlie explained and distributed large glossy photo prints.

"The techs finished with Dr. Mesko's image and morphed it into some different sets. We'll get to the database and project it on Karen's large monitor. There we can look at the complete range; I printed the six I thought might be the best for our canvassing."

In a matter of minutes, Karen started the retrieval process. The first set assumed he would not radically alter his basic appearance: baldhead (but now completely shaved) and the original goatee. This image was aged around a couple of different scenarios: someone who aged well and looked younger than his actual age: next normal aging: last someone who suffered from smoke and sun damage.

Some different assumptions fashioned the next set: he let his hair grow, got rid of the goatee, and changed to a full beard, dyed hair: then the entire group of beardless men was aged.

Charlie appreciated the complexity; the guy dropped out of sight more than ten years ago. He thought it best to assume Mesko wanted to disappear and drastically changed his appearance. Now the problem became the high number of options, and he knew too many pictures could confuse a witness.

The squad all agreed at some point Mesko had worked in the Sector as a qualified psychologist with clients; they were making many assumptions with few facts. Charlie needed some action. "First, let's hit all the institutions with patients or clients who are full-time residents. If we strike out, then we knock on the door of every psychologist and psychiatrist practicing out of a private office and in a 50-mile radius around the city. It would be impossible for him to practice in the city and not have contact with one or more of these people."

Wes hesitated. "Charlie, I've a problem with this approach. This damn Robin knows his way around people who are intellectually challenged or mentally disabled and the associated care facilities because he got the recordings.

But we don't know it was Dr. Mesko. There are a lot of medical staff and even administrators who had an opportunity to record. On top of all this, Mesko has vanished. And nothing indicates he ever came back into practice and rubbed shoulders with the people you want us to canvass. Are we wasting our time?"

"Well give me an alternative."

"Why not go public and get the morphed images splashed on national news for a couple of nights; it'll be faster, and we get a wider audience, possibly someone who knew him at the time of his disappearance.

Second, let's dig deeper into the Pattersons and the Sharmas. We've only started our research into their histories. Why of all the rich and famous were they selected? What, if anything makes them unique? I know you did some background work on this, but we always get interrupted and never get too deep. Shouldn't we spend more time on these two families?"

Charlie thought about the suggestions for a few minutes. "In reverse order, I agree: time to crawl over the families and see how he was able to spy on them and gather all the info undetected. Karen since you started digging into their family histories, you might as well include their staff and the outside firms they hire; that'll allow Terry to concentrate on the motor vehicle searches.

 I'll use my contacts and solicit some help from the press who maintain extensive archives of social events, charity balls and relate parties. I want to identify any events where both families are prominent. OK?

Now your first recommendation. I don't want to go public. If Dr. Mesko is Robin Hood, I don't want him to know about our progress. In some remote location Monk's tied up, and if Robin panics he'll kill him and disappear. My guess in three or four days the main delivery will arrive.

One last thing: the Chief got us a couple of extra bodies to help search the property records and sales or rentals of cabins, primarily rural property. Robin requires a spot where he can work undisturbed. It's unlikely to be registered under the name of Mesko. We'll use the best pseudo or alias combinations Manuel created. That is what we have, so we have to run with it."

"Ok Charlie, I know you are right I'm just so damn frustrated. I'll select about 12 of the morphed images to use; I'm afraid the whole array will be too confusing, too many choices. And you know we are all committed. This is 24/7 until we find the match."

"Thanks Wes. Karen, can you stay for a few minutes?''

"Want some more coffee? Just let me get the door, and we can talk. Karen I'm going to step out of bounds for a few minutes..........Karen, you have to walk away."

"Walk away? What is this all about?"

"I'll ask you to stop for a minute and accept this as coming from a friend and not a supervisor...OK?"

Karen never responded just stared and waited. Charlie didn't hesitate. "It's you and the Chief. You need to walk away. I think you're stronger than the Chief, and you know it can only end in disaster unless you walk. He's not going to leave his wife, not at this stage in his life and career; it doesn't matter how he feels about her or you. Neither of you wants to end your careers with this as your legacy."

Karen's emotions surfaced. "Who asked you? You're the last person to be providing insight into personal relations............goddamn it ....I guess everybody knows....shit."

"No, at this point, not everybody knows but soon. Look I told you this is not your supervisor talking. You're right I'm not an expert, but what I see is not a happy ending. I think you've the strength to do this... .tell him it won't work .....bury yourself in this case and then use all your accumulated days for a long holiday in Australia."

Karen wiped the tears away. A silent watering, no sobbing just a damp set of red eyes.

"The Chief and I talked about breaking up a couple of times then we reconcile; it's so hard. We are such a good fit, I mean beyond sex; we can finish each other's sentences. The two of us communicate with a glance; we're from the same …….."

Charlie let her talk and watched her pay the price for some comfort and love, she (and the Chief) needed and found. The price would be high for both of them. Finally, she stopped, wiped her face and forced a grin.

"I'm finished. Out of steam. I know you're right. I'll tell the Chief …….time to walk and this time I mean it…thanks Charlie."

She made for the door.

"Karen there is one thing. Don't tell the Chief I gave you the advice."

"I understand. Now it's my turn. All of us have voted, and the decision is: you must donate your jacket to the Salvation Army. It's too big and too ugly to be constantly on your shoulders."

# # #

By using an electronic package, the material, a set of morphed images and a questionnaire, was distributed throughout the Sector in minutes. The targets were the offices of all health related facilities, doctors' offices, and the psychologists' national registry. Unlike the sound bites inquiry, this canvass targeted the executive level and human resources personnel, those sectors responsible for hiring. A response was mandatory.

It became the most aggressive canvas in the history of the Sector, detectives quick to pursue any slow responses. They regularly encountered absent staff or busy managers, but they pushed hard, and the replies rolled in, all consistent: never saw the man.

Charlie began to feel that this clue would not be enough, and he saw the concern on Wes's face as the responses piled up.

# # #

"Terry, what about the motor vehicle license search?"

"Charlie, I'm using all 12 images for a comparison to the registry mug shots. This means all male drivers in a 100-mile radius. The search is almost finished and so far no hit."

"Not fucking possible. The son of a bitch has to drive, and he's too smart to get caught without a driver's license, too big a risk."

"Charlie maybe he no longer lives or works in the Sector. Maybe he used to work here, and moved and is just back to play his games. I think we have to expand the search and go national. Our focus is too narrow."

"OK, expand the search beyond the Sector but do it by region so that the adjacent Sectors are the first. I still believe he's here in our Sector. And, I think we're close but somehow not on track. What else? The best clue to date and we're fading. What are we missing?"

# # #

Late in the evening and an exhausted Karen stared at the one name she was sure would be their next step toward Robin. It surfaced in the family research, which she and Terry had conducted at various stages; the damn job made more complicated as Charlie switched assignments and then reassigned his detectives.

However, between the two of them, they completed a detailed search of all staff and services both families used in the past three years. One company came to the front: Maids & Gardens. Both parents used this company numerous times both for work on their large outside yards and inside their homes, whether for regular house cleaning or special occasions. The significant number of temporary staff the company employed and their shabby record keeping resulted in a slow and awkward search.

The company surprised Karen with their cooperation and willingness to use overtime to assist in her search. She wanted names of staff who had been assigned to both families. The result: five people who had been assigned a significant number of times to both families; the other link:

these people worked both in the yard and later inside the house, an excellent experience for documenting security and habits.

Four of the staff were women and still employed by the company. The fifth: a man who no longer worked for the business, had not for some time. Karen confirmed that his home address was a fake and the rest of the personal data was false. The company apologized; they employed so many temporary workers that on occasion they did slip up; to compound the problem: no photo on file. The manager apologized and agreed their recordkeeping and hiring practices demanded tighter control. Karen labeled him a good confessor who would go far in that company's hierarchy but essentially a liar; the lack of detail on temporary staff was probably a standard process and always would be. In any case, she did have a name: Henry Messer.

This link in the puzzle confirmed their thinking: he had scouted the families. Tomorrow morning she would talk to other Maids & Gardens staff about this Messer. She was not optimistic about what useful information would result; the people in the office could not even remember him. He was just one of many who flowed through their offices, worked for a couple of weeks, got his pay and may or may not return for another assignment.

CHAPTER 30: BILL THOMPSON

Uncle Willie, now Commissioner of the Prisons Division, never stopped an old habit of random wandering through a prison, talking to convicts and guards, not any profound discussions, just casual interchanges, lots of humor, on occasion a nugget, and always gossip. Fort Green used to be Willie's prison. As former warden, he knew all the corridors, gates, and most of the guards and convicts. Outside a few prisoners shuffled around the exercise yard, no groups, just isolated walkers; the decommissioning of the prison had destroyed the regular routines and old habits; he stopped to talk to Mallory.

"Snowman, I hear you passed the S1 Interrogation and are heading for a Farm."

He did not bother to tell him: Jessie had asked for his advice. The former warden advised Jessie to clear Mallory. The white haired convict with the yellow fingers was used to short discussions with Willie, who had been Warden all the years Mallory served.

"You're right Commissioner. I'll be gone in a few days. I'm pleased to be moving on and out of here."

"You heard Willard, our financial hustler, was executed today?"

"Yah, the bastard never stopped hustling, right to his last breath. In here he screwed some convicts out of their last dollar with his goddamn Omega scheme."

Willard had sold crushed aspirin powder as an antidote to S1 Interrogation drugs; his promise: Omega powder would allow you to complete an S1 Interrogation under your own control.

"He classified as a repeat offender with a multitude of financial hustles which drained the lifesaving of many families over numerous years."

"I know. Most of us thought Willard was a real prick, without honor. No one is sorry for him. We're looking forward to the Farm and Half Way Houses. It sounds as if there may be some hope for rehabilitation."

Uncle Willie watched him walk across the yard and line up at the door providing entry back into the prison. He liked Mallory and hoped he could take advantage of this opportunity. The Snowman would never know how close he came to an S3 memory scan and a repeat offender label. Should this convict be told? The ice around the Snowman was extremely thin. Mallory craved excitement and action. However, his next action could be his last.

Willie kept walking, guards opening doors without any requests from him. They knew his routine and respected the man. A few more discussions and he found himself in the staff cafeteria. The kitchen staff left out a large container of coffee and a plate of cookies for a self-serve snack routine. The place was deserted except for Emma Collins at a table near the coffee. He poured his coffee and joined her at the table.

"Emma, have you slept in the last five days?"

"Yes, a few hours here and there." Then she tried to divert any discussion about herself.

"I can't believe the change in Jessie. Overnight or it seems like overnight he's grown into the leadership role the Judge wanted. He clears barriers in minutes, he's ahead of us on most issues, anticipating and, in general, being a positive role model for the staff. I understand he assisted you with creating temporary Farms and Half Way Houses for your projected excess inventory. You must be very pleased with this resource and his revised attitude. Maybe it's self-confidence."

Uncle Willie knew that Stephen threatened Jessie's career but never told Emma, not necessary, the results counted.

"Yes I'm more than pleased; he even talked to the community leaders in the neighborhood where our Farms and Houses are located. I know the Judge is beaming."

For a few minutes, they both were silent and drank coffee. Finally, Bill opened.

"Young lady it would be best if you would get eight hours sleep today; you can't do everything. We're back on schedule, and the extra executions were validated. You don't look good. I know about your excess workload before Dr. Jerry King; then his appointment meant more pressure because you worked with his bad decisions. The delay, the recovery analysis and now a restart added to your burden. I think I should ask the Judge to provide some relief for you. You know Dr. King was not your fault."

"I try to sleep, but within a few hours I'm up and have to work. At University, Jerry King and I became close friends, and I do feel sorry for him. I don't know what came over him. When I knew him, his only focus was research and his teaching; students loved him, packed the lecture hall when he presented. I sometimes wonder if the publicity and celebrity status of Dr. Max didn't generate some envy and a desire to be considered on the same level.

Jerry is brilliant, but Max is a few steps ahead of everyone. Whatever the reason for Jerry's recklessness and poor judgment, he almost destroyed Stephen's career, and we're lucky innocent men were not executed.

I fought with him, ugly screaming arguments but I didn't take it the next step. You did; you went to the Judge; I should have, instead of assuming Jerry had an agreement with the Judge."

"Easier for me; I was never the man's friend and little to lose; if they fired me, no problem. I'm already drawing a pension. Don't feel bad; he used to be a close friend. And even I assumed he'd informed Stephen."

Another prolonged silence, which ended abruptly when she lost control. Uncle Willie's kind words touched the exhausted woman. Emma's elbows rested on the table, and she lowered her head onto her hands; this was her starting point for a series of quiet sobs, tears hitting the table, the crying soft and steady. It all happened so quickly Bill never had a chance to respond. Almost as quickly she wiped her face and put her mask back on.

"Bill I'd appreciate it if you would not mention this to anyone; we only have a few days left. If at any time I feel I not capable of doing the job, I will step aside, this I promise you."

"Emma, I trust you; this stays with us. Do you want to talk about it?"

"No, nothing but fatigue. Thanks, it appears I can handle my professional life but am good at destroying my personal life. I seem unable to coordinate or manage both simultaneously.   Sorry for running." With those comments, she left Bill at the table with his coffee and an untouched cookie.

He was not in a hurry. The name on the door may read 'Bill Thompson', but he would always be Uncle Willie to the convicts and guards. He thought about his next move, which was against Sector policy and could potentially cost him more than his current job. The Snowman should be informed as to how close the vote had been and how close an S3 memory scan sat in his future.

As he walked back down the long corridor, he thought about Emma, a young lady in turmoil. Had Jerry King been a former lover who rekindled a flame? Was this the reason for all the chaos during King's tenure? Did they reunite? You had to admit King was a very handsome man and a smart son of a bitch.

CHAPTER 31: Charlie's Log: AN EPIPHANY

Color me black. My rationality is spinning out of control. On edge, poised to do something reckless or stupid, lashing out at the world.

Before going home, I tried a vigorous workout. Too cold for an outside run. I used the treadmill, then someone wanted a squash game, followed by a few weights and finally the hot tub. Generally, at this stage, it all comes together for me, or I see things in a new light. Not today. No epiphany.

Monk needed me, but my thinking stuck in one gear, dominated by rage and frustration; I could not relax and think clearly. Part of the mess due to Red. I couldn't shake her; my thoughts continued to return to her, and I could not fathom her attitude. In a matter of hours, I converted from a passionate lover to some leftover embarrassment. An endless loop: first rage about Monk and then frustration about Emma.

Wes and the team completed each canvass, and we had nothing, no one even came close to selecting any of our morphed images, none of the psychologists or psychiatrists even remembered the name. Mesko had vanished. The motor vehicle search extended to include all males regardless of age within a 300-mile radius: same results.

Robin knew the families and their routines well enough to select a victim, bypass security and capture his target. Each family had employed a cleaning service, Maids & Gardens, who utilized many temporary staff to deal with peaks in their business.

 For the families, this meant strangers in their homes and gardens. Unfortunately, almost all the very wealthy in the city used this service, the biggest in the city. Karen reviewed the Patterson and Sharma families and came up with one name Henry Messer. I agreed with Karen: both of us convinced he was Robin. But after isolating the name, we came to a complete stop, all searching an absolute void. As an employee of Maids & Gardens, Henry worked in both homes a number of times.

 Were we clutching at anything, which confirmed our thinking? Was Henry just a bum who lived on the street and not a master criminal?

# # #

Early next morning I started the bacon before brother Sam burst through the door; he was in a somber mood.

 "Morning Charlie, you don't look good. I assume there is nothing new on Monk."

"No, we have nothing………a frustrating bugger all."

He dropped that line of discussion, hung up his coat, and dropped some travel brochures on the table.

"Here's India: traveler's glossy brochures and the details around our travel plans. Happy reading."

"Thanks and don't worry I don't plan to join your trip. It's for my research."

 "Well to change the subject. Are you still upset with Red?"

"Just leave it, Sam ………….I've given up on that woman."

"You know there could be a valid reason she refuses to answer your calls. I just don't see Dr. King as being her type, mind you the man is her boss, and that can sometimes make a difference."

I cut it off before he went further into some damn analysis. I knew he wanted to help.

 "Sam, why don't you start the eggs and finish the bacon? I want to squeeze some fresh orange juice.'

For the next half hour, we finished making breakfast and then eating it. Sam and his wife booked a holiday trip to India and collected some the glossy brochures, which all travel agents generously give away to their clients. He showed me his itinerary; India seemed full of bright colors, temples, tigers, cows in the street, and then I spied a picture of a rather gruesome Hindu goddess. I read the description, which explained she was Kali the goddess of destruction, the destroyer of ignorance and so forth. One mean looking son of a bitch.

With his last coffee, Sam read the paper, and I glanced through the other material he had left on the counter. The city had been hosting a national conference for the psychologist community. Sam acted as a conference co-chair, but since this was the last day with no important assignments, he took a short break to have breakfast with me.

I read about a Dr. Truncheon, who had given the keynote address. I read his curriculum vitae, an impressive man with an international reputation and clients all over the world. His specialty: working with people who had undergone severe life changes; this seemed to cover a multitude of events from limb amputations to messy divorces. I became intrigued and read about some of his more high-profile cases.

An intriguing article; I drank my coffee and read, engrossed, Sam also in his world. Then my epiphany arrived; I think it was the quiet which Sam often brings. But once I fully relax my system often does its job. Sorry, can't explain any better. I read the details about the session twice, and then I jumped on Sam.

"This Dr. Truncheon. Is he still in the city? Is he available? Can you get a hold of him?"

"What the hell is going on? Suddenly you are interested in a psychologist. You interested in making a change in your life?"

He saw I was serious. "When do you want to see him…. immediately? Ok. Ok ….. I'll call right now."

Once Sam made the call and appointment for me, I explained my epiphany. He did not seem as entranced with the concept as I was. I didn't care: the idea felt good. This would be one way to vanish from society and leave no footprints.

"Ok buddy, Dr. Truncheon is still at the Ritz and is willing to talk; he'll wait in his room. I have to go and soothe a few egos: some of the conference presenters missed me and aren't pleased with my absence. I hope your hunch is valid; it's wild, but your instincts are good. Good luck ………….bye."

I called Wes and told him to bring all the morphed images to the Ritz; I never explained my hunch.

# # #

Later in the day, after our discussion with Dr. Truncheon, we met with the entire team and the technician, Matt, who had morphed all the images of Dr. Mesko.

Everyone was down. No jokers were left in the room. They all knew Monk, and they all knew his projected lifeline, with us being useless witnesses. I tried to get the picture of his two fingers and two ears out of my mind. My guess: in a couple of days a parcel might arrive at my desk, and his body discarded somewhere in the Sector.

"Everyone have enough coffee? Matt's doing some new morphing for me. While he is finishing the last few, I will explain what is going on.

At breakfast this morning I read some high gloss brochures: first, a travel brochure about the wonders of India, on the back cover a half-page picture of Kali…… a Hindu goddess of destruction and the destroyer of ignorance. I repeat a goddess, a goddess…..a bloody woman.

Second, I dug into a newspaper article about the Psychologists' conference. One of the speakers specialized in dealing with people who wanted a sex change. His presentation dealt with the selection of candidates, the preparation work and the follow up needed.

It suddenly dawned on me what a good way to disappear from society, change your sex and name. Wes and I visited with a Dr. Truncheon who specializes in sex-change operations; he didn't recognize any of our pictures but did discuss the process and personalities associated with this dramatic change. Counseling is available in many cities.

 I've asked Matt to morph our pictures of Mesko; this time from male to female and of course to age the material."

No shouts of Eureka. Not much excitement on this one, but no one challenged me; it was about what I expected.

Matt said, "I'm ready, what I want to do is project my results up on your giant wall screen. Lots of options, so I'll step through one at a time, and you shout if you want me to stop."

We all faced the wall, and the image display started. I admit it felt strange seeing the man turn into a woman. Of course, I had no idea as to what to expect, just hoped someone we encountered in our canvassing would show up on the screen. Matt flashed through about 25 images then one hit the screen that both Karen and I recognized; she was faster than me.

"Son of a bitch ....nurse Helen".

Jesus Christ, a hit!

CHAPTER 32: A ROUNDUP

This substantial clue electrified the squad. A solution? Monk saved? Charlie allowed the chatter to continue while he absorbed the unanticipated. A woman yes, but Helen a jolt.

"I want extreme caution as we move closer to Robin Hood. He's on edge, and if he suspects we're close, he'll kill and disappear. I don't know how Helen fits in. Is it this simple? Dr. Mesko got a sex change or is there another twist? Could she be his sister?"

Wes was more direct. "Charlie, stop over analyzing. Helen equals Robin Hood. Remember what Dr. Truncheon said: even after the operation and the hormone treatment, the individual will retain some of his original or innate characteristics, like strength and muscle mass. Helen may be as strong as a man.

This means she can handle the bodies, particularly with or without parts cut off. I know Monk will be a problem for anyone. Shit, at 310 pounds, how and the hell is anyone going to handle him? Unless she plans to cut him into manageable pieces…sorry Charlie, but that's how I see it."

Karen jumped in. "I agree with Wes; she's the one. Remember how Helen handled the giggler, Barry, and got him back on the couch. She never asked for help. And even though Barry is not a big man, that was not an easy lift and more than some structured technique; there is some raw strength in that frame. Helen also pulled the giggler's grip off her forearm, like peeling an orange; and, I can tell you Barry has a fierce grip."

Charlie tried to keep on an even keel and not let his excitement sway his thinking, no emotional override, Monk too important, the next hour critical, a systematic approach needed.

"Yes, no more. I know. Here is what I need: first, Terry go to the Complex, don't go in, just monitor the staff exit and parking lot. Next, Manuel, you go to her apartment complex and watch her home location; she doesn't know either of you, and this should be a safe play.

If we pick her up immediately, I doubt she'll confess or cooperate. But, we know she uses a remote location for the killing. Now with her name, I want Wes back on the property search; she either bought or rented a place in the region, something isolated like a cabin or a small farm. I mean a place where her traffic and the noise doesn't raise an alarm. I understand our time constraints, but I want the property first.

Last, I'm going to the Judge and try to get approval for an S1 Interrogation for Helen. With nothing but a morphed image, I'm not optimistic about obtaining approval; the news outlets appear to be taking turns criticizing our recent interrogations. That goddamn channel seven played up the giggler's interrogation, mixing fact and fiction, stressing he is not a felon, just an innocent kid.

So I have to assemble a good case. If our friend from legal, Mr. Brewster, is present, he'll not give a damn inch; his CYA has developed into an obsession. I'm going to assume the Judge, with Brewster's strenuous backing, will turn us down on the Interrogation.

I'm convinced the key is to find her other property; this is where she's holding Monk. In the meantime, we monitor her. We can't lose her. In fact, Manuel and Terry, you'd better each use an extra car and staff to help. We can't afford to lose sight of her."

# # #

Charlie and Karen hesitated at the front entrance of the Complex; Terry in the parking lot with another unmarked car around the back. The Judge, as Charlie guessed, had refused an S1 Interrogation for Helen; the first search for property purchased under Helen's name came up empty. Wes keep at it, now with a series of computer generated aliases, but they couldn't wait, time to confront Helen.

They anticipated she would be a tough one: smart, hard, an experienced psychologist and probably knew enough law they could not bluff her, also a fanatic. They had no leverage. All she had to do was to point out the limitations of the computer morphing software. Even though other female pictures surfaced during the morphing, they chose to follow up on her because she was convenient, Why not chase any of the other pictures? Why not treat them as possibles? This had been one of Doug Brewster's arguments.

As they walked up the long sidewalk to the front entrance, Karen could not resist. "I see you didn't take our advice. You ever consider giving that coat away? Those pockets are big and deep enough to hide a suspect; Jesus they almost hang to your knees."

"Leave it; I'm not in the mood."

Karen approached the receptionist, identified herself and asked for Helen, the response a disappointment.

"Helen's off today; she phoned in sick. Can anyone else help you?'

They retreated to the parking lot; Charlie phoned Manuel at Helen's home.

"Manuel go in and pick her up we will meet you at the station."

# # #

Back at the station, Wes had coffee for himself and Karen and hot chocolate for Charlie.

"No luck. If Helen leased or bought in the Sector, she used a different name, and it must be entirely different because we ran every damn letter combination of her name and didn't get a reasonable hit. Sorry"

Before Charlie could answer, a message came in from Manuel. "She is gone, not home. Impossible to tell whether she's fled or just gone for the day."

As they sat around Charlie's desk, Karen and Wes focused on their coffee; silence prevailed in the office in contrast to the noise and action outside. A few hours ago, they were riding a wave, and now they'd slide into the trough, and it looked like the next wave would drown them.

Karen started to speculate. "After the giggler interview, I went back to the Complex and talked to as many staff as I could. Took a couple for coffee, shared some police stories and generally tried to be a big friendly teddy bear. I wanted to hear what they said about the Complex and the treatment of the residents.

The hottest and most frequent topic of gossip: our friend Villa. They don't like him; he is stubborn with one helluva temper. There are conflicting views about his sexual orientation; one group think he is gay, trying hard to demonstrate he isn't, but most are convinced he is in the closet and afraid to come out.

The real juicy gossip comes from another smaller group. They believe Villa is having an affair with Helen. Of course, the others scream 'bullshit he's gay'.

My confusion and question: if he's gay, why hook up with Helen?"

Charlie interrupted. "Remember Dr. Truncheon's comments about remnant characteristics? What if the sex change was not a 100% successful, and our dear Helen has more male characteristics than she is aware of or we can imagine?"

"Shit, Charlie it's too wild; now you're completely off the tracks. You're proposing even though Helen is now a female, something about her attracts a gay male. What the hell are we into? An aroma? A scent? A body shape? An aura? Villa senses this through some animal instinct? He accidentally rubs against her, and it feels right? Shit, this is too crazy."

"I'm going back to the Complex. Karen, you come with me. Wes keep looking at the property lists, and also look under Villa, maybe we get a hit."

# # #

Karen went to round up Dr. Villa, and Charlie waited in the front of the building; they thought it best to interview him outside the building and away from the staff. As he walked toward Charlie, his displeasure exploded all over his face and body, each stride an aggressive statement. He wanted a confrontation, his face inches away from Charlie.

"I just told your junior help that I have no idea where Helen might be. She could be seeing a doctor; she did phone in sick; we cooperated with you people once, and later this junior detective snuck back in: wasting staff time, collecting gossip. This has to stop."

He almost shouted the sentences but did not spill a drop from the mug of hot chocolate he gripped in his right hand.

"Actually Dr. Villa it doesn't have to stop, and we'll take as long as necessary; this is a murder and kidnapping investigation. I thought you wanted the killer caught and the Complex out of the spotlight.'

"I don't need a fucking lecture. What do you want?"

"If you don't know where Helen is, do you know if she owns or rents other property other than her condo?

The doctor hesitated for a moment, just long enough for Karen to catch it and signal Charlie, who also recognized a potential lie. "No, I'm not aware of any other apartment or building she owns or rents."

"You appreciate this is a serious crime and it would best if you did not place yourself in the middle of the investigation." No response he just looked at Charlie.

"We know you and Helen are having an affair, and hence you may be privy to some information not known to the rest of us." Karen hoped her accusation might shake the son of a bitch. Instead, it led to another outburst.

"You'd better not throw those types of accusations around in public; Helen and I were close, once, for a very brief time but more as friends and not lovers. And, before you ask, I'm aware of her operation, again a private issue. Now if there is nothing else, I'll return."

Charlie was close to losing it. "Do you want to be dragged down to the station and interrogated there? There's a life at stake at this moment, and you might be able to save him; your cooperation would be appreciated."

No response. Villa just turned and walked to the front entrance, Karen moved to stop him when Charlie called her off.

"He's not going to cooperate; let's go."

He walked to the car. A confused Karen rushed to catch up. Monk's life was at stake, and Charlie walked away from a man who was obviously lying. This did not make sense.

CHAPTER 33: Charlie's Log: A RECKLESS ACT

A short drive back. Karen drove, and I thought about the options: Villa was not going to talk, for whatever the reasons. We might be able to force him, but I knew it would take a lot of time. Dr. Mesko or Helen would win the race unless I could get past Villa.

Karen continued with Villa, spouting off about the hardnosed, tight-lipped bastard. I wasn't listening because one solution kept surfacing, a reckless move, and a potential career ender. The idea now dominated as I mentally filled in all the details of each step. I knew how reckless it was; even if I succeeded, my act would probably be discovered, and I would be fired.

One important step: get the rest of the squad away from the station; there had to be no doubt I acted alone. There was no other way, even Sam would understand. Goddamn it. I didn't like the idea of throwing away my career.

"Karen I want you to drop me off at the Forensic building. Then go back and pick up Dr. Villa for interrogation at the station, put him in room 12. I want this room with only one security camera and the big couch, no cuffs or any restraints.

Also, radio in and tell the entire squad to go home and to stay at home, but be available for a call, no exceptions. I will meet you back at the station. Last, I want to deprive Villa of his favorite pastime: drinking hot chocolate. Take his mug away from him when you put him in the room. Remember no mug, confiscate it."

"Goddamn it Charlie. What're you planning? You're up to something. I'm not dumb. You can't beat it out of him, and you can't wait for him to come around. I want to help. Monk is a good one...............you said we're friends; let me a part of this."

"The price is too high for you and the rest of the squad. Best not even to talk about it. As far as you know, I'm going to start an all-night interrogation, and you're to come back in a few hours and have a go at him, Wes next, etc. Now don't ask anymore. It'll be ok, just get our group out of the station and sell the all-night interrogation as a plan to Wes He might be the stubborn one."

Karen knew enough to stop arguing. Her last comment was. "I notice the hot chocolate he likes the best is the extra creamy stuff with the dark foam; Maxies sells it. That's where Wes bought yours the other day. They have an outlet right next to the station."

 I don't know how she guessed, but she's a smart lady.

She dropped me at the Forensic building; it was passed the supper hour, and the building was nearly deserted. I hoped I did not encounter Emma. I knew drugs were stored in Emma's section.

The S1 drug cocktail mixes were prepared ahead of time; this allowed Forensic staff to respond quickly to any requests: no preparation delays. Typically after the first combination, they wait four or five hours for all the chemicals to react and stabilize. Although some interrogations are carried out here, most occur at our station; there we have a couple of rooms, room 12 being one of them, which allow an individual to relax or lie down.

At our first supper, Red told me about the delay in reestablishing their security system, and their temporary set up with a limited number of cameras and the temporary keypad locks. My luck held: the place had the under-construction look. But I was sure there would still be evidence of my visit.

If Red wanted to confess that she gave me her keypad security codes during pillow talk that would be up to her. Her birth date, for Christ sake. In fact, she even bragged about one simple code for all three keypad locks: one for her office, one for the lab and a third for the storage unit. Maybe she would not remember; just like she can't seem to remember most things about that night.

In the storage unit, the premixed S1 Interrogation drug cocktails sat stored one of three shelves, in sequence by weight range. Each bottle labeled and designated for a particular weight; mixtures created for five-pound weight increments. Bottles were stored with the lowest weight range on the bottom shelf and the heaviest on the top shelf. I was looking for a bottle labeled 170-174 pounds. After his formal complaint about

Karen, Villa's personal file remained on my desk, documenting not only his academic career but also his physical statistics.

For an S1 Interrogation, Forensic staff delivered the container to us at the Investigative building, the Station. Inventory control was tight; there was a formal sign off as one of our employees accepted the drugs and recorded the name of the accused, along with this particular container, which had a unique batch number. The Forensic tech even stayed to observe the solution got to the correct individual.

Early in our history, they did all the questioning or at least supervised the interrogation because there were concerns about possible side reactions to the drugs. But all this proved to be a non-issue, and now police carry out examinations without a medical technician from Forensics. Normally, the side reactions are mild and happen during the 24 hours after the drugs have been ingested so police personnel can deal with a standard S1. The exception now: during the decommissioning of our prisons they were searching for repeat offenders and used the Forensic staff.

I gained access to her office and the lab; she hadn't changed her entry codes, but my entrance was captured by the front hall camera and became part of their daily log.

The last hurdle: the padlock on the storage unit; had she been consistent and not changed the combination? To my surprise the unit had a glass front; so much for security: one smash with a hammer, and I would have all the drugs I needed. No need. Her birth date opened the lock, and I selected my bottle.

I locked every door on my way out, even though I knew it was foolish. Any security cameras active in their reduced security arrangement had captured my image. I didn't spend time trying to duck the cameras because I knew they there were too well hidden for me to bypass. The only one I spotted was in the front entrance hallway. The Chief will shoot me for this.

Once out of the building, I walked back to the station, with one diversion on the way. I stopped at Maxies to order one extra rich hot chocolate and one small coffee. Maxies was crowded with long order lines, not good for an impatient detective. I tried not to think about the S1 bottle in my pocket. Jesus the line was slow. I ignored my surroundings and went over every step of my plan. Villa was going to be a slippery mean bastard; I had to appease him.

By the time I got upstairs, everyone was gone except Karen, who stood in front of the viewing window of room 12. She looked at my hands and the hot chocolate but did not comment.

"Time to go home Karen; I'll call in a couple of hours, if he doesn't break before that."

Our station video recorded this comment, and the prove she'd left the station, on standby along with the rest of the squad. Before she left, she gave me the look and whispered, "Good luck."

Through the observation window, I watched Dr. Villa pacing the room. Time to execute: I poured the S1 Interrogation mix into his hot chocolate and gave it a vigorous shaking to ensure the chemicals integrated into his drink. When I walked in, he started where he had left off a couple of hours ago.

"I told you everything I know….goddamn it."

I handed him the drink. It was either a tremendous thirst or his chocolate addiction; because he immediately started gulping down the mixture.

"It's surprising Dr. Villa ….. Sometimes as we talk to people for an extended period of time the unexpected surfaces, something important they never even thought of….so why don't you relax on the couch. I'll sit on this chair, and we'll chat."

He almost ignored me as he concentrated on getting his chocolate fix; my chemicals apparently did not detract from the flavor. I sipped my coffee while he chug-a-lugged his hot chocolate. I tried to keep it light, talking about the work of the Complex: a standard procedure, or by the book, while we waited for the chemicals to take control. The drugs appeared to have an impact very quickly because he responded to some of the small talk.

"You can't believe how happy I'm that you brought in this hot chocolate. It's a vice. A habit I can't break…..I know the staff joke about it, but I don't care...my God I must've been thirsty I finished it all.........now I feel like a nap…. like after lunch."

"Well you're on a couch why not relax and lean back, and we can talk some more about Helen."

I could see he was under: a smiling man, pleased with life, a cooperating member of the community, wanting to talk. I didn't know how fast and hard to push: I started with Helen.

"How long have you and Helen been lovers?"' Jesus, was this too direct?

He smiled, unperturbed and started. "I'm gay and confused to be attracted to her, but the attraction grew the longer we worked together. Then one day after work and a few drinks she told me about her sex change; I was stunned, never guessed. But the more I studied her face, I noticed this was not a fine-featured woman……. in fact, her features closer to a man's…..even her voice deeper."

He stopped, his breathing got heavier. Jesus, I hope he didn't have a heart condition, I forgot this is the one situation, which can lead to severe side reactions. Then he started again, and I understood he must've been reliving the steamy parts.

"After her confession, more drinks and we ended up in her condo; this was the first time I had sex with a woman since my divorce. To my surprise, we were a match, and I stayed all night. Both of us wanted our affair to become public, but this was difficult at the Complex. Then our relationship kept evolving, and to my amazement, we were both in love. First, our employment did present some difficulties; the Complex wouldn't allow us to both work there; we needed a transition plan. The plan was for her to find a new job, get reestablished, and after a brief waiting period, we get married.

I'm still gay and will never change. There is only one way this marriage will work is that Helen, although physically a female, presents as a male………..that's the best explanation I can give."

He stopped again. Jesus, was he running out of steam, drug wearing off? I pushed and made an abrupt jump in a different direction. "Besides the condo what other place did you meet?"

"No place else only the condo ………it's beautiful spot, great location "

Not the answer I wanted. I needed the other address. Was Villa involved in the killings?

"Did Helen ever speak of strong likes and dislikes Things that pissed her off? The property she would like to own?"

"Oh yes after sex she became quite vocal…..she felt the super-rich had everything hand to them, and they would never understand how condescending they are, completely oblivious to their remarks and actions."

He stopped. I knew he was tiring and there were more gaps in his speech as seemed to be hunting for a word.

Finally, he restated. "She loves the country south of here …....you know the Indian Reservation, but she couldn't buy a lot there …......not for sale….....you know they only lease...........she said some spots were so isolated there was not a neighbor for miles …......this is the property she felt would allow her to relax and reenergize."

"Did she ever get a place on the Reserve?"

"I'm getting sleepy; I've been up almost 24 hours……I want to help, but it's difficult to focus…..oh yes the Reserve……the Reserve………….I don't know if she got a spot or not but one day we went for a drive, and we're on the west side of the lake, and she said this was her favorite place   …but that's all she said."

"Did you have anything to do with the kidnapping and murder?'

"Good God no and I can't believe Helen did…..I just don't think she was involved….....I thought you're harassing gay people…… and I wasn't going to help or cooperate with that type of harassment….....I don't know anymore ………….do you mind if lean back put my feet up and sleep.'

"Go ahead Doc; we're done."

 I did a bit of housekeeping and left the room. To my surprise, Karen walked out of the observation room.

"Sorry Charlie I told you I was going to be part of this. Stop staring. If you get out of the way, I'll get us access to the Reservation records, which no one, unfortunately, thought to search."

In various parts of the country, the native North American Indians manage large tracts of land known as Reservations. They maintain control over the land and the associated records.

She went to work, and I start calling the rest of the team to return. I tried not to think about the pending charges against me: first stealing the S1 drug mix, second unauthorized use of S1 on a citizen who hadn't committed a crime. Of course, I rationalized: there had not been an alternative. I finished calling the squad about the same time Karen yelled.

"Touchdown, got the bitch."

I ran over to the screen and viewed the layout of the property: a rather large isolated cabin on the west side of the Reservation about 200 yards from the lake. This had to be it. A perfect spot.

Now to plan the assault. It would be better if we could first get her off the property or at least out of the cabin, Wes could help with a plan. I could hear him running up the steps. Before he got to us, Karen looked at me and said.

"Charlie, you really are one crazy son of a bitch!"

How much did she know?

CHAPTER 34: A LURE

Charlie found time to observe and assess Wes. The question: does he allow him to be part of the takedown? Over the past couple of days, Wes appeared to have stabilized and actively participated in the planning of Pameela's police funeral. The police funeral should be a morale booster for the entire squad.

Wes and Charlie worked on the approach plan. Charlie stressed. "We've to get her out of the cabin. If she is the least suspicious, Monk gets killed; at this point, I'm not sure how much she knows about our progress, but she may have heard about our search at the Complex."

Wes had been thinking about an approach. "I agree. But the question is what'll make her voluntarily come out of the cabin? I don't see her being the type to rescue a woman with a flat tire."

"No, that won't interest her, but she is a fanatic when it comes to the rich with old money. A real fucking fanatic and this is where we aim. We need a scene, which will get her emotions to overrule her logic. We have to get her cranked up, so she forgets her situation and responds to what is in front of her. Jesus, she's already butchered two people because she hates the rich."

Wes surprised Charlie. "Here it is: a large black sedan with a little chauffeur stops in front of her cabin. The passenger a fat older man, gray hair, abuses the little chauffeur, lots of noise and the chauffeur begins screaming, a scenario from the slave days.'

"Jesus Wes, I didn't know you were such a drama queen. Let me finish. The chauffeur could be a small man with a Spanish heritage, like Manuel and the passenger a mean looking bugger, like Webster from Vice.

Manuel gets out to relieve himself beside a bush, and Webster gets out to yell and scream at him for stopping. They can't park too close but too far and she won't hear or see all the detail. A good act should be enough to have her out for salvation and retribution.

Make sure it's a big car, and the costumes are first rate. I'll call Webster to come immediately, he's a bit of a prick, but he's a good cop. You can get Manuel ready.

Now, hang on. We need a minute. Here it's: Wes, you can be part of the team under two conditions. First, all your weapons, issued and others, stay locked back at the station; second, you stayed glued to my hip throughout and don't stray. You accept?'

Wes smiled, surprised Charlie allowed him to work the case for so long.

"Yes, I accept. Let's go get the bitch."

#

Various organized teams distributed themselves throughout the woods surrounding Helen Demarce's cabin on the Reservation. The dense bush throughout the clusters of trees provided an excellent opportunity to conceal sharpshooters and the other members of the SWAT unit. Charlie was the command control, and he reinforced his demand: once outside Helen was not to reenter the cabin.

It took a few hours to set up the scam and have the SWAT staff deployed. Charlie's control center was camouflaged with a good view of the cabin and its front door; he would control the entire operation, including the SWAT team. A small gray van parked next to the cabin provided further confirmation of Helen's presence.

The black sedan passed the cabin and went down to the lake, where the passenger got out and walked around the shore, all the time drinking from a flask, occasionally releasing a senseless roar. This was a privileged personage strutting around on some personal trip. A unique image at cabin's front window confirmed that the sounds had carried to the cabin. The passenger got back in, and the car turned from the lake, it missed the first turn and ended up in front of the cabin, about 50 yards away.

The car came to an abrupt stop. The chauffeur burst out and ran to the nearest bush, where he pulled down his zipper, with his back to the cabin; the passenger followed him, cursing and yelling for him to wait and return. Within seconds, a screaming match developed. Actually,

Webster did the screaming; then he grabbed the chauffeur's hat and hammered his chauffeur repeatedly with the hat, full swings. Webster was not holding back. Each swing of the hat had Manuel uttering great sobs; Charlie was impressed and thought: an Oscar performance.

The front door burst open, and an indignant Helen came flying out, a broom in her hand, her screaming louder than Webster's. She was prepared to teach Webster a lesson in good manners, his abusive actions a blot to her sensitivities, a flagrant display of assumed prerogatives. She was surprisingly agile as she ran toward the couple with the broom raised above her head.

At less than 20 yards, she stopped and stared at the two of them, both combatants stopped and watched her approach. Later the team remembered Manuel had been a back up to Karen on a recent TV interview, although not the spokesperson but apparently a member of the team. Whether she recognized Manuel or sensed something when both Webster and Manuel stopped so abruptly, gaining their control and feelings so quickly, it did not matter. Helen's intelligence warned her: time to return to the safety of the cabin, she wheeled around, dropped the broom and sprinted to the open door.

Charlie understood his role and didn't hesitate with his command. "Take her now! She can't get back into that cabin. Goddamn it, now!"

Two sharpshooters with unobstructed views lived up to their reputations and training. The force of bullets drove Helen forward, and she died in the doorway of the cabin, her face flat down in the entry, her back marked with the killing shots, a quick and surprising ending.

Robin Hood's career ended with 21st-century weapons. Charlie and Wes sprinted to the cabin: both concerned Helen might have a partner inside the cabin. As soon as he stepped in, Charlie turned on the lights; the cabin was designed as one large room, near the far end was a large table with a shape Charlie recognized. He strolled up to the table and smiled down at the naked man who was impatient. "As you can see, I'm still alive but rather desperate to get off this table, see a doctor, and tackle a steak."

"Jesus Christ Monk, is that all you can do is complain?"

The medical staff followed behind Charlie and soon wheeled Monk out of the cabin and into an ambulance where a doctor started treating him. Charlie waited close by until the doctor was satisfied, and the ambulance left the Reservation.

 Wes and Charlie walked around the cabin as the Forensic team continued with their routines. The back wall was completely covered with a variety of high gloss pictures of Kali; below the images were some candles in what appeared to be a place of worship or an altar. There were no body parts or remnants on the altar, but Charlie guessed, at one time, they'd served as an element in her unique liturgy.

On the kitchen counter, they found a diary: a large book, with no lock, like a big logbook. Charlie registered the book with Forensics and then took it outside to read. He jumped to different parts of her history, some sections with many lines of details, other events only accorded a few words, no pattern as to why the discrepancy in her approach. He stopped at points of his interest:

First, her obsession with the wealthy and privileged started early in her life. It appeared her original attitude had been fear and respect for their position, possessions, and poise; then as her education progressed her attitude hardened into anger and envy. Did her anxiety about her sexuality supplement and intensify her anger? Charlie read some of the episodes, which featured embarrassing put-downs, real or imagined.

After she completed her postdoctoral work program, she immediately began plans for a sex change. It probably had been unnecessary to start the fire in the psychology department, but Helen did not like loose ends. She consulted with a surgeon for almost two years before the surgery, completing the psychological tests and undergoing further counseling.

The name change process was a pleasant surprise: in her state, new legislation allowed her to bury her past as part of becoming a new person. High profile psychologists lobbied for the new law, explaining how critical it was for the success of these types of transformations to completely discard all reminders of the past.

Even before the surgery, her surgeon provided the forms used to detail all aspects of her life. He explained it would be used to do an extensive check to confirm no criminal record, no outstanding debt, a detailed search down to delinquent parking tickets. A significant extra cost, but she agreed it was worth the money.

After the review and validation had been completed, she appeared before a judge. The background search certified she was not trying to escape the law, old credit companies, or any other persons. This allowed the judge to accept her application, and she obtained a new identity: a passport and driver's license among the many new legal documents. Her original name and details became a sealed record only to be accessed if authorities could present sufficient evidence. In a relatively short time, the male, Harold Mesko, vanished without a trace and Helen emerged.

To finish the process, she obtained a nursing degree, a complete change in professions. For a while, she was stable, but then all the resentment came back, never to leave her. Once she committed to a course of action, much of the anxiety declined.

She spent hours of planning the events. It was not difficult to choose the Patterson family and the Sharma's. She wanted maximum impact for her projects, and these two families were among the highest profile in the city.

The company Maids & Gardens bragged about serving the elite of the community; they employed many part-time workers because of the peaks in demand, which put a drain on their permanent staff complement. She hired on as a temporary, male; she requested outside jobs, and once her assignments included work for both target families and identified their security systems, she quit.

Helen came back three weeks later: this time to assist the permanent staff with any of the cleaning projects and to case the inside routines. Again her simple male disguise fooled Maids & Gardens, who were too busy to check the false employment data she provided. Helen was meticulous, a favorite of Maids and Gardens supervisors. Within a few weeks, even working only part time, she collected the necessary details about the home and gardens of both families.

In fact, two more families sat on her list, but for some reason, she changed plans and grabbed Monk. This seemed to be her pattern: detail plans and sudden deviations before completion.

"Wes, listen to this. Helen documents her love life:

That fucking Villa is a weak, mediocre excuse for a doctor. How did he ever get certified? The entire Complex knows he's gay and still he pretends. I should never have let him touch me. Now he won't stop. The idiot is in love.

And on and on she goes about this Villa."

"Charlie this is the same Villa who thought they would soon marry? So much for love!"

"It appears the giggler clue was one she wrestled with the most and debated its merits. But the excitement of having the police so close won out, and she included the giggler on the audio clue set; then she found it provided a bonus: the presence of our group. She observed us in action and watched our frustration.

Then another departure from the plan: Monk; but the concept was smart. She considered the Roman Catholic Church the apex of the rich and famous: either because of the money in its vaults or the way it flaunted its decorated priests amongst the poorest in the country.

When Monk first came to the Complex, she made sure they became friends; he wanted to establish a regular Sunday service or at least a weekly prayer evening. Villa, for some reason, vigorously opposed the idea; he kept having the decision delayed and eventually getting the request denied.

Monk was more than willing to help a woman move some heavy furniture at her cabin out by the lake on the Reservation; she picked him up and drove him out in her gray van. For a big man, he turned out to be the easiest acquisition, so trusting."

An extensive diary. And it would provide many of the answers. Charlie closed the book, looked out into the yard, grateful for a satisfactory conclusion. Wes read his text messages and relayed a disturbing dispatch.

"Boss, we've one small problem with this takedown."

Charlie wondered: how Wes knew about his actions back at the Station?

"What is it?"

"She was shot in the back. Helen wasn't armed. She wasn't threatening us with a weapon, and you gave the order to fire. Anyway, that's how it got reported to the Chief."

# # #

Stephen sat in his car, an impatient onlooker. Having been granted an early release from a Sector Farm, Dr. Kate currently resided in a Halfway House.

He was glad the Sector's unanticipated problem resulted in an opportunity for her. The decommissioning of all prisons meant the Sector accumulated mountains of video records: memory scans or S1 Interrogation results from each prison. Experts already recognized these files as an excellent source of future detective work, particularly for the Cold Case squad. It became evident they needed an approach to classifying and archiving the material, and all the qualified staff was busy with other prison reform tasks.

Since most people accepted her motives for the bribery incident, it was not long before someone recommended her to undertake the work of the unofficial archivist. Regional knew they needed an expert and were prepared to absorb an adverse potential public reaction to her early release. A community service but the massive undertaking was a challenge she enjoyed. Without being asked, she began to note and propose changes, to enhance both the S1 and S3 process, the lady obviously much more than an archivist.

Her early release a good sign. But regardless of her efforts and work in the next few months, she remained branded and might never be able to hold a position, which would match her qualifications. However, the university allowed Sonja, her daughter, to continue in medical school but did withdraw the scholarship. An anonymous donor paid for tuition and books: Kate did not have any doubts about the donor; would it ever be out in the open?

More good news: Sonja even started to visit her; she finally understood the sacrifices Kate made and the penalty she paid and would continue to pay.

The weather turned, and the rain retreated for a few days. Stephen got out of his car and leaned on the hood, letting the sun warm his face. He knew he was about to deliver another blow to his career. Regardless of her early release, Kate was still viewed as a criminal.

Was he a stupid teenager? Surely, he could wait until she completed community service, as he originally planned. But, this unanticipated assignment meant some extra months before she finished all the obligations. The delay loomed as too much. Maybe he'd been spending too much time with Dr. Max and Charlie. Best to drive away and forget her.

An exit door opened and Kate walked out in the company of a small group of other women; they all headed to a bus, which was to transfer them back to the Halfway House. He quickly moved towards her.

"Kate, Kate…over here."

She used her hand to shield her eyes; the sun had blocked her vision.

"Steve, my God, Steve…it is great to see you…but you shouldn't be here…you know that.."

Before she could finish, he stood in front of her and spoke softly.

"I'm not wasting any more time; we both have been denying what is between us…….you know this don't you?"

They embraced both holding tight, and then he kissed her. If Charlie had been a witness, it would have been a 'Jesus Christ' moment; for other observers, it appeared as natural and complete, like a homecoming.

Unfortunately for Stephen, a TV news truck pulled up just in time to capture the entire sequence. The reporter's original objective had been to interview some of the convicts who had been granted an early release.

But now Judge Stephen Miller would be on the 6:00 pm news, probably the lead story. The reporter commented to the cameraman.

"This entire goddamn Sector 14 appears to be populated by a group of characters with little common sense, or they don't give a shit. We have a horny scientist about to marry a teenager. A homicide detective who has pulled so much shit that they call him 'Crazy Charlie'; and, now we get the top man in the Sector kissing a convicted felon on a public street. Can you believe this: a romantic, sentimental judge?"

CHAPTER 35: FALL OUT

The Chief started as soon as the detective took a chair. "Charlie, have you dropped us into another shit storm? Dr. Villa is steaming hot and screaming at anyone who'll listen. He has already been to the Judge's office. First, he claims you drugged him; he insisted on a Forensic team to come to room 12 and collect his paper cup of hot chocolate. About 20 minutes ago, the Lab team picked up his cup and your remaining coffee. That cup and its contents will be treated as evidence against you: for administering the S1 Interrogation drugs to him. Of course, he means an unauthorized application."

Charlie never responded. This had turned into his worst case scenario: Villa guessed. He knew it might happen but hadn't had time to develop a denial strategy.

"Second, the good doctor heard about the takedown at the cabin. His accusation: you ordered an execution and not an arrest. Helen never had a chance to explain; she was shot in the back, not even armed, and didn't threaten the officers at the scene. Unless I put you under suspension and begin an official inquiry, he threatens to go public; he gave us until noon. Like I said a shit storm. You have anything to say?"

Charlie made his decision: he might as well ride it out as far as it would go. "I played him that's why he's steam; Karen told me about his addiction to the hot chocolate. A cup never leaves his side. Once he was in room 12, we stripped the cup away from him.

After a couple of hours, I came into room 12 with his chocolate fix. He started to relax as soon as he started gulping the stuff. Jesus, he never stopped drinking until he drained the cup. As well, the asshole was beat; with Dr. Reed away sick, this asshole just finished a double shift. A tired guy started to open up as soon as he relaxed. He told the whole story; he gave Helen up, and this bothers him."

"Charlie, most of this sounds like bull shit.........addicted to hot chocolate. For Christ sake, you used to be better than that; I'll wait for the lab results. I, also, have a call out to the Forensic Division to check their inventory, which might clear you.

Now go and think about the takedown problem, this Villa is a bulldog and won't let go. What else do you want to share? Anything you wish to tell me? Because once I get started everything I uncover becomes part of the public record, we can't back it out. Anything I should know? The Judge gave us the rest of the day and you know he's not rooting for Villa."

The Chief appeared to be willing to play, but Charlie thought it is best to walk alone; no need to drag others into the mess. He initiated the play, and he would play solo until the end.

"No, it's like I told you."

# # #

As soon as Charlie left the office, the Chief called Emma and explained his problem.

"So Emma you have to review your security logs and recordings. Was Charlie in your building and your office? Also need an inventory check. I need to know if you are missing any containers. And the topper: I need you answers within the hour."

"Chief this is insane even for Charlie. You know the severity of the penalties for this kind of move."

"I agree, but we've no choice. Either we conduct the investigation or Villa goes public. He thinks Charlie's reputation will ensure front page headlines. And he's right."

Emma, stunned by the news, struggled to regain her composure. If true, this would result in Charlie's dismissal from the police force, and probably a criminal charge. The Judge could not save him from these accusations. She thought about the man and their weekend; she could not let him lose everything because of his reckless moves to save a friend.

However, under the rigid law, any unauthorized use of the Interrogation drugs was deemed a grave violation of policy. The drugs were considered too important for open access, the development of a possible antidote or blockage tool being just one of the concerns.

She began to systematically address the Chief's questions. The reduction in the number of active cameras wouldn't help; A public record existed. The central camera showed Charlie's main floor entrance and his brisk walk to her floor. The cameras on her floor had not been replaced, so his action on that level had not been recorded.

Next, she looked at the keypad lock monitor; the usage history showed no false starts of entering a wrong code, no attempted break in.

The last step meant taking inventory; she called in Margie to assist and witness the counts. Margie, new and inexperienced, was not used to the routines and procedures for storing and releasing the drug mixtures. The premixed medications were all in self-contained small bottles, enough for one dosage.

A small cabinet rested on the floor, with three shelves, the mixtures graded and in sequences by weight ranges. They started at the lighter weights 100-104 pounds, Emma counted the bottles; Margie watched and recorded the numbers.

Emma continued to back-up as they worked their way across the front of the storage unit. Margie followed with her recorder, confirming the numbers on file with Emma's count. The inventory in the cabinet was small, due to the shelf life of the drugs, so they quickly completed the first shelf. They moved back to the front of the next shelf to start on the 165-200 pound mixtures. Before they started, Emma bent over to retie her shoe and accidentally bumped the cabinet.

Margie in her concern leaned forward to grab a bottle, which was falling off one of the shelves. At that exact time, Emma straightened up, and she knocked the bottle out of Margie's hand, collided with Margie's chin and drove her head back. The collision threw Emma back into the cabinet; her hand flew out and knocked off an entire row of bottles from the 165-200 pound shelf.

The resulting mess of broken glass covered the floor, blood from Margie's chin and blood from Emma's hand added to the mixture. Margie, in a vain attempt to help Emma regain her balance, stepped forward. The result was she and Emma completed an awkward and futile dance, more bottles fell; and more glass cracked under both sets of feet. Margie started crying.

"Oh damn, it was my fault; I just wanted to save the one bottle. It was falling off the shelf. When you straightened up, I was too close to you."

"Margie, get the first aid kit; I believe we both need some repairs. If we can't get your chin to stop bleeding, you might need stitches, and I guess I'm in the same boat; my hand throbs and throbs."

"God, what a mess. We'll be unable to finish the inventory count for this range of weight mixtures; all we have is shards of glass. I'm sorry."

Emma felt sorry, she certainly did not mean to injury Margie. The planned bump into the cabinet was to allow her to throw her arm back and knock bottles off the target shelf. This result certainly looked more impressive and accidental, particularly if Margie kept proclaiming it was her fault.

"Margie, this is not a significant expense, in fact, some weeks we destroy just as many because they exceed the expiry date. You made a minor mistake. Purely accidental. That is how I'll document it, an accident, nothing negative on your file. Now it appears your chin has stopped dripping blood, so you can help with my hand."

After she cleared the glass and reported to the Sector, Emma phoned the Chief, her approach and comments rehearsed and practiced.

"Chief, I've finished our review, and I'm not sure there is much here for you. First, Charlie was in the building at least the front reception area. We were to meet; but, I got hung up with the Judge and forgot to call Charlie and cancel. He didn't stay too long. That's all from our Security camera show.

The second level of security consists of the keypad locks, which have to be opened to get the drug mixture; the monitoring software didn't record any unauthorized attempts to open them. The locks will be replaced next week….. not high tech but they do record any attempts to use them without the proper passwords."

She failed to mention her indiscretion during her weekend with Charlie when she bragged about her simple approach to the three locks. The indiscretion was one thing, but her failure to change the passwords immediately after now stood as an even more serious offense or lack of judgment.

After she had finished her spiel, one thought crossed her mind: did the Chief have anything else, to confirm the charges? If further proof existed, then she had to rely on Charlie to stonewall the Chief. Surely, he would not confess and disclose how he got past the keypads.

"Last point we completed most of the inventory but not all. Our newest employee slipped and broke an entire row of bottles; the mess makes it impossible to tell how many bottles were on the shelf before the count. However, the inventory I was able to complete was correct, and it's very unlikely any were missing from our broken set.

I'm sure he visited the building to see me and not steal drugs. If he went further than a mere meeting with me, I have no idea how he got past the keypad locks and not leave a trace. I think our S1 drugs were secure and no theft took place."

"Thanks Emma, I can't clear Charlie yet; the lab is testing Dr. Villa's paper cup to determine if any of the drug mixture was in the hot chocolate Charlie brought him. Thanks."

When she got off the phone, her anxiety level erupted and hit the ceiling. The discussion with the Chief had been a series of contrived lies and omissions, completely out of character, enough to cause her grief and concerns. Now a test of the cup!

How had Charlie been so sloppy to leave the cup? Why not take the cup? It was sure to come back positive, and the questions would fly back to her. God, what now? If they pressed her, she would confess and tell everything; she could not go on deceiving people, regardless of what it would cost her.

Charlie's reckless act would have consequences for more than himself.

#

Charlie returned to the Chief's office for the next round.

"The other small problem in front of us: on your orders, two members of the SWAT team shot bullets into Helen Demarce's back. She was not armed and had not threatened anyone; no attempt was made to wound her. Your orders are on record: shot to kill if she attempts to get back into the cabin. Any comments?"

"I knew Monk was in the cabin and utterly helpless. She ignored all warnings to stop; there was a knife in the doorway. Helen left the knife there when she came out to deal with our contrived scene. I've no doubt if she got into that cabin and reached that knife, which was more like a fucking cleaver, Monk was a dead man. She would be able to lock the door and only needed minutes; once inside she would be a few steps away from Monk."

"Shit, I know you're right, and the Mayor won't push it. Our problem: Dr. Villa he has turned into a fanatic; it appears the poor bastard was in love and now can't get over the fact that he gave you the information to find her and kill her.

I'm sure he will not listen to reason …the bastard will go public calling it an execution because she threatened your best friend. Once he does that we will not have a choice, but to create a Review Board and hearing. And you know he'll ensure your former antics get full coverage."

"Hold on Chief. There is an angle. Wes and I reviewed Helen's diary and daily log. I've copied a few pages, which I suggest you give to Villa. And let him know if a Review Board starts all the details of her writing will be open to the public."

"What the hell is in there?"

"Helen writes about her affair with Dr. Villa. She considers him an asshole, just a physical relief about one degree better than masturbation; she plays him to get the flexibility she needs around her working hours at the Complex. Once he reads, this is I'm sure his attitude will change. The last thing he can stand is for Dr. Reed and the rest of the Complex staff to see and read that assessment of him."

"Leave it with me. I've no problem playing hardball with the son of a bitch. Then I need to watch the security video from Room 12, and the hot chocolate test should be back soon. Come on back at the end of the afternoon. We should be able to wrap it up by then."

Chief never mentioned the Forensic building and Charlie didn't ask.

CHAPTER 36: WRAP UP

It was the end of the day, and Charlie thought maybe the end of more than that. Damn merry go round. Another hour and he was back for more. He was back in the Chief's office, status to be determined but allowed to sit.

"I reviewed the video. It confirms most of your comments; you do come in with a hot chocolate for him and coffee for yourself. No doubt Villa's desperate for his drink, and you allow him to drink deeply before you start. He does appear to relax rather quickly after he gets his chocolate fix and begins to like you.....for Christ sake, he must have been tired.

The two of you almost become buddies as he tells you about Helen and her place. When you exit the room, you leave paper cups, your coffee, and his hot chocolate, in the room, so we have our evidence to test.

With only one camera for room 12, the recording for that room has always been problematic and not the best quality but good enough. There are 30 to 50 frames where the record gets some heavy snow, interference that makes it difficult to get a clear image; this happens near the end when you're helping him onto the couch. What was that all about?"

"I told you about his extended shift. He wanted to sleep; I had everything I needed, so I told him to go ahead. He seemed worried about spilling his drink. So I went to the couch, put his drink on the floor, and he just leaned back. There is an adjustment handle, which allows you to lower the top half and turn it into a bed. I adjusted the couch for him and left in a hurry. No time for housekeeping. I abandoned the cups and him in the room."

The Chief appeared satisfied with the explanation. "Ok, next I talked to Emma; she tells me you had a date, well not a date, but a meeting so you'd a reason to be in the Forensic building. The keypads indicate no one tinkered with them, and I know you're not a mechanical or electronic genius, so that means you never bypassed that keypad system. The last piece of news, Emma's assistant broke an entire range of S1 medication bottles. Meaning we can't complete an inventory; this making you happy?"

Charlie already knew about Red's comments because she'd emailed him apologizing for not showing up for the evening meeting yesterday. What the hells was that all about? Nothing for days and now a cover story, the sequence did not make sense. The Chief continued while Charlie waited for the last shoe. "This smells, but it is almost too much for you, too many players involved; there wasn't enough time for you to coordinate a conspiracy like this one. I'm sure you pulled something; how I don't know. Well, you can't beat chemistry, and the lab will be calling in a few minutes. They told me there was enough hot chocolate left for a series of tests."

When the phone rang, it stopped the Chief and brought Charlie's attention back to the room. The Chief answered on the first ring, an impatient man. "No details just give me the bottom line. What? Are you sure? You got outside confirmation, and they confirmed your results? Ok, write it up, sign the papers and send it up."

The Chief looked at Charlie and for the first time grinned. "I don't know how you did it, but I'm sure you pulled a fast one and drugged that prick Villa. But, to top it all off, the lab cleared you; they confirm that the cup never contained anything but hot chocolate. I don't want to know and don't ever tell me. Now get the hell out ….and Charlie, good job… you crazy bastard."

Charlie walked back to his desk and kept going to the cafeteria. Not hungry, just needed a good strong cup of coffee. Wes and Karen occupied the far corner of an almost empty cafeteria, and they waited for him to join them. Wes was most persistent. "How in the hell did you pull it off? Don't just smile. Tell us goddamn it. Ok, ok, the next supper is on me; come on, I can't live without knowing. There is no way he opened up on a few sips of hot chocolate."

Charlie, always a fast eater, finished a cookie and most of his coffee, smiled and started, safe with these two people: "Yesterday morning you bought me a hot chocolate and coffee for yourself and Karen. As events played out, I never had a chance to touch mine, didn't even take the lid off.

When we brought him in, I had Karen install him in room 12 and take away his drink; I wanted him thirsty. While she was busy rounding up Villa, I went over to the Forensic building to get a bottle of S1 medications, and I'll never tell you how I pulled that one. Before coming back into the building, I bought him a hot chocolate, emptied the bottle of meds into the cup, slipped the lid back on.

Before going into room 12, I picked up yesterday's hot chocolate from my desk, drained most of it, left about an eighth of an inch, dumped the lid and put that cup into the side pocket of my large pockets. Yes, I concealed yesterday's cup in this ugly jacket with its pockets which can hide a small dog.

I walked into room 12 with a coffee in my left hand, a drugged hot chocolate in my right hand and a regular hot chocolate cup in my pocket, invisible to the one camera in that room.

You know about his response and his cooperation; it worked, and then he got tired, sooner than I anticipated. I maneuvered my right side pocket to be away from the camera. I volunteered to adjust the couch for him, and he helped by handing me his chocolate. Next my juggling act: adjusted the couch, retrieved yesterday's chocolate cup from my right pocket and put it on the floor and finally hide his drugged chocolate into my large pocket.

If someone watched the video with a critical eye, this is where I'm most vulnerable but them technology came to the rescue. Throughout most of that interchange, the recording went snowy with interference; you could see us but not a clear picture. What was clear: I left a cup of hot chocolate and a coffee in the room when I left. Karen, who was supposed be out of the building, watched the whole thing."

Karen smiled at the two of them and revealed her secret. "I did more than watch; I expected you to pull something and would need help. When I saw it was over and you walked over to him, I just reacted. I didn't know what was going to go down, but I was already at the camera controls. You bent down beside him …that is when I bumped the receiver a couple of time…… that damn camera is so sensitive that any adjustments cause it problems and it takes about a dozen seconds to recover. I didn't know how it would play out I just hoped it would reduce the quality. And I hear it worked. You see Charlie you're not alone and don't ever think you are."

She did not wait for an answer she got up, smiled at both of them and left them staring at her back. Wes remained with some unanswered questions. "Charlie you're one lucky guy and one crazy bastard. I'm glad you are on our side. Did the Chief or Villa pick up on the additions we entered into Helen's diary?"

"No, remember most of it was her original entries, and once he read the beginning, emotions took over. And I think he had difficulty with just reading the words, let alone worrying about a minor forgery. By the way, the 'masturbation phrase' almost put him through the roof, if she was still alive, he'd have done the job for us. I hope you didn't steal that from a contemporary novel."

Wes laughed, pleased but exhausted like Karen and after he had walked Charlie back to his desk, he started for the front door. Charlie began to call him back but stopped: Wes did not appear to want company. Maybe it was time for them all to wind down and reflect on a successful day. A multitude forms and one written report to be completed. But he decided this was not the time. He did not feel like running or weights; instead, he walked out of the station, past the Forensic building toward the park entrance. He heard someone call.

"Charlie, slow down. We need to talk; please stop."

Charlie turned and stopped, "Why did you decide to be part of this?"

Emma was blunt. "I understood your motives, and I couldn't let you lose everything because of a maniac. Besides, I became part of this when I told you my access codes; I do remember; I remember everything. Isn't my role in life to save your ass? Stop playing this lone wolf routine. You think you have to do this all by yourself? That no one else is involved?

 It doesn't work that way. We have a vulnerable Judge, who allowed an S1 Interrogation of a mentally retarded young man and memory scan on a disorganized schizophrenic.....all highly irregular but done to help you.

 And, don't you know how far out on the limb Dr. Max went on Lynn's scan? After Wassant had given her the second helping of her meds, there is no way he knew or could be sure what would happen when we restarted the scan. If any time in the immediate future Lynn's condition worsens, who do you think is going to be held responsible? And Max knew his situation."

Charlie didn't want to hear any more. He turned away and started down the main path of the park. Emma grabbed his hand and held it; the move even surprised her, fatigue had destroyed barriers, like a stiff scotch, and she was operating in a more honest unrestricted manner than she had in days. A tired detective barked, not in the mood for subtleties.

An exhausted Charlie was angry. "What the hell is going on? You ignore all my phone calls; shut me out entirely, except for a couple of cryptic text messages; hang on to your ex-boyfriend as if he is the new savior. Dropped me like a rock. Why are you here? I'm not playing any more games with you. We're even. Go home."

"I'm so sorry, just listen. One of my faults is under pressure I become entirely focused on the job at hand, everything ceases to exist. I was interim Division head, relieved for a while and then reappointed, a 24/7 job. Look at me; I look like hell, I can't even remember when I last had a shower.

I prepared for the second phase of prison reform and then Jerry King took over. I disagreed with his directive to reduce the wait time between S1 and S3 to 24 hours; we argued, almost came to blows. I didn't understand his agenda. Now I think I know: he meant to prove to the world that he was more than an ivory tower academic. In his mind, he must have envisioned TV interviews and press conferences to explain his bold and brilliant move to expedite Phase Two of Prison Reform. I couldn't sleep, staff confused and upset, everyone on edge, then the bodies piled up on questionable S3 memory retrievals.

It wouldn't stop. If Bill Thompson hadn't blown the whistle, I'm not sure what I would have done; it is as close as I have ever been to a breakdown. Understand Jerry was never my boyfriend. We'd been close, and the man I knew is not the man who betrayed the Judge and the rest of us."

Emma stopped to rest, and Charlie just stared; she quickly continued. "He is gay but has never publically acknowledged his situation.

When he was doing his grad work, we discovered each other. I wanted to focus on my grades and possible scholarships but regularly fought off invitations to parties and requests for a night out; he disliked fielding questions about why he wasn't dating.

He was and still is very handsome. We made a pact: he would act as my boyfriend. This combination meant we could choose when we went out, how long we stayed and had control. It served us both, and no one uncovered the deception.

The years in France changed him. At the U when he taught a class, the lecture hall was packed, standing room only. The students loved him, not only did he know his subject but he could explain obtuse concepts and even spent time with them outside the lecture hall. I couldn't turn on him immediately; I was so stressed: I never realized Jessie failed to inform the Judge."

Not much about her explanation helped him. Only a few people used the path, and they rushed past the drained couple. Rain drops started to fall, not heavy but steady. Both of them accumulated a soaking; neither seemed to notice.

"Emma, you don't owe me anything; he was a close friend and then your boss. It makes sense you couldn't turn on him; plus you had some strong feelings for the guy, even as a friend if not a lover. Let's agree to leave it. I don't know any smart French phrases to conclude this intimate little chat. Best to just sign off, and we can work together next week."

He turned; he did not want to face her, his emotional balance already on edge with the Villa review. She grabbed him and turned him again. "Goddamn you Charlie will you listen to me? Can you hear? I told you I am sorry. I'm sorry. I don't want to lose you. I'm not stupid or arrogant and indifferent. Please, it was just the worst time in my life, and I almost screwed everything up. Come home with me. Please."

The steady tears wet her face. Charlie finally realized she was wasted, black circles beneath her eyes, hair not done up, clothes in disarray; he knew she was telling the truth. It was his turn to be open.

"I'm taking you home, and I'm staying a long time."

Neither spoke of love, but anyone watching them walk the park path would have known Charlie found a home.

THE END

From the third Charlie Taylor novel: **KILL ALL OF THEM**

There was a random scattering of clothing on either side of the bed, apparent that no one gave any consideration to the next wearing and associated appearance.

The man was so big there was very little room for the woman who was resting on her stomach. The giant of a man was on his back, snoring, both arms flung out, making him look like a cross. One arm outside the bed, the other over top of the woman. She did not complain nor did it wake her. Unfortunately, she would never wake up, not this morning or any morning.

When he did wake up, the hangover headache would not help; but Monk would have some decisions to make.

From the first Charlie Taylor novel: **KILL MOST OF THE MISCREANTS**

They are here: albeit underground, nevertheless at the Abbey.

The place is a paradox, built around 400 years ago to serve the needs of a cluster of monks, today a commercial success. The revenue from business conferences, meditation weekends, and private retreats provide a healthy profit and allows the Abbey to prosper. A central core holds most of the buildings and is surrounded by a waist-high stone wall, with exits at various intervals. One of the exits leads directly into an adjacent woodland where the walking and jogging paths continue for miles.

He tries to control the frequency and timing of his visits. It is best to blend with a crowd, best not to be conspicuous and get recognized.

There is a multitude of pathways: some concrete, some paved, some crushed rock, and where the paths enter the woodland, some reddish earth mix predominates. He walks the forest for hours; it is on these paths he can recharge and relax.

He buried them here, months ago.

The End